"Friendship hath the skill and observation of the best physician, the diligence and vigilance of the best nurse, and the tenderness and patience of the best mother."

—Edward Hyde, 1st Earl of Clarendon

Sweet Carolina MYSTERIES

Sweet Carolina
MYSTERIES

ANGELS WATCHING over ME

Gabrielle Meyer

ANGELS WATCHING over ME

Chapter One

A CRASH OF THUNDER BROUGHT Evelyn Perry's head up from her work. Outside the window of the records department at Mercy Hospital, the wind picked up and a flash of lightning split through the sky. The storm had come out of nowhere.

"Did you know we were supposed to get a storm today?" Evelyn asked her assistant, Stacia Westbrook, who also looked toward the large floor-to-ceiling window in surprise.

"I had no idea," Stacia answered.

The thunder boomed again, rattling the old glass pane. This section of Mercy Hospital was the only one to withstand the Great Charleston Fire of 1861. Over 575 buildings in the city had been destroyed on that dreadful December night, and many people had feared that the hospital would also fall victim to the flames. But this wing had miraculously survived, along with the statue of an angel that legend said guarded the main entrance. Evelyn was so thankful the wing had survived, along with many of the original documents that were still safely stored in the Vault, a small, windowless room behind the modernized records department.

"I hope it stops before five o'clock," Stacia said. "Emmett and I have plans to go on a picnic to celebrate our one-month anniversary."

Evelyn smiled to herself. Stacia was young, just barely out of college, and had started working in the records department after her graduation in May. In the three months Evelyn had known her, Stacia had dated four different boyfriends, most lasting for less than two weeks. If she didn't like one boyfriend, she'd toss him aside for the next. She was notoriously picky, often going on and on about her dates, dissecting them like she would a biology assignment. She was also as cute as a button, and her blond hair and sparkling hazel eyes seemed to draw the attention of young men with little effort. For her to celebrate a one-month anniversary was a big deal.

"Emmett must be a pretty special young man," Evelyn mused as she turned her attention away from the storm and back to her work.

Stacia sighed and put her chin in her hand, her eyes taking on a dreamy, faraway look. "He might be 'the one.'"

"Wow." Evelyn raised her eyebrows, enjoying the dating escapades of Stacia, while thanking God that she had been happily married for almost thirty-five years. "I don't miss dating, even a little."

The sky continued to darken as the rain picked up its intensity. Evelyn loved a good storm, but she lived less than a mile west of the hospital, which meant she walked to work. If the storm didn't let up within the next two hours, she'd have to call her husband, James, to come and pick her up. And since he was busy on a secret project today, the last thing she wanted to do was disturb him.

"I can't imagine being married to the same man for thirty-five years, even if he is 'the one.'" Stacia scrunched up her nose. "Isn't it boring?"

A smile warmed Evelyn's lips as she thought back to the journey she and James had shared since the day they said, "I do." "It's anything but boring," she told the much younger woman, wishing she had the words to describe all the intricacies of marriage. "James never ceases to amaze me, and thirty-five years later I'm still learning fascinating things about his personality."

"Hmm." Stacia turned back to her desk, truly seeming to puzzle over Evelyn's comment. "I guess I'll have to take your word for it."

Evelyn's desk phone rang, and the little red light started to blink. She pushed aside thoughts of the storm and of Stacia's marital misgivings and answered the phone. "Records Department, how may I help you?"

"Evelyn?" Shirley Bashore's voice came through the line.

"Hi, Shirley. What can I do for you?"

"We have a patient who's being transferred to the intensive care unit," Shirley said. "Can you come over to the ER and gather her personal belongings?"

"Of course. I'll be there in a couple of minutes."

"Thank you." Shirley hung up, and Evelyn could only imagine how busy her friend was in the ER. Shirley was one of the most dedicated nurses at Mercy. She had recently moved to Charleston from Atlanta to take care of her aging mother, and she and Evelyn had become fast friends.

"I have to run over to the ER," Evelyn said to Stacia as she logged off her computer. She never left her program running. The patient files they worked with on a daily basis were confidential and protected by HIPAA, so she was always overly cautious to log out of any computer she accessed in the hospital. "I should be back soon."

Stacia lifted her hand to wave at Evelyn, indicating she heard her.

The records department was on the main floor of the hospital, connected to the modern grand front entrance, not too far away from the gift shop. Though this wing of the hospital had been built in 1829, it had been lovingly maintained and restored over the years and was, by far, Evelyn's favorite part of the hospital. In her opinion, nothing could ever compare to the historical architecture and charm of a nineteenth-century building. But over time, as the hospital had been enlarged, the architects had done a seamless job matching the newer additions to the old. The birthing center and cancer wings were modern and amazing in their own right.

She pushed open the door leading out of the records department and stepped into the main hall. An older couple walked past with a bouquet of mixed flowers and a pink balloon that said WELCOME BABY GIRL. It made Evelyn smile to see their happy faces. Two doctors in white coats were close behind, their heads bent in conversation, and a well-dressed sales rep passed them heading in the opposite direction, her wheeled bag zipping along the floor on her way out.

Evelyn loved the hustle and bustle of the hospital. She loved the excitement, the energy, and the new challenges each day presented.

Her heels clicked on the hard tile as she walked the short distance to the ER, past a bank of elevators and a grand staircase leading to the second floor. Soft piano music from the main entrance floated gently on the air.

As always, the ER was bursting with activity. The glass doors opened automatically, and Evelyn stepped into the waiting room. She was well known to the staff and waved at the registration gals as she walked past them and into the hub of the department. Shirley stood near the nurses' station, speaking to one of the unit coordinators. She wore her blue scrubs and had a stethoscope around her neck. When she saw Evelyn approach, she turned her full attention to her with a smile.

"Thanks for coming so quickly." Shirley reached behind the desk and lifted a white plastic bag. In the middle of the bag were the words PERSONAL BELONGINGS printed in blue. Underneath were two lines, one for the patient's name and one for the patient's room number. "I'm a little anxious to get these things to a secure location."

Strands of silver weaved through Shirley's black hair, which she pulled back in a simple ponytail. The only adornment she chose to wear was a simple gold cross necklace.

"Why are you so anxious to get these things secured?" Evelyn asked, curious about the items in the bag. It wasn't unusual for Shirley to call the records department to come and collect personal belongings from patients. Often, a person came in alone, especially after an accident, and it took time to contact next of kin. Cell phones, jewelry, wallets, and other valuable items needed to be put somewhere safe until the patient or the patient's family member could collect them. The hospital safe was located in the records department and was as tight and secure as Fort Knox.

Shirley dipped her hand into the bag and pulled out a small object. "The patient we just moved up to the ICU had this in her pocket when she came in." She opened her hand to reveal a beautiful ruby and diamond ring. "It looks really valuable."

Evelyn took the ring out of Shirley's hand and looked at it a little closer. It was an exquisite piece of jewelry, large enough for a man's hand. "I've never seen anything quite like it."

"I didn't have time to look at it closely," Shirley said as she handed Evelyn the bag. "But it needs to be put into the safe as soon as possible. I'm sure Ms. Robertson would be anxious to see it secured as well."

The ER was no place to inspect such a valuable piece of jewelry, so Evelyn slipped it back into the bag. "Can I get the patient's name and room number?"

"Her name is Jeanne Robertson, and she's in ICU room 4120. The police have taken all of her personal information and are trying to locate her family." Shirley shook her head. "But right now she's all alone. She was in a pretty rough car accident and sustained some serious head and leg injuries."

Evelyn winced. "Was anyone else involved?"

"As far as I know, there was only one other person, and he's just being discharged, but the police are waiting to question him." Shirley nodded toward a man walking out of one of the examination rooms. He was dressed in a brown uniform with a delivery service badge affixed to the arm. "He was driving a delivery truck and had to swerve to miss a vehicle that had stopped to turn. When he swerved, it pushed Ms. Robertson off the road and she ran right into a tree. Unfortunately, she wasn't wearing a seat belt."

"Oh my," Evelyn said. "He must feel awful."

If the man's troubled face and rounded shoulders were any indication, he *did* feel awful.

"I hate to run," Shirley said, "but we're short-staffed today and I'm needed."

Evelyn smiled and put her hand on Shirley's arm. "No worries. I'll take Ms. Robertson's things back to the records department and get them put away until she's ready for them."

"Thanks, Evelyn." Shirley grabbed a clipboard from the nurses' station and headed toward a patient room.

The bag was heavy as Evelyn walked back to the sliding glass doors. She passed the delivery man, who glanced at her. His gaze slipped to the bag with Jeanne's name on it and then to Evelyn again. He opened his mouth like he was going to speak, but a police officer approached and captured his attention.

All the way back to the records department, Evelyn could only think of two things: she needed to get the ring secured as soon as possible, and she prayed Ms. Robertson would recover to reclaim her things.

The rain continued to pour outside the hospital as Evelyn reentered the records department. Stacia was on the phone, answering questions about how a person could get their records released to another hospital. Two other staff members were also at work, Pam and Rick. Pam was speaking to a patient at the front desk who was asking for a copy of her daughter's immunization record, while Rick was inputting data into a computer. As the manager of the department, Evelyn oversaw a staff of five. Three of them, Stacia, Pam, and Rick, were full-time, and the other two were part-time.

Evelyn took the white patient bag into the Vault. It was the original records room, built in 1829, and was full of dozens of file cabinets. The red brick walls and maple floors were a throwback, but it was the original light fixtures that made Evelyn feel like she was walking into a different era.

She had spent several weeks at the beginning of the summer organizing the room, after years of putting off the task. The disorderly, dusty files had been in need of some attention for as long as she could remember, but there had always been some other project to be completed. There was plenty more organizing to do, but at least the dust had been tamed, thanks to the help of a couple of student interns from the College of Charleston. It made Evelyn feel a little bit lighter to know that part of the daunting task was finished.

The hospital safe was also located in this room. It was a huge walk-in, with a heavy, black metal door. Only a handful of hospital staff members had access to the combination, including Evelyn.

After opening the safe, she put the bag on a shelf and took out the ring once again. She stepped back into the room and inspected the ring under the antique lighting. A brilliant oval rose cut ruby sparkled in the center. It had to be at least three carats with smaller diamonds encircling it and set in a thick silver band. Evelyn had educated herself about antique jewelry when she and James looked for engagement rings. With their love of history, they had both wanted something old and unique. They had settled on a WWII-era ring, much like her mother's.

"Knock, knock," a woman's voice met Evelyn's ears a moment before Joy Atkins poked her head into the Vault. "I heard about the ring. Oh, is that it?"

Joy was the manager of the hospital gift shop. Since news traveled fast at Mercy, Evelyn wasn't surprised to see Joy—or Anne Mabry, another friend and volunteer extraordinaire at the hospital, who stepped into the room right behind Joy.

"I ran into Shirley when I was dropping off a bouquet of flowers to one of the nurses in the ER," Joy said, her blue eyes wide with interest. "She told me about the ring and said you were putting it into the safe. I thought I'd come and see it since my shift just ended."

"I have it here." Evelyn held up the heavy ring. The ruby caught the light and sparkled.

Joy and Anne came closer to look at it.

"Do you think it's real?" Joy's dark hair was worn in a short and simple bob, which she often tucked behind her ears. She smelled like the candles she sold in the gift shop, and she was wearing a pretty earrings and necklace set she more than likely purchased from there.

"It looks real to me," Anne said in a distracted tone as she looked closely at the ring. She wore her blond hair a little longer, close to her shoulders. Though she was always dressed well, it was her perpetual smile that made her stand out in a crowd. No matter where she went or what task she was given, Anne was often smiling.

"My goodness," Joy said. "It's immense."

"And old." Evelyn turned the ring in her fingers. "Do you see the band? It's made of silver, which was popular during the 1700s. And the rounded shape, with the flat bottom, is called a rose cut ruby. It was common from the 1500s up to the 1800s."

"Does it have an inscription?" Anne asked.

"There is an inscription." Evelyn squinted and looked closer. "'LPOC,'" she read.

"LPOC?" Joy frowned. "What does that stand for?"

"I don't know." Evelyn shrugged. "Maybe someone's initials?"

"It doesn't look as worn as you would expect for something so old." Anne reached out and lightly touched the ruby.

"I can't imagine it would be worn often," Joy mused, "especially in this day and age. Can you imagine how conspicuous you would feel walking around with this on your hand?"

"What about the woman who owns it?" Anne looked at Evelyn. "Do you know anything about her?"

Evelyn shook her head. "Just her name."

"I heard she's unconscious." Joy shook her head. "She had serious head trauma from her accident. It could be days or weeks before she regains consciousness—if she ever does."

"Is she expected to live?" Anne asked.

"Shirley didn't tell me much." Joy lifted her shoulder. "But it doesn't sound good."

"We'll need to add her to our prayer list." Evelyn stepped into the safe and put the ring back into the bag.

"And we should add the man who caused the accident," Joy said. "I heard he's pretty shaken up about the whole thing."

"Can you imagine the guilt?" Anne pressed her lips together. "Poor man. He must feel terrible about what happened."

The ladies were quiet for a moment, and then Evelyn stepped out of the safe and closed the door tight. "James purchased my engagement ring in an antique shop, and ever since then, old rings have intrigued me." She held up her left hand for them to see the WWII-era ring. "I like to think that the person who owned this before me had a long and happy marriage. Sometimes it's hard to learn the history behind jewelry, but when you do, it can be fascinating. I think I'll do a little research into the ring, just for fun. It's not every day we have something so beautiful come into Mercy."

"If you learn anything interesting," Joy said, "please let me know."

"And me," Anne added. "I'm sure there's a great story behind that piece of jewelry."

Evelyn followed the ladies out of the Vault and into the records department.

Joy glanced at the clock. It was past three, which was when she usually went home. "I'm off. I have a meeting this afternoon with my garden club. I'll see you two tomorrow."

Evelyn and Anne waved at Joy as she left.

"And what about you?" Anne asked Evelyn. "Anything fun planned for after work?"

"I don't know." Evelyn shrugged. "James mentioned to me this morning that he had a surprise project he was going to work on today and that I needed to clear my schedule for this evening."

Anne's eyebrows rose high. "That sounds exciting. What do you think he has in mind?"

"I have no idea." Evelyn lifted her hands. "I'm completely clueless."

"Did he mention anything over the last couple of weeks that might give you an idea?"

"Nothing I can think of. I've been racking my brain all day, and still nothing. But he seemed very excited, so I've been kind of excited all day too."

Anne smiled. "Now you've got *me* excited. I can't wait to hear about it."

"I'm sure I'll have lots to tell you in the morning." Evelyn's desk phone started to ring.

"I'll let you go. See you tomorrow."

"Bye." Evelyn waved at Anne and then took a seat at her desk.

She still had a couple of hours of work ahead of her, but the reminder of James's surprise had her wishing she could go home early. What in the world could he be up to?

Chapter Two

THE RAIN HAD STOPPED, BUT the sky was still dark and menacing as Evelyn left Mercy to walk home. James had called and offered to pick her up, but she had her small travel umbrella in her purse if she needed it. Besides, after sitting at her desk for most of the day, she craved the exercise.

Warm, earthy smells wafted up to her nose as she walked the familiar distance from the hospital to her front door. She passed Rainbow Row, the pretty houses painted in soft pastels, then Charleston City Hall and the Cathedral of St. John the Baptist, until she arrived at her home on Short Street. The narrow, two-story house she and James shared was painted a cheerful creamy yellow with lots of white trim and Charleston Green shutters. The familiar dark green was purported to have originated after the War Between the States when the United States government sent buckets of black paint to help the war-torn city of Charleston rebuild. But the citizens didn't want everything to be painted black, so they added the now famous green to the paint and Charleston Green was born. It graced almost every house in one manner or another in the historic district, and was appropriate for Evelyn's home, built in 1870.

Evelyn waved at a neighbor as she walked up the short flight of concrete stairs to her stoop. Her street was quiet, with historic homes, most of them Charleston Single Houses, much like hers. The style was quite popular on the peninsula in the early years when the long, narrow lots were laid out. Evelyn's house, like the others, was only one room wide and originally boasted a two-story piazza on the side, which had been enclosed by her parents when they bought the home in the early 1960s. The piazza was now a long hallway, running the length of the house, which Evelyn entered.

An unfamiliar noise met her ears the moment she stepped into the house. She frowned as she hung up her purse on the coat-tree near the door and set her house keys in the antique calling card dish on the hall table. Immediately to her right was the dining room, which they only used when they had company for dinner. Next to the dining room was a small hallway and the stairs, which went up to the second level and down to the basement. On the other side of the stairway was the kitchen, and then the living room was at the back of the house. The noise she heard was coming from the kitchen.

"James?" Evelyn asked.

"In here," he called back. "Come see what I've been doing, Evie."

There was a hint of excitement and anticipation in his voice. Evelyn slipped off her shoes and walked down the pine-plank hallway to the kitchen. The room could be closed off with pocket doors, but they rarely ever pulled the doors closed, since the kitchen had no natural light and depended upon the bank of windows in the hall.

Evelyn was not prepared for the sight that met her eyes when she walked into the kitchen.

James stood in a pair of faded denim jeans and a worn T-shirt, his tool belt hugging his waist. Dust covered his beard, which he had recently trimmed, and sweat glistened on his brow. But it was his pleased-with-himself grin that caught her attention. "Surprise!"

Where the old Formica laminate countertop had been earlier in the day, there was now nothing on the top of Evelyn's base cabinets. The old stainless-steel sink and the dated appliances were also no longer standing in the kitchen. Only the 1960s cabinets remained where they had been placed by Evelyn's parents so long ago. Evelyn had sanded them and painted them white when she and James took ownership of the house soon after their wedding, but that was the only real change she'd ever made to the room.

"What's going on?" Evelyn wasn't sure if she should be excited or alarmed.

She had no kitchen.

"I'm giving the kitchen a little face-lift." James grinned. "It's the last room in the house we haven't really worked on, so I thought I'd use the last few weeks of my summer vacation to bring it up-to-date."

James was a history professor at Charleston Southern University and would be heading back at the end of the month to resume classes. He usually spent his summer break playing golf, fishing, and doing odd projects around the house. Over the years, they had slowly updated the work that her parents had done by painting walls, refinishing the wood floors, and changing out bathroom fixtures—but they had never done anything major. They had often talked about remodeling the kitchen, but Evelyn had always hoped they could hire out the work and maybe take a little vacation during the worst of it. She'd spent years with her parents as they remodeled the house the first time and had no good memories of that experience. Fights, chaos, messes, and the worries over financial burdens had created a lot of tension between her parents. Evelyn had often worried they'd get divorced and had decided long ago that remodeling a house wasn't for her. Hiring it out was one thing—doing it themselves was quite another.

She was speechless. All she could do was stare at the mess and wonder how long it would be until she had a kitchen sink again.

Her husband's smile began to fall. "Well? What do you think?"

"Where is everything?"

"I hauled it out to the back of the house. A dump truck will be here in the morning to take it away."

She didn't want to disappoint him or throw a bucket of cold water on his enthusiasm, but Evelyn liked cleanliness and order. Already, there was a fine sheen of dust on all the surfaces, and when she glanced through the doors and into the living room, she could see all her dishes, cookware, and miscellaneous kitchen supplies stacked haphazardly in crates along the wall. How would they function this way? Unhappy memories of her childhood resurfaced, and she could feel the anxiety starting to creep in.

"H-how long do you think it will take?" she asked, still trying to maintain her composure at this surprise.

James set his hands on the edge of the cabinet sitting between them. "I head back to work in three weeks, so I'd like to get it done by then, if possible."

"Do you think it can be done?"

"That's the plan. But we'll need to order the countertop and the appliances soon so they arrive in time."

They had always dreamed of putting in granite countertops. Evelyn had even been perusing design magazines for ideas, but she hadn't settled on anything in particular. Could she make up her mind in time to place an order?

When she met James's gaze, she saw the hope and anticipation in his eyes and knew she would have to make the best of this situation. Yes, it would be a major inconvenience, and yes, it would test her patience—not to mention her anxieties from childhood—but it was a gift from her husband and she didn't want to make the job more difficult than necessary for him. It took a bit of effort, but she smiled.

It was all the encouragement James needed. His grin returned, and he rounded the cabinets to come stand next to her.

"I have so many ideas." His hands were animated as he spoke. "I think we should leave the same footprint, since it offers the best use of the space, and the cabinets are in great condition. They just need a fresh coat of paint, new door panels, and updated hardware. We've set enough money aside to get whatever appliances you'd like, as long as they fit the dimensions of the space."

As James continued to share his thoughts and ideas, a seed of excitement was planted in Evelyn's chest. Maybe this inconvenience would be worth the effort.

"I've made an appointment at the kitchen design store tomorrow after you get off work," he said. "They'll have countertop samples and cabinet door options for us to look at. The sooner we get things ordered, the sooner the kitchen will be finished."

"And you plan to do all the work on your own?" Evelyn asked, hoping he had plans to hire out the work.

James offered a good-natured scoff. "Of course I'm going to do it all myself." He was a jack-of-all-trades type and Evelyn had always been confident in his abilities, but he wasn't getting any younger and he was undertaking a big job.

"Are you sure?" she asked.

"Evie." He took her hands in his dusty ones. "I don't want you to worry about a thing. This is my gift to you. I've got this covered." He gave her a quick kiss and then continued to share his ideas.

Evelyn took a deep breath, determined to trust her husband with this project.

Yes, they were about to embark on a difficult task, but at the end of it all, she'd have a brand-new kitchen and a good reason to invite some of her friends over to celebrate.

How hard could it really be to live without a kitchen for two or three weeks?

A crack of thunder forced Evelyn to open her eyes the next morning as she lay in her four-poster bed. She slept on the side facing the two double doors leading out onto a narrow deck overlooking the walled garden. Usually, it was bright summer sunshine that greeted her in the morning. But not today.

She tried not to let the overcast weather dampen her spirits. Mornings were generally her favorite time of the day. She always woke up early enough to study a short devotion in the sitting room attached to the master suite and then get dressed and make a bowl of oatmeal and a pot of coffee before heading to the hospital by eight.

But today felt a little off. Usually, James was in bed next to her, preferring to rise a bit later during the summer. But this morning his side of the bed was empty, and when she rolled over to glance into the bathroom, it was dark and he was nowhere to be seen.

Another crash of thunder filled the air—or at least, it sounded like thunder. Evelyn pushed aside the bed covering and stepped onto the rug. She grabbed her robe from the foot of the bed and pulled it on as she walked to the french doors nearest to her.

Down below, at the back of the house, stood a large truck. One man was tossing pieces of Evelyn's kitchen counter into the back of the truck—which was making the loud noise that had woken her up—while another was positioning her old appliances onto a platform that looked like an elevator. The men were not being quiet, by any means, and Evelyn was afraid they'd disturb the neighbors.

A quick glance at the clock told her it was too early to be making so much noise.

She slipped on her house shoes and padded out of the bedroom and down the steps. "James, those men will wake the neighborhood," she said as she rounded the corner.

But James wasn't in the kitchen.

Evelyn frowned. Where had her husband gone?

The noise continued outside, so Evelyn walked down the hall and entered the living room. A large fireplace dominated the space, but it was the bank of windows on the side, and the two french doors at the back, that made it one of her favorite rooms. The natural lighting lent a warm and welcoming feel to the room, even on overcast days like today.

James stood on the back stoop, watching the men as they loaded the kitchen castoffs. Evelyn's presence must have caught his eye because he turned and grinned at her through the window, and then he opened the door. "Good morning," he said. "How did you sleep?"

She didn't want to tell him she'd slept rather poorly. Her dreams had been filled with unwanted memories of her childhood and all sorts of things that could go wrong with the kitchen project. Instead, she chose to smile and give him his morning kiss. "I've slept better."

"I'm sorry." He seemed a little distracted as he turned his attention back to the garbagemen.

"Do they have to be so loud?" she asked, peeking around James's shoulder to the house next door. "Someone will call the police to complain."

"They're almost done."

The man tossing the countertop into the truck threw the last piece in and then started to help the other one load up the appliances.

"See." James nodded at the truck. "The loudest part is over."

"And none too soon." A light turned on in another neighboring house, and a curious face poked out a back door.

Rain began to fall on the walled-in garden, making dark splotches on the stone patio pavers. The vine-covered walls and arbors, along with the fountain and wooden benches, were also getting wet.

"Let's get inside," James said to Evelyn. "I looked at the forecast, and it sounds like we're in for another stormy day."

They went back into the house, and Evelyn looked at the piles of kitchen items James had stacked in the living room yesterday. "Where's the coffeemaker?"

"Um." James surveyed the crates and squinted. "That's a good question."

"And my oatmeal?" she asked hopefully.

He shrugged. "Even if we found it, there's no stove to cook it on." His eyes brightened. "But you could make it in the microwave. I held on to that for now." James left her side and went to one of the piles. The microwave was buried under several crates, but at least it was visible and easy to find.

"Don't worry about it now." Evelyn went to her husband and put her hand on his arm to stop him. "I'll just leave a bit early and grab something at the hospital coffee shop."

"Are you sure?" He frowned. "I don't want to interrupt your routine."

Evelyn chuckled. "It's a little late for that."

James wrapped his arms around her. "I promise to have a make-shift kitchen set up for you in the dining room by the time you get home today."

She snuggled into his embrace. "A makeshift kitchen?"

"I'll set up the coffeemaker, the microwave, and the toaster oven. I can send out a text to the church and see if someone has a college-dorm-sized refrigerator we can borrow. And we can eat off paper plates and use plastic utensils for a couple of weeks. Tomorrow you can have your coffee and oatmeal, just like usual."

Evelyn was starting to get into the spirit of things. "Tonight I'll bring home some takeout for supper." It would be a treat, since they didn't eat out often.

James nodded. "See. We can do this. We might even have a little fun."

Fun might not be the right word to describe the next few weeks, but it wouldn't last forever.

"We can do anything for two or three weeks, right?" James asked.

"Of course we can."

"Good." He kissed the top of her head and let her go. "Now go get ready for work and don't mind me. The garbage truck is returning tomorrow for our cabinet doors, linoleum flooring, and the old light fixtures. I have a lot more demolition to do today. It could get loud and messy."

Evelyn tried not to cringe. "I'll be out of your way as soon as possible." She was eager to get to work and do a little more research on the ruby and diamond ring in the hospital safe. She paused on her way out of the living room. "In all the excitement of the remodel, I forgot to tell you about a beautiful ring that came in to Mercy yesterday."

"Oh?" As a history professor, James loved hearing about antiques and old mysteries.

"If I had to guess, I'd say it's from the sixteenth or seventeenth century. It's a rose cut ruby in a silver setting."

"That old? What do you know about it?"

"Not much. The owner was unconscious, and she's in the ICU. I hope to carve a little time out of my day to do some research. I've never seen a ring quite like this one before."

"Take a couple of pictures and text them to me if you get a chance." They loved researching and learning about history together, especially antique jewelry. "I'll see if I can help identify its age."

"Okay." She wished he could stop by the hospital to look at the ring himself, but she wouldn't ask him to take time out of his busy day.

The rain started to pour in earnest outside the windows as Evelyn walked down the hall. She would have to drive to work, which was just one more thing to disrupt her daily routine, but she refused to let it put her out of sorts.

When she reached her bedroom, she quickly found the outfit she would wear for the day. She often chose a simple pair of slacks and a button-down blouse. Today, she would wear a sunflower pin she had received as a gift from a church friend. Her pin collection was vast, and she rarely wore the same pin twice in one month. The sunflower made her think of bright, warm days and would be a good reminder to keep a smile on her face, despite the poor weather.

Evelyn firmly believed that attitudes were a result of an individual's choices—and she was choosing to stay positive, especially when she remembered the beautiful ruby and diamond ring in the safe at Mercy.

As soon as she had a minute at work, she would do a little research.

The thought put an extra bounce in her step and a smile on her face.

Chapter Three

THE HOSPITAL PARKING GARAGE WAS unusually full for a Tuesday morning. Evelyn rarely had to deal with parking her car and wasn't impressed with the situation now. She had to drive around for several minutes, up and down the various ramps, to find a spot—but she refused to let it frustrate her. When she finally found a place to park her car, it was on the top level, and she had to pull her umbrella out of her purse so she wouldn't get wet. It would have probably been faster just to walk to work, but it hardly mattered now. The rain was pouring so hard, she kept her head down and focused on avoiding the puddles that had gathered on the unforgiving concrete.

A large truck turned the corner and Evelyn stepped to the side to get out of the way, but as the truck passed it hit a puddle, and muddy water sprayed her pants.

Evelyn stopped in her tracks and stared down at her legs. The truck driver continued on, seemingly unaware of the mess left in his wake. Frustration bubbled up in Evelyn's chest again, but this time, she struggled to push it aside. Could nothing go right this morning?

She hurried the rest of the way, down several flights of stairs and under the covered walkway, to enter the building. Once she was inside, she lowered her wet umbrella. Under the glow of the lights, her pants looked even worse than they did outside. She would have gone home to change, but she was already late and didn't feel like fighting the storm or the parking lot again. And she didn't want to call James to bring her a new pair of slacks. He had more important things to worry about today.

With a sigh, she decided to spot-clean her pants in the ladies' room when she had a chance. But first, she needed a cup of coffee. Everything always looked better with a little caffeine running through her system. And the best place in the hospital for coffee, and a sympathetic ear, was the gift shop.

Thankfully she didn't have far to go.

"Good morning, Evelyn," Joy said when she spotted Evelyn's entrance into the gift shop.

The small store, positioned in the grand lobby, smelled of flowers, candles, and Raphael's coffee, which Joy ordered from her old neighborhood in Houston, Texas. She brewed several pots a day and offered a free cup to anyone who asked. Evelyn didn't usually stop by the gift shop for a cup until midmorning, because she had her first serving at home.

"You're here earlier than usual." Joy stood behind the counter unpacking a box of small figurines. She smiled at Evelyn but then must have noticed the look on Evelyn's face. Her smile fell and she said, "What's wrong?" Her gaze traveled the length of Evelyn's clothes, and she winced. "A run-in with a puddle?"

"Could I get a cup of coffee?" It was the only thing Evelyn could say for now. She was afraid if she started to complain about her morning before she had some coffee, she might not be able to stop.

"Sure." Joy left her small project and went to the coffeepot. "It just finished brewing."

Thankfully, there was no one else in the shop at this early hour. Joy always came in an hour before the store opened to get her paperwork done, arrange displays, and have her own cup of coffee.

"So, tell me what's going on." Joy handed Evelyn a cup of the steaming brew.

Evelyn inhaled the steam and closed her eyes briefly before she took a sip. Joy made the best coffee in the hospital, but Evelyn was fairly certain it was her friend's compassion that made it sweet.

"James decided to remodel our kitchen," Evelyn began. "He's planning on doing it all himself, and he wanted it to be a surprise, so I didn't have any time to mentally prepare myself."

"And I know how much it takes for you to embrace change."

It was one of Evelyn's worst traits. She liked things to stay neat and tidy—but most of all predictable. Change and upheaval were two things she tried to avoid at all cost. That was one of the reasons she and James had purchased her family home and why she had worked at Mercy for over thirty years. Consistency and stability were very important to her.

"Don't you want him to remodel the kitchen?" Joy asked. "I thought you were excited about the prospect."

"I am—I do want to remodel it. But it would've been nice to hire it out and maybe go on vacation so we could avoid the disruption to our daily lives. If nothing else, it would've been helpful to prepare myself for the chaos in advance. And James knows this about me. It took me three weeks to decide on the new rug for under our bed—and I just chose a simple gray one with no patterns or designs."

Joy smiled and put her hand on Evelyn's. "Did you and James fight this morning?"

"No." Evelyn shook her head and told her friend why she was in such a state of frustration, starting with the rude wakeup call and ending with the mud puddle disaster. "I know James is doing this out of the kindness of his heart, and he probably figured I've been talking about this remodel for so long, I was ready. But he only has three weeks before he returns to work, and he wants me to make a lot of big decisions very quickly."

"Do you think that maybe he knows this about you and he's trying to encourage you to step out of your comfort zone?"

Evelyn laughed. "That sounds about right. James is patient, to a fault, but he also wants what's best for me." She sighed. "At least I have a job to keep my mind occupied."

"And something to investigate." Joy leaned forward. "Did you learn anything new about the ruby ring?"

Evelyn shook her head and took another sip of her coffee. "I hope to do a little investigating today, after I get some work wrapped up." She glanced at the clock over the counter and saw that it was two minutes to eight. "Which reminds me, I better get going. Everyone will be arriving soon. Thanks for the coffee and conversation, Joy."

Joy smiled. "My pleasure."

Evelyn walked the short distance to the old wing and into the records department. Stacia was already there working with Pam and Rick, who were at their desks inputting data.

Stacia sat in the front of the room and glanced up to smile at Evelyn. "Good morning."

"Good morning." Evelyn went to her desk and set down her purse and her cup of coffee.

Stacia turned in her swivel chair. "A man came in here a couple of minutes ago with a strange question."

"Oh?" Evelyn took a seat and flipped on her computer. They received any manner of questions on a daily basis. "Did he need someone's records?"

"No." Stacia frowned. "He was asking if I knew anything about a ring."

Evelyn paused and gave her full attention to Stacia. "A ring?"

"He said it was a ruby and diamond ring, and he was wondering if we were holding it for a patient who was brought into the ER yesterday."

"Who was he?"

"I don't know." Stacia shrugged. "I've never seen him before. I thought he was coming in to deliver a package. He was wearing a brown delivery uniform."

A vision of the man in the ER the day before popped into Evelyn's head. "Was he a really tall man with curly hair and brown eyes?"

Stacia nodded. "Actually," she said as she squinted her eyes in thought. "His name was embroidered on his jacket now that I think about it—but I didn't really pay attention. It was Will, or Wayne, or something starting with a *W*, I think."

What was the delivery man doing in the records department? "Did he say why he came looking for it here?"

"No. He just asked me if I knew anything about a ruby and diamond ring and if it was being held in this department."

"What did you tell him?"

Stacia lifted her hands. "I told him I didn't know anything about a ring, but if it was being held here for a patient, it would be in the safe back in the Vault." She pointed toward the old records room.

Evelyn closed her eyes briefly.

"Shouldn't I have told him where the safe is?" Stacia asked.

"I'd prefer we don't tell people," Evelyn conceded. "But I guess no real harm is done. Did he say why he wanted to know about the ring?"

"No. After I told him I didn't know anything about it, he asked if I had a supervisor. I told him your name and gave him the records department number so he can call if he has any questions." She glanced toward the office door. "I'm actually surprised you didn't run into him in the hall. He stepped out just a couple of moments before you came in. You might still be able to catch him in the lobby."

Evelyn shook her head. "I'm already running late today. If he wants to talk about the ring, he can call me, but I can't give him any information. The ring is the property of a patient. I'm not at liberty to discuss his or her personal information with anyone."

Stacia nodded and went back to her work.

But Evelyn wasn't so fast to dismiss the delivery driver. If what Shirley said yesterday was true—and she had no reason not to believe Shirley—then the driver was at fault for the accident that had landed Jeanne Robertson in the ER. What did he have to do with the ring? How did he even know of its existence, since Shirley said the ring was in Jeanne's pocket? And why would he think he had the right to inquire after it?

There were so many questions swirling around in Evelyn's head about this ring. She couldn't wait until the patient was conscious and could tell her more about it.

Evelyn's day continued in the same vein as it had started. It seemed that whatever could go wrong did go wrong. It wasn't until lunchtime that she finally had the chance to put aside her work for a little break. She had plans to meet Joy, Anne, and Shirley for a quick lunch in the hospital coffee shop, but she didn't have to be there for at least ten minutes.

Pushing away from her desk, she stood and stretched, rubbing the lower part of her back to get out the knots. Her curiosity about the ruby ring had continued to mount all day, so she went into the Vault and opened the safe to look at it a little closer.

She was no expert, but the ruby and diamonds looked like excellent quality. The silver band had quite a bit of luster for being so old. But it was the engraved *LPOC* that had her most intrigued. What did it mean, and who put it there?

After she set the ring back in the safe, she went to her desk and opened up an internet browser. She typed in RUBY RING, LPOC in the search bar and hit Enter. Immediately, the search pulled up hundreds of possibilities, but it was the first link that stood out to her.

THE EIGHT RINGS OF THE LORDS PROPRIETORS OF CAROLINA.

Evelyn's heart rate picked up speed as she clicked on the link and saw an emerald ring with a circle of diamonds set in a silver band. It had many of the same qualities and appearance as the ruby ring in the safe and was one of the eight rings of the Lords Proprietors of Carolina. Could the ruby ring be part of a collection of eight rings? What would be the odds?

She read the article and then pressed PRINT, her excitement mounting with everything she was learning. Even if this ring wasn't part of the original set, it was still a fascinating piece of history she'd never heard about. She clicked on another article and read even more about the rings. All too soon, she glanced at the clock and realized she was late for lunch. The other ladies would love to see what she had found, so she quickly printed off the last article she'd read. Only Jeanne Robertson could answer her questions, but Evelyn hadn't heard yet if she was conscious. Maybe Shirley could shed some light on her condition.

Evelyn went to the printer and grabbed the papers. "I'm taking my lunch break," she said to Stacia. "I'll be back in an hour, and then you can take your break."

Stacia put her hand up in an okay gesture and continued to work at her computer.

The hallway was busy when Evelyn stepped out of the old Angel Wing and into the newer lobby. She had to wait for a man in a wheelchair to pass, and then she walked across the lobby to the coffee shop tucked into the corner. Her pulse was thrumming with excitement as she located her three friends, already seated at a table near one of the floor-to-ceiling windows in the little eatery. The rain was still falling and the world outside was a riot of colors. Beautiful grass pathways, often referred to as the Grove, made for a picturesque view out the windows. If it had been nice out, they might have eaten their lunches on one of the many tables just beyond the hospital walls.

"There you are," Anne said when she spotted Evelyn. She smiled and patted the seat next to her. "I saved you a spot."

Evelyn took the seat and set the papers on the tabletop. The others had already stopped at the counter and ordered their drinks and meals, but Evelyn was too excited to take the time to get something to eat.

"Look what I found," she said, nearly bursting with the anticipation of sharing her amazing discovery. She realized, too late, that she had interrupted their conversation. "I'm sorry."

The other three laughed and Shirley said, "No worries, Evelyn. I was just telling them that our accident patient woke up today."

"Jeanne Robertson?" Evelyn's excitement continued to escalate. "She's conscious?"

Shirley nodded. "She regained consciousness this morning."

"How is she doing?"

"She's had a few evaluations, and everything looks really promising. They're planning to move her from the ICU to a general bed on the second floor later today."

"That's wonderful to hear." Evelyn couldn't wait to visit with her, especially in light of the discovery about the ring. "Do you think she's ready for some company?"

"Probably tomorrow," Shirley said as she placed her hands around her coffee cup. "She's sore, as you can imagine, and still pretty shaken up about the whole thing."

Evelyn understood perfectly. "I'll plan to see her tomorrow, when she's feeling a little more prepared for visitors."

"What did you have to tell us that was so important?" Joy asked, her blue eyes shining with interest. "Does it have to do with the ring?"

"Yes." Evelyn spread out the papers she had printed. "If the ring is what I think it is, then it's part of a collection of eight rings given to the Lords Proprietors of Carolina by King Charles II in 1663. That year, the king signed a charter granting all the land that is now North and South Carolina to these eight men."

"I know a little about the Lords Proprietors," Joy said. "Weren't they somehow instrumental in helping restore Charles II to his throne after the English Civil War?"

Evelyn nodded enthusiastically. "That's exactly right. These men were the eight biggest supporters of the king, and they all put their lives on the line to see that he was restored to the throne. As a way of thanking them, he granted them a charter to the Carolinas, gave each of them new titles, land in England, and pensions, and elevated them within the English government."

"Many places in North and South Carolina are named after those eight men," Anne added. "Sir Anthony Ashley Cooper, 1st Earl of Shaftesbury, was one of the Lords Proprietors."

"Is that why the two rivers on either side of the Charleston peninsula are named the Ashley River and the Cooper River?" Shirley asked.

"Yes." Evelyn continued to nod. "Apparently, when the king granted them the charter to Carolina, he also had eight rings made, one for each lord." This was the part that excited Evelyn the most. She pointed to the page that explained the rings in more detail. "Each ring was made from a jewel in the king's collection, and each one was different. There was a diamond, a garnet, an amethyst, an emerald, a pearl, a sapphire, a peridot, and a ruby. Each was encircled by tiny diamonds and each was engraved with the letters LPOC for Lords Proprietors of Carolina inside the silver bands."

The other three ladies stared at Evelyn.

"And it was the ruby ring that was given to Sir Anthony Ashley Cooper," Evelyn said. "He was the closest to the king and was given the task of creating the Grand Model that laid out the city of Charleston, as well as the Fundamental Constitutions of Carolina."

"Do you think the ruby ring in the safe is the actual ring owned by Sir Anthony Ashley Cooper?" Anne asked.

"I don't know." Evelyn shook her head. "But it sounds an awful lot like the original ring, doesn't it?"

"Did you learn what happened to each of the rings?" Shirley asked.

"That's where it gets really interesting."

"*That's* where it gets interesting?" Joy asked, laughter in her voice. "This is already amazing—I can't imagine it getting better."

"Each of the rings has been passed down from family member to family member—except the ruby ring." Evelyn looked from one friend to the next. "Sir Anthony Ashley Cooper and Edward Hyde, the 1st Earl of Clarendon, were both Lords Proprietors, but they had a longstanding rivalry. As the king's favor increased with Cooper, it decreased with Hyde, and eventually Edward Hyde was banished from England in 1668. It was around this time that the ruby ring was stolen and has never been seen again."

Anne's eyes were huge as she stared at Evelyn. "Are you serious?"

Evelyn nodded.

"What happened to the seven other rings?" Shirley asked.

"I don't know—I would assume they're still in the possession of the original families, but I can't be certain."

"Wow." Joy let out a breath. "How will we know if this ruby ring is authentic?"

"That's why I'm anxious to talk to Jeanne Robertson," Evelyn explained. "She has to know more about this ring. I'm hoping she can shed some light on the mystery."

"Surely she knows the history of the ring," Anne offered. "It belongs to her."

"Maybe she doesn't." Shirley shrugged. "Just because it belongs to her doesn't mean she knows its history. Just think about all those people on *Antiques Roadshow*. Do you know that television show?"

Evelyn nodded. The show had aired for quite a while on PBS, but she hadn't seen it in some time.

"Most of the people who bring their antiques to the *Roadshow* experts don't know their history or their value until someone tells them." Shirley took a sip of her coffee. "That might be the case with Ms. Robertson."

"If that *is* the case," Evelyn said, "then maybe I can help her find out the truth behind the ring. But," she added with emphasis, "I can hope she knows exactly where the ring came from and that she can tell me everything I want to know."

Joy grinned, and Anne shook her head in laughter.

"That would be nice, wouldn't it?" Shirley asked.

"For now," Joy said, "you need to get some lunch, Evelyn Perry." She nodded toward the front counter. "Go on before your lunch hour is wasted."

Evelyn *was* hungry, since she hadn't had her oatmeal that morning, but even if she didn't have time to eat lunch, the time with her friends was not wasted. She could sit and talk about history for hours and walk away feeling full.

If only Jeanne Robertson were there to answer all her questions, then maybe she could satiate her curiosity too.

Chapter Four

THE NEXT AFTERNOON, SUNSHINE POURED through the windows of Mercy Hospital as Evelyn walked down the long hall on the second floor of the building. A soft smile tilted her lips as she praised God for bright warmth. Thanks to James, who had set up the makeshift kitchen he promised, she had not only had her morning coffee and oatmeal, but she had also spent time doing her morning devotions. It always amazed her how a little time in the Word and in prayer could affect her disposition for the day.

As she walked toward room 2350, she pressed her hand against the pocket of her trousers to reassure herself that the ruby and diamond ring was still where she had placed it earlier. She wished she had a better way to carry it, but she didn't want it out in the open. Right after lunch, Shirley had called to tell her that Ms. Robertson was ready for a visitor. Evelyn had immediately put aside all her work and slipped into the safe to retrieve the ring. She couldn't wait for Ms. Robertson to shed some light on the ring's history.

When room 2350 came within sight, a nurse stepped through the door and into the hall. Evelyn had never seen this particular nurse at Mercy before, but that wasn't unusual. The hospital employed hundreds of people, and new ones were hired every day. She was a pretty young woman, probably in her late twenties, with dark brown hair and matching brown eyes. Her purple scrubs looked brand new, and her bright smile suggested she was eager to please. The lanyard name badge around her neck showed her picture and her name, MADISON CUMMINGS, RN.

"Is Ms. Robertson awake?" Evelyn asked.

"She just finished her lunch," Madison said. "She's a little tired, but she's still awake."

"Thank you." Evelyn walked around Madison and entered Ms. Robertson's room.

It struck Evelyn that there were no balloons or flowers or any other indication that friends and family were thinking about Ms. Robertson. Hadn't her family been contacted? Surely they had been by now. So why were there no gifts? Shades at the window kept out the bright sunshine and cast the room in a shadowed, grayish hue.

Ms. Robertson lay on her bed with her head raised just a bit as she watched a home remodeling program on television. A large bandage covered the left side of her forehead and her short, curly hair was pressed flat on the right. Her left leg was in a cast from hip to heel, and it was elevated. She looked to be in her early sixties, though it was hard to tell, since her eyes were swollen and a large purple bruise pressed across her left cheekbone.

When she caught sight of Evelyn, she sighed. "What now?" she asked. "Why can't I get a moment to myself? You people want me to get better, but no one lets me sleep. Every ten minutes someone is in here poking and prodding, testing and evaluating."

Evelyn didn't come any farther into the room. "I'm sorry, Ms. Robertson. I have no wish to upset you. My name is Evelyn

Perry. I'm from the records department. I'm not here to run any tests. I can come back at a different time if you'd like to rest."

Ms. Robertson lifted the remote and turned off the television. "You're here now. You might as well tell me why you've come."

Evelyn didn't want to make Ms. Robertson uncomfortable or to trouble her in any way—but she also wanted to know more about the ring. She took a seat on a hard vinyl chair next to the bed.

"And call me Jeanne," Ms. Robertson said.

Evelyn offered a smile, hoping to put Jeanne at ease. "When you came into the ER I was put in charge of your possessions and I placed them in the hospital safe."

"Good," Jeanne said. "I've been wondering where my cell phone went. Could I have it back, please?"

Evelyn nodded. "I'll see that all your things are returned to you as soon as possible." She dug into her pocket and pulled out the ring. "But I'm here right now specifically because of your beautiful ring. It appears to be very valuable, so if you'd like for me to keep it in the safe for the duration of your stay, I'm happy to do it."

"My ring?"

"Yes." Evelyn opened her hand to reveal the ring lying on her palm. "It's such a magnificent piece of jewelry. I was hoping you might be able to tell me a little about it."

Jeanne studied the ring but made no move to take it from Evelyn. Finally, she shook her head. "That's not my ring."

Evelyn's eager smile turned into a confused frown. "This was in your pocket when you were brought into the ER."

"I've never seen that ring before in my life." It was Jeanne's turn to frown. "I don't own any rings. Jewelry is a waste of good money, if you ask me."

Evelyn slowly pulled her hand back and looked down at the ring.

"And look how big the band is," Jeanne continued. "That looks like it's made for a man's finger, not a slender finger like mine."

"This isn't your ring?" Evelyn's voice revealed her incredulity. "But it was with you when you were in the accident."

"I don't know where that ring came from." Jeanne was starting to get agitated as she repositioned herself in her bed. "If you don't have anything else for me to deal with, I'd like you to leave, please."

Evelyn stood, her mind running through all the possible scenarios regarding the ring. If it wasn't Jeanne's, then how did she come into possession of it? And if it wasn't hers, then who did it belong to?

"I'm sorry to have bothered you," Evelyn said. "I'll see that your cell phone and other personal belongings are returned to you as soon as possible."

Jeanne gave a slight nod of acknowledgment and then turned her television on again.

Instead of having answers, Evelyn had more questions than before. She left Jeanne's room and stepped into the bright hallway again. Maybe Shirley got it wrong. Maybe the ring wasn't in Jeanne's pocket when she was brought into the ER. But, then, where had it come from?

With renewed curiosity, Evelyn walked down the hall and went to the grand staircase. A couple of minutes later, she entered the ER.

Thankfully, it wasn't as busy as usual and she was able to quickly locate Shirley sitting at the nurses' station.

Shirley greeted Evelyn with a big smile. "Did you get a chance to speak to Ms. Robertson?"

Evelyn nodded, but she couldn't help the frown that tilted her brow.

Shirley's smile disappeared. "What's wrong?"

"Can I talk to you in private?" Evelyn didn't want anyone to overhear them speaking about a patient or the priceless ring resting in her pocket.

"Of course." Shirley stood and tilted her head toward a corner of the ER. When she seemed satisfied that they had enough privacy, she leaned forward. "What happened?"

"I went to visit Jeanne and show her the ring, but she said she's never seen it before. She claims it's not hers."

Shirley studied Evelyn's face for a second, as if comparing the information Evelyn had just given her with the information she already knew. "I'm the one who removed the ring from Ms. Robertson's pocket. I know, for a fact, that she came into the hospital with that ring in her possession."

"She says it's not hers. Could there be another explanation?"

Shirley glanced over Evelyn's shoulder. "Wait a second. I have another thought, but I need to ask Dr. Barnhardt."

Dr. Chad Barnhardt was one of the ER doctors on staff at Mercy. Shirley approached him as he stepped out of an examination room, and after a couple of seconds, he glanced in Evelyn's direction. Both he and Shirley walked across the short space back to Evelyn.

"Hello, Evelyn." Dr. Barnhardt didn't smile, but Evelyn didn't expect him to. He was a kind man, but he was also cool and analytical. Already, she could see that his mind was working on this problem. "Shirley tells me Ms. Robertson denies the ownership of the ring we found in her pocket the other day."

Evelyn nodded. "She says she's never seen it before."

"I think I can answer this question quite easily." He was a tall man, with silver at his temples. Evelyn had to look up to study his face as he spoke. "Dr. Tennyson consulted with me yesterday regarding Ms. Robertson's evaluation. It's not unusual for a patient with a head trauma, such as Ms. Robertson's, to experience short-term memory loss of the twenty-four hours before or after an accident—and it appears to be the case for Ms. Robertson. Upon evaluation, Dr. Tennyson said Ms. Robertson does not recall the accident or anything else that occurred on Monday."

"But how would that explain her not knowing about the ring?" Evelyn didn't understand.

"If she came into possession of the ring within the twenty-four hours before her accident, then it's only natural that she doesn't remember it."

"But did she?" Evelyn looked from Dr. Barnhardt to Shirley.

"It's just an educated guess," Dr. Barnhardt said. He nodded at Evelyn, indicating he was finished with their conversation. "If you'll excuse me."

"Thank you," Evelyn said. "I appreciate your help."

"My pleasure." He turned and left.

Shirley glanced at Dr. Barnhardt as he walked away. She shook her head. "That man has about as much personality as a cactus."

Evelyn only smiled.

Shirley came close to Evelyn's side and shrugged. "Maybe Dr. Barnhardt's theory explains the reason Ms. Robertson doesn't recognize the ring."

"Maybe." Evelyn pressed her hand against the ring in her pocket, an idea forming. "But maybe there's a way I can help jog her memory." She would need to retrieve Jeanne's items from the Vault and ask her a few more questions. Hopefully the woman would be more receptive to a visitor after she had time to rest.

At exactly five o'clock, Evelyn left the records department with Jeanne Robertson's possessions in hand. The white plastic bag bumped Evelyn's leg as she walked up the grand staircase to the second floor.

Evelyn hadn't looked inside the bag, but if she had to guess, she would assume there was a purse, a pair of shoes, and a few odds and ends taking up the bulk of the space. Could there be clues inside the bag that might help Jeanne remember what happened two days ago? It was Evelyn's hope that something might prompt some memory or that the women might find information about what Jeanne had done in the twenty-four hours prior to the accident.

That was, if Jeanne allowed Evelyn to pry. She didn't know why, but the ring had so captivated her imagination, she wanted to learn all she could about its origins. And, if it truly didn't belong to Jeanne, Evelyn would need to try to find the owner. Until she knew for certain it wasn't Jeanne's, she wouldn't get the police involved. But if

Jeanne continued to deny her ownership, then Evelyn would have no choice but to call them and hand it over to the authorities.

She just hoped it wouldn't come to that.

"Knock, knock," Evelyn said as she opened Jeanne's door. "May I come in?"

"Why not?" Jeanne said.

Evelyn entered the room and found the nurse, Madison, helping Jeanne sit up. A supper tray was on the nearby table, with roasted turkey, mashed potatoes, and gravy. Evelyn's stomach began to growl. For a second, she contemplated what she might make for supper but then remembered that she did not have a kitchen to cook in and felt a little deflated.

It would probably be takeout again tonight.

"Oh," Jeanne said, "it's you."

"Hello, Jeanne." Evelyn offered her warmest smile. "I came to return your things to you."

Jeanne's face brightened, just a bit. "My cell phone?"

"I'm not sure what all's in the bag," Evelyn said. "Where would you like me to set this?"

Jeanne waved it over. "I'll take it."

Madison had finished helping Jeanne and was now positioning the tray table next to the bed. Evelyn watched Jeanne as she opened the bag and pulled out her purse.

A watch also slipped out of the bag, as did a pair of shoes and socks.

Jeanne ignored all of it except her purse. "I sure hope it's in here. I've been meaning to call my boss, but I don't have his number memorized."

"What kind of work do you do?" Evelyn was determined to get as much information out of Jeanne as possible.

"I work from home as a systems analyst." Jeanne glanced up. "I help companies assess the suitability of information systems in terms of their needs and assist as a liaison between software companies and computer programmers."

Evelyn was impressed. "It sounds like a very sophisticated job."

Jeanne just shrugged as she continued to search through her large purse for her phone.

"And where is home?" Evelyn asked.

"Atlanta." Jeanne's eyes lit up. "Aha!" She pulled her cell phone out of her purse and tried to turn it on, but her face fell. "The battery's dead." She sighed. "And I don't think I have a charging cord."

"What kind of phone do you have?"

Jeanne told her. It was a phone similar to Evelyn's, and she carried a charging cord in her purse. Since she planned to head home right after visiting with Jeanne, she had her purse on her shoulder. "I'd be happy to loan you the use of mine." She didn't even wait for Jeanne to accept her offer but took her purse off her shoulder to dig for her cord.

"Really? That's awfully nice. Thank you."

"I'm happy to help." Evelyn located the charging cord and plugged it into the wall behind Jeanne's bed. She handed the other end to Jeanne, who plugged in her phone and set it on the bed next to her.

"I appreciate that," Jeanne said with a nod. "I don't check in with my boss often, but there were a few emails I needed to return after I got home from Charleston. He's probably wondering why I haven't emailed him back yet."

"You were only planning to be in Charleston for a couple of days?"

"Only one day." Jeanne paused and frowned but didn't say anything.

"What brought you to Charleston?"

Jeanne continued to frown as Madison moved her supper tray into position.

When Jeanne finally looked at Evelyn, she shook her head. "I don't remember why I came, to be honest with you. I just know I was only going to be here for a day—or maybe overnight." She paused and stared at her supper plate for a moment. "Isn't that strange? The drive from Atlanta takes over four hours, and I don't come here often. Maybe once or twice a year. Why would I only plan to be here for a day?"

"What usually brings you to Charleston?"

"I have some family here. An uncle, who recently passed away, and a cousin." She paused again. "But why would I come now? I used to visit with my uncle, and I hadn't seen my cousin in years until my uncle's funeral. And then after my uncle died, I told myself I didn't have any reason to return to Charleston."

"Perhaps there are some clues among your belongings." Evelyn didn't want Jeanne to get suspicious of her intentions, so she treaded lightly.

Madison remained busy tidying up the room, but she appeared to be just as interested in this line of questioning as Evelyn.

When Evelyn caught her eye, Madison gave her a concerned look. "She doesn't remember what happened."

"I'm sitting right here," Jeanne said to Madison with a raised eyebrow.

"I'm sorry, Jeanne." Madison's cheeks colored pink. "Are you starting to remember anything from before your accident?"

Jeanne touched the bandage on her forehead and made no move to start eating her meal. Her face revealed a hint of panic as her chest rose and fell deeply. "No. And I don't like that at all. I have a really good memory. I can recall, in detail, many events in my life—but I don't even remember leaving my house in Atlanta or the drive to Charleston. I definitely don't remember what I did here before the accident." She glanced at Evelyn. "What time did the accident happen?"

"I was called into the ER to retrieve your belongings around two thirty. By that time, you were already stable and transferred to the ICU, so I'm thinking that perhaps your accident happened an hour or so before that. It should be written in the police report."

A nurse popped her head into Jeanne's room and glanced around until her gaze landed on Madison. "You're needed in room 2360. Can you come?"

Madison looked from Evelyn to Jeanne, as if disappointed that she couldn't stay to hear their conversation. But it was obvious she was done assisting Jeanne for the moment, so she nodded. "Sure."

After Madison was out of the room, Evelyn decided to reiterate her idea from before. "Perhaps we can help you retrace your steps by looking for receipts in your purse. Do you keep receipts?"

"Of course. I keep everything." Jeanne opened her purse again and took out her wallet. "I put them in here, and at the end of each week, I file them." She unzipped her wallet and pulled out about a dozen receipts. "My head hurts too much to read the tiny print." She handed the pile to Evelyn. "Do you mind?"

Evelyn took the receipts and looked at their dates. Only two were from the day of the accident, and both were from establishments in Charleston. The others were all receipts from Atlanta. "There's a City of Charleston Parking receipt with the time stamp of 10:43 a.m. and a restaurant receipt on East Bay Street at 12:39."

Jeanne worried her bottom lip and squinted. "Why can't I remember any of it?"

"The doctor said that it's common to lose your memories of the time directly before and after a head trauma like yours."

"Will I get my memory back?"

"I'm not sure."

Jeanne met Evelyn's gaze. "Why are you so curious about what happened to me the day of the accident?"

Evelyn wouldn't lie to her. "I'm curious about the ring. I think it's a very valuable and rare piece of jewelry. If we can't prove it rightfully belongs to you, then I'll need to hand it over to the police. And if it is yours, I'd hate for you to have to deal with all the red tape later on when you want to get it back."

"Do you really think the ring is mine?"

"It was in your pocket when you came into the ER."

"May I see it again?"

Evelyn took the ring out of her pocket and handed it to Jeanne.

"It is beautiful." Jeanne turned the ring around to read the inscription. "And what does LPOC stand for?"

Evelyn told Jeanne about the Lords Proprietors of Carolina and her theory about this ring belonging to Sir Anthony Ashley Cooper, 1st Earl of Shaftesbury.

"Really?" Jeanne lifted her eyebrows. "That's pretty amazing if it's true."

"I was hoping you might know more about the ring."

Jeanne shook her head. "Sorry." She ran her thumb over the ruby and looked up at Evelyn again. "I don't know anything about the Lords Proprietors, and like I said before, I don't own any jewelry. I'm not married and have never really seen the need to spend money on frivolous items. But if this is my ring, I'd sure like to keep it. Do you really want to help me figure this out?"

"I'd be happy to." Evelyn smiled, thankful Jeanne wasn't upset at her intrusion. "I'll do a little research into the restaurant and the parking meter on these receipts. If you remember anything, please call me right away." Evelyn wrote her cell number on a scratch pad. "I'll come back tomorrow and see how you're doing."

"I appreciate your help." Jeanne handed the ring back to Evelyn. "For now, would you please keep this in the hospital safe? I wouldn't want anything to happen to it."

"Of course." Evelyn took the ring and slipped it into her pocket again. "I'll put it back before I leave for home."

Evelyn said goodbye and left Jeanne to eat her supper.

They hadn't unraveled the mystery yet, but Evelyn was determined not to give up until they did.

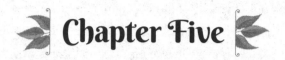

Chapter Five

THE AIR WAS HOT AND humid as Evelyn walked home from work that evening. There wasn't even a trace of a breeze, and her skin quickly grew damp with perspiration. She wanted nothing more than to put her feet up in the cool living room, with James at her side, and watch a fun romantic comedy together.

But her hopes for a little rest and relaxation quickly evaporated when she walked through the front door and saw dust hanging thick in the air.

"Evie, is that you?" James called from the kitchen. "I have another surprise for you!"

Evelyn groaned. She wasn't sure she wanted to know what the surprise might be—especially if it meant more work and mess.

Slowly, she hung her purse on the coat-tree and put her keys in the calling card dish. Whatever surprise he had in mind had created a thick layer of dust on everything. She ran her finger along the hall table, and it left a mark in the dust. The whole downstairs would need to be cleaned, including the walls and trim, the fabric on the furniture, and the windows. It would take hours. There was no way she could sit in the living room and relax knowing this dust was all over everything.

"I think you're going to love this," James said as he stepped into the hall, a grin on his face. He was covered in white from top to bottom. It coated his head and beard and made him look like he had silver-colored hair.

Evelyn forced herself to smile and followed him into the kitchen.

"See." He pointed to the back wall where he'd cut a hole. "I'm going to finally put a window in the kitchen."

The hole was like a gaping wound in the side of the house. Pieces of splintered wood stuck out around the edges and the humidity poured into the house, making the dust stick to her skin.

"What do you think?" James asked. "Doesn't it let an amazing amount of light into the room? We've always wanted more natural light in here."

It did add a great deal of daylight to the once cave-like kitchen. It also gave her a view of the front lawn of the house next door. "Do you have the window, or will you need to put plastic up over the hole for now?" Just thinking about how vulnerable she'd feel with a flimsy piece of plastic covering the hole made her shiver despite the heat.

"I have the window. I ordered it a couple of weeks ago and picked it up today. It's actually one of the reasons I wanted to wait to start this project." He nodded toward the back of the house. "It's on the patio. I was just waiting for you to come home, so you could help me hang it. I'd like an extra pair of hands."

Evelyn nodded, though she had her doubts. She had never helped to hang a window before—and she wasn't too keen on the idea of working in the heat outside. But it would be nice to have a window in the kitchen. And, if James knew what he was doing, he could surely instruct her.

"Okay. Just give me a few minutes to change. And when I'm done helping you, I'll need to go through the house and dust everything."

James made a face and shook his head. "I don't think it'll pay to clean everything until I'm done. It's bound to get dusty again."

Memories of the mess she'd grown up in returned, and she felt that same anxiety start to bubble up in her stomach. "I can't live in this filth, James."

"It's only for a little while."

"Two or three weeks isn't a little while. Besides, I'd like to watch a movie in the living room, but I can't sit on the furniture if there's a layer of dust over everything." Her anxiety continued to mount. What might be next? Would she come home and find an entire wall missing? "Why couldn't you have put a tarp over the kitchen doorway to keep all the dust inside?"

James was an inherently patient man—to a point—and Evelyn could tell he was struggling to keep calm with her now. "To be honest, I didn't even think about the dust. I thought, instead, about how excited you'd be to have a window in the kitchen."

"I am excited for the window. But I'm also exhausted from work, and I'm not excited about spending the evening cleaning."

"I'm exhausted too." He indicated his dusty appearance. "But I can look beyond this temporary inconvenience at the bigger picture."

"Are you saying I'm incapable of seeing the bigger picture?" She knew the bigger picture. She knew what it was like to live in filth—and she hated it. Maybe she was too particular, but she had good cause.

James crossed his arms. "I'm saying that you've been a lot more focused on the tiny details, and frankly, it's getting a bit tiresome to hear you complain. This is a gift—not to mention a lot of work. Each time you complain, it makes me wonder why I even started this project."

"I didn't ask you to do this, James. I would have been a lot happier if you had discussed it with me first. And maybe planned to hire it out."

He stared at her. "This was meant to be a gift, Evelyn—a surprise. I knew if I did it myself, we could afford nicer appliances and a few more extras."

"Unfortunately, it's turned into a headache."

James didn't say anything for a moment, and she knew she had hurt his feelings. She tried to calm her emotions and took a deep, steadying breath.

"What do you want from me?" he asked, turning up his dusty palms. "It's too late to go back now."

"I'd like for you to tell me your plans. If I had known you were going to cut a gaping hole in our house, I could have at least prepared for the shock. Maybe even put up a piece of plastic, or a sheet, or something, to keep the dust from infiltrating into the rest of the house."

"If I had told you, then it wouldn't have been a surprise."

"I'm okay with that. You know I don't like surprises. I just need time to prepare."

He studied her, his lips pressed together. "Fine."

"Fine. I'll go upstairs and change—"

"Don't bother helping with the window. I'll see if John from next door can help."

"I can help—"

"Don't worry about it, Evelyn." His voice was flat as he took his cell phone out of his pocket. "Go on upstairs and put your feet up. I'll dust the house after the window is put in place."

Evelyn hated to fight with James. They didn't do it often, but when they did, it always left her feeling unsettled. She couldn't go upstairs and put her feet up to relax knowing there was strife between them. And, even though she was upset, it really wasn't James's fault. Yes, she wished he had discussed his plans with her, but how could she blame him for wanting to give her a gift?

"You don't need to call John to help with the window," she said, "and you don't need to dust the house for me. You're already doing more than your fair share." She didn't have a hard time admitting when she was wrong—but it wasn't her favorite thing to do either. "I'm sorry for overreacting. I do appreciate all the hard work you've put into this project already." She moved toward her husband, and despite his dusty shirt, she wrapped her arms around him. "I'm sorry."

He slipped his phone into his back pocket before embracing her in a tight hug. "You don't need to apologize. I've been married to you long enough to know you like to prepare as much as possible. I'll be better about giving you a heads-up before I do anything big."

"Thank you for this gift, James. Just ignore me when I get uptight."

He kissed her and then pulled back to smile again. "I almost always do."

Evelyn made a face at him.

James laughed. "I promise to get this done as fast as possible, Evie."

"I know you will." She reluctantly pulled out of his embrace. "Give me a couple minutes, and I'll be ready to help you hang that window."

As Evelyn walked up the stairs, she was thankful her husband was a kind and patient man, and that a little humility on her part allowed them to forgive each other.

They would need all the patience and forgiveness available if they were going to survive this kitchen remodel.

The next morning, Evelyn was busy at her office desk when the door opened into the records department.

"May I help you?" Stacia asked as she rose and greeted the person who entered.

He was a handsome young man who looked like he could have fit as easily in the 1950s as today. His white button-down shirt was rolled at the sleeves, and he wore a thin black tie. Covering his eyes were black horn-rimmed glasses. When he caught sight of Stacia, his mouth turned up in an arresting smile. "Hello."

"Hello," she said with a sweet voice.

Evelyn chuckled to herself as she saw the instant chemistry between the two.

"How are you—" He paused and looked at her name tag. "Stacia Westbrook?"

"I'm okay," she said, her voice tilted and teasing. "May I help you, Mister...?"

"Hunter O'Reilly." He put his hand out for Stacia to shake. "I'm a reporter with the *Charleston Times*."

"Oh my." Stacia's Southern drawl deepened with fascination. "What brings you into the hospital today?"

"I'm looking for Evelyn Perry."

Evelyn's eyebrows rose in surprise. What would a newspaper reporter need with her?

Stacia motioned toward Evelyn. "This is Mrs. Perry."

It took a second for Hunter to turn his gaze to Evelyn, but when he did, he put on his reporter persona again, and he nodded a greeting. "Hello, Mrs. Perry."

"Hello, Mr. O'Reilly." Evelyn stood from her desk and approached the front counter. "How may I help you?"

Hunter pulled a small notepad out of his back pocket and removed the pencil he wore over his ear. "I'm here in regard to a ring. Do you have time to answer my questions?"

"A ring?" Evelyn frowned.

"The ruby and diamond ring you have in the safe here in the records department." He said it matter-of-factly, as if there was no question. "I have a source who gave me the information, and I did some research on the ring. I'd like to run the story in the weekend edition of the *Charleston Times*. Could you answer a few of my questions?"

Several questions rose in Evelyn's mind as well. "Who told you about the ring?"

Hunter pressed his lips together and shook his head. "Sorry. I never reveal the names of my sources. What kind of a journalist would I be if I gave away all my secrets?" He winked at Stacia, who was hanging on his every word.

Evelyn crossed her arms. "I'm not at liberty to speak about the ring."

Hunter leaned against the counter and flashed a charming grin. Evelyn was fairly certain the young man was used to getting his way and wasn't above using any means necessary—even flirting with a sixty-year-old married woman.

"Come on, Mrs. Perry. You wouldn't turn away an up-and-coming reporter, would you?"

"I would."

"I wouldn't," Stacia said. "I know a little about the ring."

"Stacia!" Evelyn's voice rose higher than she intended.

"What?" Stacia asked.

"Please return to your work," Evelyn said to her employee. "And you are not to speak about the ring—or any other personal property of our patients—to anyone." She'd have to have a conversation with Stacia later. The young woman knew better, but it seemed that the charismatic reporter had her losing sight of her responsibilities.

Stacia returned to her computer—but not before turning to smile at Hunter one more time.

"Mr. O'Reilly," Evelyn began. "I am not at liberty—"

"Aren't you curious what I know about the ring?" He continued to lean against the counter, his easygoing manner and suave countenance making him both likable and infuriating. "I think you'll be pleasantly surprised to hear what I have to say."

Curiosity waged a war with propriety in Evelyn's mind. She *did* want to know what the reporter had dug up about the ring, but, at the same time, she couldn't give away any information. "I would greatly appreciate knowing what information you've gathered," she said. "But I cannot—and will not—give you any. I'm legally bound to protect every patient in this hospital."

"So Jeanne Robertson is still a patient here?" He poised his pencil over his notepad. "Could you tell me her room number so I can speak to her myself?"

"This conversation is over, Mr. O'Reilly."

"Now wait," he said, loosening up a little. "I really think you'll want to hear what I know about the ring."

It took all her willpower to say what was necessary. "I can wait until the paper is printed on Saturday."

He grinned at her, as if appreciating her intelligence. "Touché."

"I really cannot give you any information. I'm sorry."

"I understand." He sighed. "It doesn't hurt to ask. And I have a couple of other leads—but I think I have all the information I need to run the story anyway."

Evelyn really did want to know what he knew. She could wait a couple of days to read the paper, but it would be nice to have a little heads-up. "I'm sure it will be interesting."

He lifted his eyebrows over his horn-rimmed glasses and wiggled them. "You bet it is." Hunter glanced over his shoulder and then leaned in. "I know where the other seven rings are."

"You do?" Evelyn's heart rate picked up speed. Would he tell her?

"There's a man in England who claims to be a descendant of Charles II—"

"Charles II didn't have any children," Evelyn said. "His brother took over the throne upon his death."

"No *legitimate* children," Hunter said. "But he claimed over a dozen children by seven different mistresses, some of whom he made into dukes and earls. Four present dukes descend from King Charles II in unbroken male lines, and even the late Princess Diana was descended from two of Charles II's sons. Prince William, Diana's son, will be the first descendant of Charles II to take the throne when he inherits it one day."

"Really?" Evelyn had no idea.

"As I was saying," Hunter continued, "there is a man who claims to be a descendant of Charles II—a man by the name of Lord Marshton. It's rumored that he's been collecting the rings of the Lords Proprietors of Carolina for the past decade and has been able to acquire seven of the eight."

"Are the rumors true?"

"From what I can find—yes, I believe they are." Hunter slipped his pencil over his ear again. "He's been looking for the elusive ruby ring from the very beginning, and until Jeanne Robertson came into possession of it, no one knew where it was."

How had the news traveled so quickly—and how did this reporter know so much about the ring so soon?

"What does Lord Marshton plan to do with all the rings?" she asked.

"Apparently, he inherited one of his ancestral homes and is struggling to keep it up. Once he has all eight rings, he plans to put them up for auction and use the money for upkeep on the manor house."

"And how did you learn all this information?"

Hunter grinned again and wagged his finger at her. "Nice try, Mrs. Perry, but you've already gotten more information out of me than I was originally willing to give you."

Evelyn smiled. "You can't blame me for trying."

"Ha!" Hunter laughed and put his notebook back into his pocket. "I plan to inquire after Jeanne Robertson's room number, and then I plan to ask her about the ring."

"Be my guest," Evelyn said. "If she chooses to tell you about it, that's her decision." Evelyn was fairly certain the reporter wouldn't get any more information than he already had, since Jeanne didn't recall anything about the ring.

"And what about Stacia?" Hunter asked, turning his attention back to the young woman. "Can she give me a little more information?"

Evelyn shook her head. "She's not at lib—"

"What kind of information would you like?" Stacia asked.

"How about your phone number, for starters?"

Stacia lowered her eyelashes. "And why would you need that?"

"To see if you'd like to get together sometime soon—maybe over a nice meal on the waterfront?"

It didn't take Stacia long to hand over her cell phone number. Hunter took it and winked at her. "I'll be calling soon."

"I hope so." Stacia's cheeks were a becoming shade of pink.

Hunter smiled and tipped his chin at Evelyn. "Thank you for your time."

Evelyn shook her head as the young reporter left the office. When he was gone, she turned to Stacia. "Watch that one closely."

"Oh, I know how to handle him."

"And don't forget your HIPAA obligations. You're not allowed to discuss any information regarding patients at Mercy Hospital without their express permission."

Stacia smiled to herself and turned back to her computer. "Believe me, Mr. O'Reilly won't be thinking about work when he's out with me."

Evelyn almost rolled her eyes, but she refrained and instead just chuckled.

She went back to her desk, wondering where Hunter O'Reilly had heard about the ring. Only a few people in the hospital even knew it existed.

"Hey, Stacia," she said.

"Yes?"

"Did you happen to mention the ring to anyone?"

Stacia swiveled on her chair to look at Evelyn. She shook her head. "No one."

"Did anyone come into the records department and ask about it?"

"Just that delivery truck driver."

"No one else?"

Stacia frowned and shook her head.

"Okay." She smiled and nodded at Stacia to let her know she could return to her work.

Had the delivery truck driver tipped off the reporter? But why? And how did he know so much about the ring?

Or was it someone else entirely? There was no telling who Jeanne spoke to on Monday before the accident.

Maybe Evelyn should ask for the police report and find out the name of the driver. If nothing else, she could call him and see if he was willing to discuss what he knew.

But first, she would need to look into Jeanne's receipts. They were lying on Evelyn's desk right where she'd left them the day before. She hadn't had time to research them since arriving at work, but maybe now would be a good time. She would call the restaurant and ask if anyone remembered seeing Jeanne eating there on Monday. And she would locate the parking meter to see what businesses might be in the general vicinity. Perhaps she might gain another clue and have a better understanding of the events leading up to Jeanne's accident.

It was apparent she wasn't the only one interested in learning more about the ring.

Chapter Six

AT TEN MINUTES TO FOUR, Evelyn's office phone rang. The internal system light blinked, telling her the call was from someone within the hospital, but she didn't bother to glance at the number before she picked up the receiver. "Records Department, Evelyn speaking."

"Mrs. Perry?" It was a woman on the other end. "This is Jeanne Robertson."

Evelyn's complete attention focused, and she turned her gaze away from her computer screen. "Yes. Hello, Jeanne. What can I do for you?"

"I just remembered something—and I thought you'd like to know. It's about the restaurant I went to on Monday."

Excitement shifted up Evelyn's spine. "I can be in your room in less than five minutes."

"You don't need to come to me—"

"I've been sitting at my desk since my lunch break. I could use an excuse to stretch my legs."

"Oh, all right."

Evelyn hung up and grabbed her cell phone and Jeanne's receipts. "I'm running up to the second floor. I should be back soon," she told Stacia and Rick, who were making copies.

"Got it," Stacia said.

It took less than five minutes for Evelyn to climb the stairs and arrive at Jeanne's room. When she did, she was greeted by the nurse, Madison, who was just leaving.

They almost bumped into each other, and Madison yelped, putting her hand over her chest. "You frightened me."

"I'm sorry." Evelyn moved to the side so Madison could pass her. "It seems we keep running into each other."

Madison smiled but didn't offer a response as she walked down the hall toward the nurses' station. She tossed a glance over her shoulder but then continued on.

Evelyn knocked on Jeanne's door and let herself in. "Hello," she said when she saw Jeanne sitting up. The bruise on her face was turning several different shades of green and yellow, and the bandage on her forehead was smaller today. "You look like you're improving by leaps and bounds."

"I'd like to leave," Jeanne confided, "but the doctors think it's best if I stay for continued monitoring." She shrugged. "They're still concerned about blood clots and infection."

"I'm sorry to hear that." Evelyn didn't know how Jeanne felt about faith or religion, but she couldn't help but add, "I've been praying for your recovery."

"I appreciate that."

Evelyn took the seat next to Jeanne's bed. "What did you remember about the restaurant?"

Jeanne picked up her cell phone, which was lying on the bed next to her. "I was going through my messages to see if I could find anything helpful, and I came across a text from my cousin Roy, who lives here in Charleston." She held up her phone to show Evelyn the text. "Apparently, for some reason, Roy and I made plans to meet up for lunch on Monday at Blossom's on East Bay Street."

Evelyn reached for the phone. "Do you mind if I read the text?"

"Be my guest." Jeanne handed the phone over to her.

The text was pretty straightforward. Roy had sent it to her on Monday morning, and it simply said, WOULD YOU MEET WITH ME AT BLOSSOM'S RESTAURANT AT 11:30? I'D LIKE TO DISCUSS UNCLE TONY'S DECISION.

Under Roy's text was Jeanne's response:

I'M WILLING TO MEET, IN HONOR OF UNCLE TONY'S MEMORY, BUT THERE'S NOTHING YOU CAN DO TO CHANGE HIS DECISION. I'LL SEE YOU THEN.

"This is the only correspondence you could find?" Evelyn asked, handing back the phone.

"Regarding my reason to be in Charleston? Yes." Jeanne set the phone by her side again. "I was also visited by a reporter earlier today who said you sent him to me."

Evelyn lifted an eyebrow. "I did *not* send him to you."

"Well, it doesn't really matter. I couldn't tell him anything he wanted to know, but I said I might call him if I thought of something."

"I didn't think you could tell him anything." Evelyn nibbled her bottom lip. "Do you remember meeting with your cousin at Blossom's?"

Jeanne shook her head. "I don't."

"Would you be willing to call him to ask why you met?"

It took a moment, but Jeanne finally sighed. "I have no wish to speak to him—but if it helps me put the pieces together again, I could swallow my pride and give him a call."

Evelyn nodded with encouragement.

Jeanne picked up her phone again and pressed a few buttons. She activated the speaker, which allowed Evelyn to hear both sides of the conversation, and looked out the window to the bright day beyond the hospital.

After a few seconds, a man answered. "Did you have a change of heart?" he asked.

Jeanne took a steadying breath. "Roy, I was in a car accident on Monday."

There was a pause on the other end of the phone. "Are you serious? Where are you?"

"Mercy Hospital, here in Charleston."

"You're still in Charleston? What happened?"

"I don't recall." Jeanne glanced at Evelyn. "I've been told I was pushed off the road by a delivery truck that swerved to miss someone in a turning lane. But I don't remember anything from the accident—or the day of the accident."

Another pause. "You don't remember meeting me for lunch?"

"No. But I saw the text about Blossom's Restaurant. Did we meet there?"

"You really don't remember?" Roy's voice was incredulous.

"I don't even remember why I came to Charleston to begin with." Her voice was impatient, and her face was set into hard lines. "I'm hoping you can shed some light on the issue for me."

Roy snorted. "I'm sure you are."

Jeanne shook her head and looked outside again. "I didn't think you'd be helpful—even with me being in the hospital."

"What's it worth to you?" Roy asked. "You've never given me anything freely, so I assume you believe that everything has a price tag. What will you give me?"

Pain and sadness radiated off Jeanne's bruised face. Whatever had come between her and her cousin, it was deep and aching. "I'd just like to know why I'm in Charleston." Her voice became vulnerable and shook, just a bit. "I'm scared and confused, Roy. A little compassion is all I'm asking for."

Roy didn't say anything for a couple of seconds, but then he sighed. "I'll come and see you. I don't live far from Mercy. I can be there in less than ten minutes."

"You'd come and see me?" Jeanne's eyes filled with tears.

"Sure. You're the only family I have left, I guess—obligation and all that. I'm already on my way, Jeanne. I'll see you soon."

Jeanne hung up the phone and kept her face turned toward the window for a heartbeat. She wiped her eyes and then looked at Evelyn. "Hopefully we'll have more answers soon."

Evelyn rose. "I should go and let you have some—"

A knock at the door interrupted her.

"Hello," a deep male voice called into the room. "May I come in?"

Jeanne frowned but shrugged. "Sure."

The delivery truck driver entered Jeanne's room, a bouquet of flowers and several balloons in his hands. He was a tall, broad-shouldered man, with light brown hair. He wore his brown uniform, complete with a brown baseball cap. His eyes, which were wide, scanned the room and fell on Jeanne. Remorse and guilt rolled off him.

"Hello, ma'am," he said, his voice catching. "I'm Wayne Preston." He thrust the gifts forward. "I brought you a few things to brighten your room. I wish I could do more."

Jeanne continued to frown as she studied him. "Are you the man who pushed my car off the road?"

Wayne swallowed hard. The mixed bouquet of flowers shook in his hands. "Yes, ma'am. I am. And I'm here to tell you how sorry I am."

Evelyn went forward and offered a smile as she took his gifts and brought them to the deep windowsill. She set them down, turning the bouquet to put the prettiest flowers toward the room.

Jeanne glanced at the flowers and balloons but didn't thank Wayne. Instead, she pressed her lips together and didn't say a thing.

"It's very nice of you to bring the gifts," Evelyn said, needing to fill the empty, awkward silence. "The flowers are beautiful."

Wayne nodded at Evelyn and then took off his cap. He gripped it in his hands, wringing it like he would a wet washcloth. "I'm real sorry, Ms. Robertson. I've relived that day in my mind a thousand times, trying to figure out what I could have done differently to prevent this accident. It's eating me alive. I didn't know how long to wait before I visited you to apologize." He paused and then looked at her closely. "They say you can't remember anything that happened that day. I-is that true?"

Jeanne just scowled at him.

Evelyn could see that Jeanne was struggling to talk to the man responsible for her accident and memory loss, so Evelyn said, "May I ask what happened?"

"Yes, ma'am." Wayne licked his lips. "I was driving east on Broad Street, near the intersection of Broad and Legare, when a car unexpectedly stopped in front of me to turn left. My instinct was to swerve right and miss the car, but when I did, Ms. Robertson, who was driving beside me, also had to swerve right. Her car went off the road, and she ran into a tree. The police said she didn't have her seat belt on and she was going pretty fast."

"Are you suggesting it's my fault I'm in such a state?" Jeanne asked, her voice raised. "If I'd been wearing a seat belt or hadn't been going so fast, I might not be in this hospital?"

"No, ma'am," Wayne said quickly. "I take responsibility for what happened, and I'm real sorry."

"As you should be." Jeanne pressed her lips together again.

"I have a nearly perfect driving record," Wayne said. "And I've been reprimanded by my manager for this accident. They're working with the police and your insurance company to rectify the situation."

"Yes, I know," Jeanne said. "I've been speaking to my lawyer."

"I just wanted to come and apologize," Wayne said. "I've got a wife and kids at home, and I need this job right now. I don't want to cause more pain or discomfort for anyone." He put his hat back on and said, "It's probably best if I leave."

"Thank you for coming," Evelyn said to Wayne. "It was a very kind gesture."

Wayne nodded at Evelyn and then looked one more time at Jeanne before leaving the room.

"I'm sure it was very hard for him to come here," Evelyn said, trying to lighten Jeanne's mood.

She snorted. "Harder than lying here, in pain, with memory loss?"

Evelyn chose not to answer—but then she remembered that Wayne had come to the records department asking about the ring the day after the accident. Perhaps she could catch up to him and ask what he knew about it.

"I'll be right back," she said to Jeanne. "I'd like to ask him something about the ring."

"Be my guest." Jeanne waved her away.

Evelyn left the room, hoping she hadn't missed her opportunity to talk to Wayne.

Wayne was just at the top of the grand staircase when Evelyn finally reached his side.

"Mr. Preston," she called to him.

He turned, his countenance still heavy from his meeting with Jeanne.

"Please," Evelyn said, "may I have a quick word with you?"

"Of course." He moved away from the steps and rejoined her in the hall near a large floor-to-ceiling window overlooking the Grove. "What can I do for you, ma'am?"

"First, I want to say how very sorry I am for everything you've been through these past few days." Evelyn shook her head, sad for everyone involved. "Accidents are called accidents for a reason, so try not to be too hard on yourself. It could have happened to anyone."

Instead of showing relief at her reassuring words, the look of guilt and shame in Wayne's eyes only intensified. He didn't meet Evelyn's gaze for a moment as he stared down at the floor.

"But I'm not here to speak to you about the accident," Evelyn said quickly, seeing that the mention of it brought him more grief. "I'd like to ask you what you know about Ms. Robertson's ruby ring."

Wayne's head snapped up, and he stared at Evelyn. "What do you mean?"

She studied him for a moment, trying to read his expression and response. "My assistant told me that you came into the records department the day after the accident inquiring about the ring."

After a second, Wayne swallowed and then shook his head. "I-I'm sorry, but I don't know anything about a ring."

Evelyn frowned. "But, my assistant—"

"I need to be getting along." He started to back away. "I shouldn't have taken this long. I'm already behind schedule. Good day, ma'am."

Before Evelyn could utter another word, Wayne Preston was down the stairs and out of sight.

She stood there, wondering why he would lie about inquiring after the ring. Wasn't he the delivery driver who had come into the records department? He'd met the description Stacia had given. Then why not simply tell her the truth?

Unless he was hiding something. But what could that be?

Evelyn turned back toward Jeanne's room and noticed Madison standing near one of the patient rooms, a chart in hand—though she wasn't focused on the chart. Instead, she looked like she'd been eavesdropping on Evelyn and Wayne's conversation.

As soon as Madison noticed Evelyn's attention, she turned her back and fumbled with the chart in her hands.

"Is something wrong, Madison?" Evelyn asked.

Madison shook her head and then stepped into the patient's room, her movements awkward and clumsy.

Something wasn't right—but Evelyn couldn't put her finger on what was going on with the young nurse.

She returned to Jeanne's room and found the woman staring out the window from her bed. Jeanne turned her head quickly but then deflated, as if disappointed to see Evelyn and not someone else.

"Oh," Jeanne said. "It's just you."

"I'm sorry. I thought I should come and say goodbye before your cousin arrives." Evelyn began to back out of the room again. "I'll leave—"

"Please." Jeanne held up her hand to stop Evelyn. "Can you stay with me while he's here?" She let out a heavy sigh. "Our visits never go well. It would be nice to have someone in the room so we don't try to wring each other's necks."

Evelyn couldn't deny that she'd like to be there to hear what Roy had to say. And if it gave Jeanne any measure of relief to know she was present, Evelyn would gladly stay. "Of course."

"Thank you." Jeanne pulled the bedding up tight around her waist and then ran her hands over the blanket to ease out the wrinkles.

The second hand on the clock seemed to stall as Evelyn took a seat on the vinyl chair beside Jeanne's bed. She tried to start a couple of conversations, but Jeanne was distracted and kept looking at the door every time there was a noise in the hall.

Finally, the door opened and a middle-aged man entered the room. He was of average height, fairly lean, and clean-shaven. He wore a simple short-sleeved button-down shirt and a pair of khaki shorts. His hair was cut close to his head, and his eyes were curious as he met Jeanne's gaze. But as he took in the state of her condition, they opened wider in shock.

"What happened?" he asked.

"Hello, Roy." Jeanne folded her hands on top of the blanket. "This is Evelyn Perry. She works here in the records department."

Evelyn rose to shake Roy's hand. "It's nice to meet you."

Roy nodded, but his gaze and attention shifted back to his cousin. "Are you okay?"

One of Jeanne's eyebrows lifted. "Can't you tell by looking at me that I'm not okay?"

"I mean, will you be okay?"

Jeanne shrugged. "In time."

"Tell me what happened. Is it true you can't remember anything from Monday?"

"It's true." Jeanne recounted what she knew of the event and how it had transpired. She also told him about her memory loss. "So that's why I called you. I hoped you'd be able to tell me why I came to Charleston."

She didn't offer her cousin a chair, so he continued to stand near the entrance to the room, where the door was still open. Evelyn had a good view of the hall from where she was sitting and she noticed Madison approach, but the nurse didn't enter or walk on by. Instead, she stood just outside the door, working on a chart. If Roy wasn't standing in Evelyn's way, she would close the door to offer them privacy.

The more Evelyn witnessed the new nurse's actions, the more questions she had. Who was she? Where did she come from? And why did she seem so curious about Jeanne's affairs? Maybe it was nothing. Maybe Evelyn was simply suspicious of anyone associated with Jeanne Robertson right now.

"I suppose I can tell you what I know," Roy said as he crossed his arms over his chest.

"I would really appreciate your help." Jeanne's voice was low and vulnerable. And, if Evelyn was correct, she could see a hint of pleasure in Roy's face at his cousin's situation. He smiled, almost as if he was gloating that he knew something she didn't.

"If you remember correctly," Roy began, "Uncle Tony died a few months ago."

"My memory loss doesn't go back that far," Jeanne said with a little snark.

"And on Monday morning," he continued, "the will was finally read."

Jeanne frowned and looked off into the distance. "I remember— we met in his lawyer's office, here in Charleston."

Roy nodded. "And we learned that most of Uncle Tony's estate was used to pay the nursing home care costs."

"All but a few of his possessions," Jeanne filled in—and in that moment, her eyes lit up. "Including his ruby and diamond ring."

"Ah." Roy shook his head derisively. "There's the old fighting spark in your eyes."

"I didn't even know about the ring until the will was read," Jeanne added, almost to herself.

"Neither did I. He never mentioned it to me before."

Jeanne squinted, as if she was remembering something. "And when the lawyer told us the ring was being left to me, you became angry."

Roy's jaws pressed together as he stared at his cousin. "I can see that everything is returning."

"Almost everything," Jeanne said slowly. "Except, I don't remember what happened after I left the lawyer's office."

"You went to the North Harbor Trust to retrieve the ring from Uncle Tony's safe-deposit box."

Jeanne squinted, as if trying to remember. "And that's when you texted me and asked me to meet with you to discuss his decision."

"You shouldn't have gotten the ring." Roy's voice rose in anger, and he didn't seem to remember—or care—that Evelyn was in the room. "I was the one who moved to Charleston to look after him—I checked in on him regularly, made sure he went to his doctor's appointments, and even had him over to our house for the holidays, though he was a cantankerous old man who made our lives miserable. You only saw him once or twice a year and rarely checked in on him at all. I made sacrifices to see to his care—and what did he leave me? His run-down, beat-up car."

Jeanne didn't speak as she stared at her cousin.

"What happened to the ring?" he asked.

"It's in the hospital safe. As soon as I'm released, Evelyn will see that it's returned to me."

Roy glanced at Evelyn and then back to Jeanne. "And what will you do with it then?"

"I haven't decided. And as for Uncle Tony's decision," Jeanne said, "it was his ring, and what he did with it was up to him. Maybe he thought I'd appreciate its history and value it more than you would."

Roy snorted. "What do you need with the ring? You're wealthy enough as it is. I'm the one who sacrificed my job in Savannah to move here and take care of him. My bank account has suffered ever since."

"Maybe he knew I'd keep it and you'd want to sell it. Maybe it has historical value to our family."

"Even if neither one of us ever heard of it before Monday?" Roy scoffed. "You don't deserve the ring, and I'll do whatever it takes to get it from you."

Jeanne narrowed her eyes. "Are you threatening me?"

Roy's voice dropped even lower. "I'm warning you. If I have to sue you, I will. That ring belongs to me." He stared at her for a long moment, and then he turned on his heel and left the hospital room.

Jeanne didn't try to stop him.

Evelyn was quiet as she sat next to Jeanne's bed.

"Something doesn't feel right to me," Jeanne finally said. "I still can't remember what happened after I found out about the ring. I don't remember going to the bank or having lunch with Roy or where I went after lunch, before the accident." She pressed her hands to her eyes. "And my head is aching, just trying to think about all of it."

"You don't need to worry about any of that right now," Evelyn said as she rose from her chair. "You need to focus on getting well, so you can go home. I still have the parking meter receipt, which might be another clue. And since I enjoy solving a good mystery, I'll do whatever I can to help get to the bottom of whatever happened that day." She paused and then leaned closer to Jeanne. "Did you feel threatened by your cousin? Because if you did—"

"Roy's all talk," Jeanne said, waving her hand toward the door, as if to push him aside. "How could he sue me? The will was clear. Besides, he doesn't have two nickels to rub together to hire a lawyer."

Evelyn wasn't so certain. There was something ominous about Roy's warning, and she didn't like it one bit.

Chapter Seven

IT WAS FOUR THIRTY BY the time Evelyn walked back down the grand staircase to the main level of Mercy Hospital. The encounter with Wayne Preston and then with Cousin Roy left an uneasy feeling in her gut. With each new revelation came more questions. At least now she knew the ring did, in fact, belong to Jeanne, but what happened between Roy and Jeanne at lunch? And how did Wayne come to learn about the ring—enough to ask about it the next day? When Evelyn questioned him about it, why had he become so evasive?

And who told Hunter O'Reilly about all of it?

Evelyn fingered the parking meter receipt in her pocket as she walked through the lobby, toward the coffee shop in the corner. The scent of fresh baked goods drew her, but it was the sight of Madison Cummings, just entering the little shop, that solidified Evelyn's decision to stop. There was something about the nurse that made Evelyn curious, and she wanted to get to know her story a little more.

Madison stood in line at the counter, wearing a pair of scrubs with her hair up in a messy bun. She was studying the menu board on the wall and didn't notice Evelyn approach.

"Hello, Madison," Evelyn said to her.

The younger woman jumped and turned. She was the edgiest person Evelyn had ever come across.

"Oh," Madison said as she placed her hand on her chest. "I didn't know you were there."

"That's why I said hello." Evelyn smiled, hoping to put the woman at ease. "Do you mind if I join you?"

Madison opened her mouth, but nothing came out at first. She fidgeted and then said, "I was thinking I would take my coffee to go. I'm just getting off a long shift."

"That's too bad. I was hoping to get to know you a little better. Are you new to Charleston?"

"I am."

"What brought you here?"

"I'm just a temp nurse," she said with a shrug. "I like to travel around."

"It must get lonely to move from place to place, forced to make new friends all the time."

"I'm a people person," Madison said with an overly bright smile. "I enjoy meeting new people."

"Have you been to many places?"

"My fair share."

"That must be exciting. Do you stay in the United States, or do you travel internationally?"

Madison moved ahead in line and glanced toward the lady behind the register. She seemed reluctant to answer Evelyn. "I've done both."

"And where is your favorite place to work?"

The young woman glanced nervously at the line again and then back at Evelyn. She didn't seem eager to share more information than was necessary.

"You know," Madison said, "on second thought, I think I'll just head home without the coffee." She yawned and put her hand over her mouth. "I'm still not on Charleston time, and I'm ready for bed." She stepped out of line. "Goodbye."

Evelyn started to apologize for being too pushy—but Madison rushed out of the coffee shop so quickly, she didn't have time to even say goodbye.

And worse, Evelyn had the distinct feeling that Madison didn't want her to know anything about her. Why not? Was the young woman running or hiding from something? It never occurred to Evelyn to wonder why a person would want to be a temp nurse, moving often from one place to another. Maybe some of them did it to run from their past.

The thought intrigued Evelyn as she walked back to the records department a few minutes later, a hot cup of coffee in one hand and a fresh-baked scone in the other. Was Madison Cummings running from a sordid past—or even a bitter love story? Had she witnessed a mob-related crime and been placed in the witness protection program? Or maybe it wasn't a troubled past. Maybe she was an undercover police officer, come to learn the truth about the ruby and diamond ring.

Evelyn smiled to herself. She didn't often let her mind turn to fanciful things, but ever since that ring showed up at Mercy Hospital, she could think of very little else.

Maybe Madison Cummings was simply a young woman eager for adventure and travel.

She was pondering these things as she entered the records department and found Stacia at the front desk.

"Sorry, I was gone longer than I expected," she said to her assistant.

"No worries. I held down the fort while you were away."

"Anyone else come and inquire after the ring?" She was half-joking, half-serious.

"Not that I know of. Why? Did you expect someone?"

Evelyn shook her head and set her coffee and scone down on her desk. She took the parking meter receipt out of her pocket and looked at it a little closer.

"What are you looking at?" Stacia said as she came to stand next to Evelyn to glance at the slip of paper.

"An address." Evelyn pointed to the stamp on the receipt that told her where the meter was located in Charleston. "This is in the historic district. I'm thinking about driving there this evening to see what businesses are in the area."

"What kind of business are you looking for?"

"A lawyer or a bank or something like that. I really don't know. Maybe I can make a list of businesses and show it to Jeanne to see if any of them ring a bell."

"Or," Stacia said with a smile, "we could google the address and see what businesses are in the area."

Evelyn chuckled. "Sometimes I forget how convenient technology is."

Stacia laughed and pulled her cell phone out of her back pocket. She opened the map app and typed in the address on the receipt. Within a nanosecond, a map popped up on the phone and each business was listed over the corresponding building.

"Voilà," Stacia said as she handed her phone to Evelyn.

"Thank you. You just saved me a lot of time." Evelyn ran her finger over the phone's screen, looking at all the different businesses in the area. There were lots of restaurants and boutique shops, as well as other companies, like an insurance company, a travel agency, and others.

"I wonder what Jeanne was doing in this area," Evelyn mused, almost to herself—and then her eyes landed on a business that looked very appropriate and promising.

"Sinclair Antique Jewelry," she read out loud to Stacia, her voice rising with excitement. "Do you think that's where she went?"

"There's only one way to find out. Give the jeweler a call."

Evelyn pressed the icon and the store's address, phone number, and service hours popped up. She glanced at the time on the phone. It was already a few minutes to five. "It's almost time to go home, and James is expecting me. The jeweler doesn't close until seven. Maybe I'll drive over there a little later and check out the shop for myself."

Stacia took her phone back and returned it to her pocket. "I have a date tonight."

"Oh?" Evelyn said. "With Emmett?"

"Goodness, no." Stacia made a face. "We broke up last night. I'm going out with Hunter O'Reilly, the reporter from the *Charleston Times*."

"You broke up with Emmett last night, and you're going on a date with Hunter *tonight*?" Evelyn couldn't keep the incredulity from her voice.

"Of course. What else would I do with my evening?"

Evelyn could think of a dozen productive things Stacia could do but chose not to respond.

She was just happy she had James to go home to.

A loud noise met Evelyn's ears the moment she entered her house after work. It almost sounded like a saw of some kind, though she couldn't imagine what James might be cutting into today. When she set her keys on the side table, she found another layer of dust. It was on everything, and a quick glance toward the kitchen door told her James hadn't bothered to put up a tarp to prevent it from infiltrating the whole first floor again.

Instant frustration welled up in Evelyn's chest. "James!" she called out.

The saw didn't stop, so she walked down the hall toward the kitchen.

Last night she had spent two hours cleaning up the mess he had made from cutting the hole in the wall. Now all her work was for nothing. It was even more infuriating that James had told her that would happen.

"James!" she called again, this time coming around the corner into the kitchen.

Her husband was awkwardly positioned with the top half of his body inside the base cabinet directly under the new window, a power tool in hand. He wore hearing protectors as he cut out an opening in the bottom of the cabinet. Sawdust gathered in a pile while something like smoke floated up from the saw, billowing in the room.

Evelyn stood for a couple of seconds to watch him, wondering what in the world he was doing.

Finally, James finished the job and removed himself from the cabinet. When he stood, he took off his hearing protectors and turned. His face lit up. "You're home."

"What are you doing?"

James glanced at the hole he just made. "I thought we should move the sink here near the window."

"What's wrong with where the sink has been for the past sixty years?"

"Wouldn't it be nice to stand at the window when we're doing the dishes?"

"Not if it means filling the house with dust again." Evelyn's voice rose higher than she intended. She forced herself to take a steadying breath and then proceeded with more calm. "I thought you said you would warn me before you made any more big decisions."

"It's just a little mess, Evie. I can vacuum it up in a second."

"There's dust all over the house again—"

"That's not from anything I did today." He motioned toward the hole in the cabinet. "That's all the mess I made."

"Then why is there a layer of dust over everything again?" Evelyn felt shameful tears threatening the backs of her eyes. "After all the work I put into cleaning last night—"

"I warned you. The dust can hang in the air for hours before it settles. If there's dust on everything today, it's probably still from yesterday's mess. I told you not to waste your time—"

"I can't do this anymore." Evelyn hated her inability to deal with this situation. It made her feel as defenseless and vulnerable as it had when she was a child. "I'm sorry, but I need stability and sanity in my home. I can't worry each day that I'm going to come home to one more random hole in my kitchen." She motioned toward the bottom of the cabinet. "And how long will this change take? Won't you have to completely redo the plumbing? Do you even know how to run plumbing?"

"I watched a YouTube video today."

"I don't need the sink near the window. It's just fine where it is. I want this kitchen finished—and the sooner the better."

He stared at her for a moment. "Are you sure?"

"Yes." She sighed. "I just want all this to be done. Please don't make more work than you had planned. Keep the sink where it's at—didn't we already order the countertop with the sink in its current location?"

"I called the granite shop, and they said we have until Friday to change the specifications."

Evelyn shook her head. "Please. Let's just stick to the original plan."

James slowly nodded. "Fine. If you're happy with where the sink is now, we'll leave it there."

"Thank you. Can we fix the hole?"

"We can fix anything."

Evelyn's shoulders loosened. "Good," she said. "I just want to be done." She glanced around. There was random construction garbage lying around, tools to put away, and the floor could use a good vacuuming with the large shop vac they had purchased.

"I'll take care of this," James said, as if reading her mind. "Why don't you go out and pick up something for supper? Maybe order from one of your favorite restaurants downtown."

Evelyn thought of Sinclair Antique Jewelry. Maybe she could pop in while she was out getting supper for them. "Are you sure?"

"Absolutely. Take your time. I'll get this place cleaned up, and then you and I can enjoy an evening off together. Maybe go to a movie or out to a park just to get away from the mess for a while."

Her heart felt light and hopeful. "Really?"

James nodded. "We could both use a break." He put his hands on her shoulders and turned her around to leave the kitchen. "Go grab us something to eat, and when you get back this will all be clean."

He walked with her to the front door where she grabbed her purse and her keys. Then he gave her a kiss, and Evelyn left the house.

She took a deep breath when she was on the front stoop, the door closing behind her.

Her car was parked in the back, so she walked along their short driveway and got into her vehicle. Since she was able to walk to work and they did most of their shopping on the weekends, she and James only owned one car. During the school year, James usually drove the car on his forty-minute commute to Charleston Southern University, though he was able to use public transportation when needed. They had talked about getting a second vehicle over the years but didn't feel the cost was justifiable. Besides, they didn't have a lot of extra space to park a second car, and Evelyn was happy walking to work or using public transportation herself.

Now, however, she got into their stylish midsize Camry and pulled onto Short Street to head toward the jewelers. She'd go there before picking up supper, just to make sure she arrived before they closed for the evening.

It was less than a mile to the jewelry store, which was nestled in the French Quarter on the corner of State Street and North Market Street. It took longer for Evelyn to find a place to park than it had for her to drive there. Downtown was busy this Thursday evening. The weekend crowd usually started to pull into town on Thursdays, and by Saturday, it would be almost impossible to park anywhere within the historic district.

Finally, Evelyn found a spot a couple of blocks away from the jeweler and then had to walk to the shop. She passed several beautiful buildings, many of them boasting ornate ironwork balconies and tall, shuttered windows so common in this section of town. There were many prominent art galleries, restaurants, and other businesses in this district. It was a popular destination for locals and tourists alike. The entire area had originally been located within the walled city of Charleston and had been part of Sir Anthony Ashley Cooper's Grand Model. A heavy contingent of French immigrants had settled the area, thereby giving it its designation.

Sinclair Antique Jewelry was located on the main floor of a four-story building. The large plateglass windows in the front were filled with eye-catching jewelry that sparkled and shimmered in the early evening sunshine. Evelyn couldn't help but stop to admire an especially decorative necklace, which, if she would have to guess, would probably date back to the Edwardian era.

Cars passed on State Street and North Market and pedestrians ambled by, some with shopping bags, others with backpacks, and still others with briefcases.

Evelyn opened the front door and was greeted by the sound of a bell overhead, indicating her arrival.

Long, glass-topped counters filled with jewelry graced both sides of the shop. Above, soft lights glowed down and made the jewels sparkle. Potted ferns, oriental rugs, and dark walnut trim gave the shop a luxurious feel.

"Welcome to Sinclair Antique Jewelry," a woman said when Evelyn entered. "My name is Abigail Sinclair. How may I help you?"

Evelyn closed the door behind her and walked to the center of the shop where she met up with Abigail. No one else was in the store, and it appeared as if Abigail was the only employee. Perhaps someone else was in the back, though it mattered very little to Evelyn.

"Hello," Evelyn said to Abigail. "I'm wondering if you could answer a few questions for me."

"It would be my pleasure." Abigail was a pleasant-looking woman with a short, pixie-style haircut. She wore a simple gray pantsuit ensemble with a white shirt under her jacket and a pair of short black heels. "Are you looking for a particular piece of jewelry?"

"I'm actually here to inquire about a customer who might have stopped here on Monday."

Abigail frowned. "Oh?"

"I work in the records department at Mercy Hospital. On Monday, a patient was brought into the ER after a car accident. She had a ring in her possession, but unfortunately, she's suffering from amnesia and cannot recall where she might have visited right before the accident. We have reason to believe she might have come here."

"Seriously?" Abigail's face revealed her shock. "I've heard of amnesia, but I've never actually met anyone who has suffered from it."

Evelyn nodded. "Unfortunately, it's a very real problem for some people, including our patient."

"We had several women come into the store on Monday. Could you tell me why she might have stopped here?"

"She had an old ruby ring—"

The moment Evelyn mentioned the ruby, the look on Abigail's face shifted from shock and empathy to anger and irritation. "Was her name Jeanne Robertson?"

Evelyn nodded. "Do you remember her?"

Abigail crossed her arms. "I had the unfortunate occasion to meet her, yes. She came in here on Monday morning."

Evelyn wanted to hug Abigail in glee. She had uncovered another piece of the puzzle. But Abigail's attitude and general demeanor regarding Jeanne didn't warrant even a smile on Evelyn's behalf. Instead, Evelyn found herself frowning. Clearly, the encounter between Abigail and Jeanne had left a sour taste in Abigail's mouth.

"Do you recall what time Jeanne stopped here?" she asked.

"It was midmorning, maybe around eleven or so." Abigail dropped her arms by her sides. "But I have no wish to discuss Ms. Robertson's situation. She was deeply insulting when she was here, and I told her to leave and never come back."

Evelyn's eyes opened wide. "I'm sorry to hear that."

"Why are you trying to help her?" Abigail asked. "What's this to you?"

"The ring was given to me to put into the hospital safe in my department. When I did a little research, I discovered the letters *LPOC* on the inside of the silver band. If it's the ring I think it is, it has significant historical implications for Charleston. And because

Jeanne is a patient at our hospital, I took an interest in helping her."

Abigail lifted an eyebrow. "Is she as rude to you as she was to me?"

Evelyn smiled. "She's uncertain about what happened on Monday. I promised I would help her put the pieces of the puzzle together."

Abigail studied Evelyn for a moment. Finally, her anger subsided and she relaxed—just a bit. "You seem like a nice lady, so I'll answer your questions. But I'm only doing it for you," she added quickly. "Not for that Robertson woman. She doesn't deserve my cooperation."

"Thank you," Evelyn said. "I appreciate any help you can offer."

"What would you like to know?"

"First," Evelyn began, "I'd like to know if the ring is from the seventeenth century. Could it be one of the rings from the Lords Proprietors of Carolina?"

Abigail slowly nodded. "I believe it is—and that's what I told Ms. Robertson. I'm actually quite familiar with the history of the rings gifted to the Lords Proprietors of Carolina from King Charles II. That's why I was so shocked when Ms. Robertson brought it in here. It's been missing for hundreds of years. When I started to ask Ms. Robertson where she got it, she became rude and suspicious— like I was going to try to steal it from her or some such nonsense."

"Did she tell you anything about the ring? Did she know any of the history?"

Abigail shook her head. "Not that I remember. She didn't know any more than what I told her—but I could see the dollar signs forming in her eyes as I shared the history."

So, Jeanne's story was partly true. She didn't appear to know anything about the ring before it had been given to her. "Did she ask you what it was worth?"

Again, Abigail nodded. "I gave her an appraisal and then I offered to buy it from her—which is what I often do when I find a rare piece of jewelry. That's my business after all, but she became insulting and accused me of trying to rip her off. She said my appraisal wasn't accurate and that I was trying to buy the ring for under its value." Abigail's face filled with anger again. "I'm a professional, if nothing else, and would never try to undercut someone for my own profit. My reputation means everything to me. I gave her a fair appraisal value and then made a fair offer." Her voice rose as she spoke. "Ms. Robertson was rude and demeaning. I told her to leave and never come back." Abigail pressed her lips together for a moment. "Regardless of her behavior, the ring is remarkable and one of a kind. If she ever decides to sell, I would like a chance to make another offer—as long as she doesn't insult me again."

"I'm not sure if she will sell it." Evelyn glanced at the clock on the wall. It was getting late, and if she wanted time to enjoy James's company tonight, she'd need to get going. She still had to pick up something for supper. "Thank you for your help. Is there anything else you can remember from that morning? Anything that might help us put together the events that led up to her accident?"

Abigail was quiet for a moment as she thought. "She was distracted by her phone. It looked like someone was texting her. And she was agitated, but whether that was from excitement over her recent inheritance or because of something else, I can't say for certain. She did tell me she would get a second opinion, and I told her to be my guest. I stand by my appraisal, though I told her if she put the ring on auction, there was no telling how high the bidders might go. You can't predict something like that."

"And that's all?"

"Yes. She left here with her feathers ruffled, and I was happy to see her leave." Abigail balled her fists. "It's a shame that a ring as rare and valuable as that ended up with a woman who has no concept of its importance."

The last thing Evelyn wanted to do was cause Abigail more unrest. "Thank you for your time, Ms. Sinclair. Do you mind if I call you, should I have other questions?"

Abigail nodded. "That's fine."

Evelyn expressed her thanks and then let herself out of the jewelry shop.

The more she investigated, the more she discovered about Jeanne Robertson's personality and character. And the more she discovered, the less she liked.

Chapter Eight

By the time Evelyn returned home, her stomach was growling—especially because the food she had picked up at a seafood restaurant on the waterfront smelled delicious in the to-go containers on the passenger seat. She had chosen lobster bisque, cheddar biscuits, and Caesar salad. It had taken all her willpower not to grab one of the warm biscuits from the bag on her drive home.

"James," she called from the back door when she walked into the house. "I'm home."

There was no sound coming from the kitchen. Maybe James was upstairs taking a shower, getting ready for their evening out. Evelyn set her purse on the table near the back door, a bounce in her step. She walked through the living room, down the hall past the quiet kitchen, and then set the takeout on the dining room table in the front of the house. There was a layer of dust on the table, on the chairs, and even on the windows.

Evelyn walked back down the hall to get a dishcloth from the crates set up in the living room. But when she passed the kitchen, she noticed that everything was exactly as it had looked when she left. The tools, garbage, and even the sawdust from the opening James had made in the cabinet were all still in a pile on the ground. He hadn't cleaned anything, and she'd been gone for over an hour.

She went to the living room and found a dishcloth. Since there was no kitchen sink to wet the cloth, she went to the small bathroom under the stairs. It was a tiny room with space for a very small sink and toilet. She could just barely stand up straight in the room and James had to bend whenever he entered, but it served a purpose.

Evelyn put the cloth under the faucet and turned the knob—but nothing came out of the spout. She turned the other knob and nothing happened.

There was no running water.

"James!" she called again. "Did you turn off the water?"

Still no reply.

She might as well go upstairs and find out where he went. Maybe the water worked in one of the bathrooms on the second floor.

Evelyn trudged up the stairs, dry dishcloth in hand.

But James was not upstairs, and the water wasn't working in either of the second-floor bathrooms. She stood in her master bathroom, her hands against the counter, and looked at herself in the mirror. Evelyn hated to be crabby or out of sorts, but every time she turned around, there was another inconvenience she had to deal with because of this kitchen remodel. To top it all off, her husband was now missing. She wasn't terribly concerned that he wasn't in the house. No doubt he had a good reason for leaving—and she had the vehicle, so he couldn't have gone far. But what would have called him away?

Back down the stairs Evelyn went to grab her cell phone from her purse near the back door, the lobster bisque and cheddar biscuits getting cold on the dusty dining room table. She pulled her phone from her purse and dialed James's number.

Within a couple of rings, he picked up. "Hey, Evie." His voice sounded heavy and concerned. "Are you back?"

"I am—but where are you?"

He sighed. "We ran into some trouble with our water."

"I already found that out on my own."

"I'm in the basement with a plumber."

"You're what?" Evelyn walked out of the dining room and into the stairway hall then down the steps leading into the basement where their laundry room was housed.

"I turned off the water today, thinking I was going to move the sink's plumbing, and when I went to turn it on again, it wouldn't work."

Evelyn walked into the laundry room where she found James standing near the plumber, holding a flashlight for the man as he worked.

James was still holding his phone, but when he saw Evelyn, he slipped it into his pocket. He was still wearing his old jeans and T-shirt, which were dirty and stained. He hadn't showered yet and didn't look like he was anywhere near ready to be done working for the evening. Any hope Evelyn had of enjoying a nice hot meal and then spending the evening relaxing with her husband was slowly draining away.

James shook his head, clearly upset. "I thought I could manage the plumbing myself," he said. "But it looks like I made more of a problem than I anticipated."

The plumber glanced at James and chuckled. "You're not the first. Probably watched a YouTube video and thought you could handle it."

James didn't bother to answer.

94

Water had pooled on the tile floor near the plumber's feet.

"What happened?" Evelyn asked.

"I turned off the water main today," James said, "and took apart the pipe leading into the kitchen. I had planned to move it for the new location, but when you said you didn't want me to, I came back down here to put everything back together. Turns out I didn't do it correctly, and when I turned the water back on, it started to leak. Thankfully, I was able to get Randy here to come by on a moment's notice."

Evelyn nibbled her bottom lip, not wanting to ask the question most pressing on her mind. How much would an emergency visit from the plumber cost? And—more importantly—how long would it take?

"Can I speak to you?" Evelyn asked James.

The plumber glanced at James, a knowing look on his face.

James handed the flashlight to Randy and followed Evelyn out of the laundry room, up the stairs, and into the hall. The aroma of lobster bisque met her there, making her stomach growl.

"How long before we have water again?" she asked.

"Randy said it could take an hour or two—if he has the right parts."

An hour or two would put them close to bedtime, which meant they probably wouldn't get away for the evening.

"And how much will this cost us?"

James sighed. "It won't be cheap."

Evelyn put her hand on the stair railing. She didn't want to blame James—it was a mistake, one he was probably regretting more than she was.

"I don't think I can sleep tonight without cleaning up this mess," Evelyn said. "And how will we do that without any water?"

"I have an idea." James put his hand over hers on the railing. "Is there someone nearby you're comfortable staying with for a couple of days, until I can get this mess under control? Then I can keep working into the evenings and get this done even faster. You can ignore the mess, and I'll have it all cleaned up before you get home."

His suggestion sent an unexpected pang of regret through her chest. They'd never willingly spent time apart—other than for an occasional business meeting that might call one or the other out of town for a night or two. For thirty-five years, they'd slept side by side, through the good times and the bad. Why was she letting this project get the better of her?

"It would only be for a night or two," he said quickly, no doubt reading the look on her face. "I know this is hard on you—and there's not a lot I can do about the dust or the unexpected setbacks, like the plumbing. If you go somewhere else you can get a little rest and not have to worry about what's going on here."

"Not worry?" Evelyn met her husband's kind gaze. "That's all I'll be thinking about if I go away."

James smiled. "I don't want you to go, Evie, but I also don't want you to be uncomfortable. I really think it would be best if you go away for a couple of days."

Evelyn wasn't so sure, but she couldn't deny it sounded lovely to walk away from the mess for a while. Maybe, if she did go, she'd come back in a better frame of mind, ready to help tackle the project instead of getting upset at every little thing.

"Maybe Joy would be willing to have me stay with her for a couple of days. But only if you're sure."

"I can handle being on my own for a couple of days—but I won't like it." He winked at her, and she knew he was trying to make it easier for her to go.

"I love you, James Robert Perry."

She would give Joy a call. And though she was certain Joy would be happy to have her as a guest, Evelyn would count the hours until she could come home and be with her husband again.

Less than two hours later, Evelyn stood at Joy's front door. James had driven her over after they had eaten their supper. He hadn't been able to clean up and shower, so he had opted not to stop and say hi to Joy. Since the plumber was still working at their house, he decided to head back home to get more work done. He waved and pulled away.

Within seconds, Joy was at her door, an energetic spaniel at her side. She opened the door wide, a smile on her face. "Come in, come in."

Evelyn's heart was heavy, and she couldn't deny she was a little embarrassed too. "I feel a little foolish to ask this favor of you."

"Nonsense!" Joy ushered her into her beautiful entry. "I hope you don't mind another guest. My daughter asked me to take care of Mopsy for a couple of days while she's having her floors redone." Mopsy's excitement was evident as she jumped and ran in circles, her nails clicking on the tiled floors. "You're always welcome here, Evelyn," Joy said, "for any reason."

Joy closed her front door behind Evelyn and put her hand on Mopsy's head to calm and steady the spaniel. "I made up the guest room for you, and you're more than welcome to stay as long as you need."

The aroma of fresh-baked cookies and Joy's signature coffee floated into the entryway from the kitchen. Everything was neat and orderly, and as clean as could be. Evelyn felt her stress and worries melting away. Mopsy's enthusiastic joy at having a guest put a smile on her face.

"Why don't you go on up to the guest room, set your things down, and then meet me in the kitchen?" Joy put her hand on Evelyn's shoulder.

Evelyn had told Joy that they were remodeling their kitchen and she needed a couple of days away from the mess, but no doubt Joy had a lot of questions—especially because James hadn't come in to say hello.

Evelyn nodded and walked up the open staircase, which was back outside on the main-floor piazza. Mopsy followed close at her heels, but Evelyn didn't mind. She liked the companionship and loved having the furry little creature close at hand.

Upstairs there were two bedrooms with built-in bookcases and a shared bathroom. The guest room was at the back of the house, above the kitchen. The walls were painted a warm, creamy yellow, and the wood floors gleamed. A soft white rug was cushy under her feet as she set her small suitcase on the quilted bed. Darkness had fallen over Charleston, and here, at the back of the house, overlooking Joy's courtyard, it was quiet and still.

At least, as quiet as Mopsy would allow. The dog trotted around the end of the bed a couple of times, as if checking out the space to make sure all was well.

"You silly dog," Evelyn said as she bent and stroked Mopsy's brown and white head.

A few minutes later, the two of them went back down the stairs and joined Joy in her spacious kitchen.

"I hope you don't mind having a constant companion," Joy said as she nodded toward Mopsy. "She'll follow you around the house until the moment you leave."

Joy left the kitchen and put two steaming mugs of coffee on the small dining room table and then came back to move cookies off the pan and onto a plate. She motioned for Evelyn to take a seat in the dining room.

"I don't mind at all," Evelyn said as she sat in one of the chairs, able to see Joy in her kitchen. "I've often thought James and I should get a pet, but it's probably a good thing we don't have one right now."

Joy stopped filling the plate with cookies and looked at Evelyn, concern in her brown eyes. "I hope you're not having troubles with James."

"Oh, no!" Evelyn shook her head quickly. "James and I aren't having troubles—at least, not directly."

"Good." Joy's entire countenance eased, and she brought the plate of cookies from the counter to the table. "I'm happy to hear that. I was so worried that you and James were fighting."

"I should have shared more with you before I came," Evelyn conceded. "But I thought we could catch up once I got here."

"I'm just so glad it's not marital problems." Joy took a seat on the white chair, and her kind face radiated warmth. She was truly a good and wonderful friend, and Evelyn was so thankful she had decided to move to Charleston when her husband, Wilson, had passed away. Their one and only child, Sabrina, had come to Charleston several years ago. When Joy found herself alone, she knew it was time to leave her old life behind to be with Sabrina and her granddaughters, Mallory and Eloise. After she found work at Mercy Hospital, she and Evelyn had become friends. Joy tended to be quieter than Evelyn's other friends, but that gentle, soft-spoken personality allowed her to listen and hear things others often missed.

"It's not marital problems," Evelyn admitted, "though it has been putting a strain on our relationship." She sighed and wrapped her hands around her coffee mug.

"The kitchen remodel?"

Evelyn nodded. "I'm grateful he's doing the project, and I know I'll love it when it's finished, but it's bringing up so many negative emotions in me. Every time I turn around, I'm losing patience, getting frustrated, and fighting with my husband."

"That seems like a fairly common side effect of remodeling," Joy said. "I've heard several couples say that house projects are a source of contention between them. And when it's a big and inconvenient project, like a kitchen, it's only natural for it to add stress to your life and relationship."

"I know—but I don't want it to." Evelyn sipped her coffee and smiled down at Mopsy, who flopped onto her belly, right over Evelyn's feet. "I remember my parents fighting a lot when I was a child—and it was usually over the house. I hated hearing it and would hide away in my bedroom, under the covers, with a book so I could escape—and now here I am again, running away, trying to escape from the same thing. I feel weak and childish."

Joy reached across the table and squeezed Evelyn's hand. "It's okay to step back and take a deep breath. Is James upset that you left?"

Evelyn shook her head. "It was his idea."

A smile lit up Joy's face. "See. There you go. James is a good man. He knows what you need."

"I just wish I wasn't so weak."

"Struggling with something doesn't mean you're weak, Evelyn." Joy folded her hands on the top of the table. "It means you're human. God uses all sorts of difficult situations to strengthen our character. He could be teaching you a whole host of lessons through this situation. Don't beat yourself up if you need a little break. It's during the quiet moments that we have the time to reflect on what God is trying to tell us. As long as you use this opportunity to learn a lesson, then none of it is wasted."

Hope curled up in Evelyn's heart and lay there to rest. Joy was right.

"These cookies smell delicious," Evelyn said.

"Help yourself." Joy took a sip of her coffee. "I made a whole batch for us to enjoy."

"Thank you for opening your house and your heart to me." Evelyn smiled at her friend. "It means more than you'll ever know."

"It's my pleasure, Evelyn."

Mopsy chose that moment to lift her head and offer a friendly bark.

"And Mopsy's too, apparently." Joy chuckled.

Evelyn's laughter bubbled up from her chest, and she realized it had been far too long since she'd felt this happy and carefree.

But she didn't want to reserve her good mood for her friend alone. Maybe one of the lessons God was teaching her was that despite her circumstances, she could still have happiness and contentment, and she could share it with everyone in her life. Both at home and at work.

She thought about Jeanne Robertson, lying in her hospital bed, alone, with very few people showing any care or attention for her. Perhaps God had brought Evelyn into her life to help her find a little happiness and contentment as well.

Chapter Nine

THE NEXT MORNING, EVELYN AND Joy walked from Joy's house to Mercy Hospital. It was a short walk, just what Evelyn needed in the brilliant sunshine. The day was fresh and bright with possibilities. She felt rested, invigorated, and ready to tackle the last workday of the week. She and Joy had made plans with Anne and Shirley to have supper that evening together at a favorite restaurant, and James had called her before she left for work, asking if she'd meet him tomorrow at the appliance shop to pick out her new refrigerator, stove, and microwave.

When they entered the front lobby, Joy went toward the gift shop and Evelyn went toward the records department. She was an hour early, but that would give her plenty of time to get some morning tasks completed before her other staff came in to work.

Evelyn was humming a favorite hymn to herself as she lifted her lanyard to run her badge in front of the keypad near the door to her office. The lock clicked open, and Evelyn turned the knob. She flipped on the light and then stopped in her tracks.

The door to the Vault was standing ajar.

Strange. Evelyn kept the door closed and locked at all times—even when she was working in the office. Not only because it contained historical records but because it housed the hospital safe.

Granted, the safe was secure, but Evelyn didn't want to take any chances.

Quickly, she set down her purse and the to-go mug of coffee Joy had prepared for her earlier and walked across the room to the Vault door. Her mouth slipped open when she saw that the lock on the door had been tampered with—and broken.

Her hands were shaking, and her heart was pumping hard. Everything inside of her wanted to run into the Vault to see if there was any damage, but her common sense won over and she rushed to her desk to fumble with the phone. She pressed the SECURITY button and, within a heartbeat, there was a calm voice on the other end of the receiver.

"Security, how may I help you?"

"This is Evelyn Perry, Records Department Supervisor. I believe there's been an intruder in the Vault."

"I'm dispatching security officers to you immediately, Ms. Perry," the young woman on the other end of the phone said. "He should be there within minutes."

"Thank you." Evelyn hung up the phone, her pulse still thrumming through her veins. Her second instinct was to alert her friends. She picked up her cell phone and opened a group text with Joy, Anne, and Shirley.

IT LOOKS LIKE SOMEONE BROKE INTO THE VAULT. I'M WAITING FOR SECURITY TO COME AND CHECK IT OUT.

It was the only thing she needed to text. There was no reason to invite them to come—she knew that if any of them were available, they'd be there in a flash.

Joy was the first to show up—even before Security arrived. Her eyes were large as she stepped through the office door, which Evelyn had purposely left open. She glanced toward the Vault.

"Have you gone in?" Joy asked.

Evelyn shook her head. "I'm waiting for Security."

"Who could have done this?"

"I have no idea." Evelyn paced in front of her desk, tossing a glance over her shoulder at the open door. "I don't even know the extent of damage. Why would someone want to break into the Vault?"

Shirley came bustling into the room next, though her face was calm and stoic. It seemed that very little upset Shirley, which made her a perfect nurse and caregiver. She offered Evelyn's nerves some much-needed peace as she surveyed the room and showed no signs of deep concern. "I heard about the break-in. Have you been in the Vault yet?" she asked.

"No. I'm waiting for Security."

"Where are they?" Joy asked as she poked her head out the door and looked right and then left down the hallway.

"Why don't we go into the Vault and look ourselves?" Shirley asked.

"I'd rather not tamper with anything until Security gets here." Evelyn glanced at the clock. It had only been three minutes, but it felt like a lifetime.

"That's probably a good plan." Shirley walked over to the Vault's door and, without touching it, tried to peek inside. "It's pretty dark in there. I can't really see anything."

"Here they come," Joy said with a measure of relief as she came back into the office. "The security officers are walking down the hall, and Anne is right behind them."

Evelyn walked to the door to greet the two men who were dressed very much like police officers. They wore navy pants and blue shirts and had radios strapped to their belts with the mouthpieces up near their shoulders for easy access. The men were tall and broad and gave Evelyn the sense of protection she needed at a time like this.

Anne, who was dwarfed by the security guards, rushed up behind them, her face filled with concern and worry. "Are you all right?" she asked Evelyn.

Evelyn nodded. "I'm completely fine. A little shaken up, but fine."

"What seems to be the problem, Evelyn?" Officer Seamus McCord was a former deputy sheriff, with striking blue eyes and a fierce sense of protection for everyone and everything in Mercy Hospital. He had been at Mercy for years and had assisted Evelyn several times in the past with various tasks and concerns.

"I came into the office about five minutes ago," she told Seamus. "Everything seemed normal from the outside, but when I turned on the light, I saw the Vault door was open and the lock broken." Her heart was still pumping a little harder than normal.

"Anything else out of the ordinary?" Officer Rafe Jagger asked. He stood a little taller than Seamus. He was also younger and newer to Mercy, and Evelyn didn't know him as well.

"Nothing that I noticed," Evelyn said, though she glanced around the office one more time to make sure. Her desk, Stacia's desk, and the others looked exactly as they usually did. All the paper files, in the dozens of shelves along the wall, also looked untouched—though it could take weeks and weeks to discover if a file was missing. Most everything they did now was on the computer and the files on the shelves were slowly being transferred to digital copies.

"We'll go in and inspect the Vault," Seamus told the ladies. "Sit tight until we know it's safe for you to enter."

Evelyn nodded.

As the two officers slowly walked through the opened door and into the Vault, Anne, Shirley, and Joy crowded around Evelyn. They stood in a tight knot, all of them trying to get a peek into the room.

Seamus flipped on the lights. The door was open wide enough for Evelyn to see records strewn all over the room.

"All those files," Joy lamented to Evelyn. "Look at that mess."

It didn't seem possible, but it appeared as if whoever got into the Vault had torn it to pieces. Papers were everywhere. But it wasn't just the fact that the records were disorganized—some of the paper and photographs were so old, they could have been easily destroyed in this senseless act.

"It looks like it's all clear," Seamus said as he walked back into the office space. "If you'd like to come in, you may."

Evelyn was the first to enter the Vault. It was worse than she'd first suspected. Almost every filing drawer was opened, and the majority of the files were torn out. But it was the hospital safe that drew her attention.

"It looks like whoever got in here was after the safe," Seamus said. "It's been tampered with, but it doesn't appear to have been broken into. I don't have the combination, so if you'd be so kind as to open it, Evelyn, I'd appreciate the chance to inspect it."

"Of course." Evelyn quickly turned the dial in the prescribed combination, and the lock gave way. She opened the heavy door and stepped back.

After a few moments, Seamus came out. "Looks secure, though you might want to check."

Evelyn stepped into the safe, and though she didn't have its contents memorized, it looked untouched. Her real concern was Jeanne Robertson's ring, but it was still there.

"As far as I can tell, everything is in its place." Evelyn walked out of the safe, closed the door, and locked it.

"Other than a broken lock and some files thrown around," Seamus said to Evelyn, "does it look like anything else is vandalized or stolen?"

Evelyn walked around the room, her dismay at the disorderly files mounting, but she shook her head. "No."

"Maybe someone was just trying to cause trouble," Office Jagger suggested. "A prank?"

"But why?" Shirley asked. "It doesn't make any sense. And how did they get past the main door into the office without breaking it open?"

"Perhaps they're an employee or they stole an employee's badge," Seamus offered. "I don't think it was a prank, though. It looks like whoever came in here was trying to get into the safe. Maybe, when they weren't successful, they took out their anger and frustration on the files."

Evelyn wasn't so sure—though it seemed plausible.

"Wait," Joy said, her voice shaky. "What's this?" She pointed to a piece of paper on the top of a filing cabinet.

It was a yellowed sheet of paper. Evelyn picked it up and found an old patient file with smudged and faded ink on one side. On the other was a note scrawled in fresh black ink:

Next time I'll get into the safe and take what's rightfully mine. Don't try to stop me from getting the ring or the destruction will be worse. You'll regret meddling, Mrs. Perry.

Evelyn dropped the paper back onto the file cabinet, her heart skipping a beat.

"Who would say and do such a thing?" Anne whispered.

Seamus walked over to the file cabinet and looked closer at the note.

His face was grave. "Things just got a lot more serious," he said. "We don't take too kindly to threats of any kind here at Mercy Hospital."

"Isn't there a video security system in place?" Anne asked.

"There is," Seamus said. "But the cameras aren't in every room. We've got them positioned in the high-risk areas, such as the lobby, ER, nurses' stations, gift shop, and the like. We don't have one here in the Vault or even in the records department office, since most of the current records are all digitized and this wasn't designated a high-risk area."

"Even with the safe here?" Shirley asked. "That seems like a pretty obvious place for a camera."

"Most of the things usually stored in the safe don't have much value," Evelyn explained. "And very few people even know it's here."

"We do have cameras in most of the hallways," Officer Jagger added. "We can have someone check the footage from last night to see if there's anything suspicious."

Seamus looked very serious as he addressed Evelyn. "You can rest assured that we will do everything possible to uncover the perpetrator. If you see anything suspicious or get any leads, please let us know."

"If you can come up with a possible list of suspects," Officer Jagger said, "that would also be helpful."

"I will." Evelyn nodded. "Thank you."

"And I'll take this note with me for evidence." Seamus put on a pair of black gloves and gently lifted it. "Good day, ladies."

The officers left the records department just as Stacia was coming in. Her mouth gaped as she passed the tall gentlemen and both nodded a greeting at her.

"What's happening?" Stacia asked Evelyn the moment she laid eyes on her.

Evelyn quickly told Stacia the story while Anne, Shirley, and Joy began to gather up the papers and photographs that were lying on the floor in the Vault.

"Who would do such a thing?" Stacia asked, her eyes wide with shock.

"That's what we need to figure out," Anne said. "Evelyn, who do you think would do this?"

The first person that popped into Evelyn's mind was Jeanne's cousin Roy. He had threatened Jeanne that he would do whatever it would take to get the ring.

"Do you think the villain is after the ring?" Stacia asked.

Villain was such a strong word—but it fit the crime.

"Yes," Evelyn said. "He or she said so in the note." She looked at Anne and said, "Jeanne's cousin has the most at stake where the ring is concerned. He believes it's rightfully his."

"Then he should be at the top of the suspect list." Joy set a stack of papers on top of a filing cabinet.

"Who else knows that the ring is in the safe?" Anne asked. "Anyone could be a suspect where the ring is concerned, if they were desperate enough."

Evelyn tried to focus. Had she told anyone else that the ring was in the safe?

"There was a delivery truck driver in here the day after the accident, inquiring about the ring," Stacia offered.

"Yes." Evelyn nodded. "Wayne Preston. He was the man who caused Jeanne Robertson's accident." Could he be ruthless enough to break in and leave a threatening note?

"Anyone else?" Shirley asked. "Think about all your interactions this week."

"Yesterday I went to a jeweler who had spoken to Jeanne about the ring," Evelyn said slowly. "I might have mentioned it being in the safe to her."

"And what is the jeweler's name?" Anne asked as she took a scratch pad and pencil off a nearby table.

"Abigail Sinclair." Evelyn told them all she knew about the jeweler and her interest in the ring.

"Who else?" Joy asked. "Besides all of us standing here."

Evelyn racked her brain and then she looked at Stacia, a certain reporter's name coming to mind.

Stacia shook her head and stared back at Evelyn. "He didn't do it."

"Who?" Shirley asked.

"There was a reporter who stopped in here yesterday," Evelyn said. "He knows about the ring in the safe."

"He didn't do it," Stacia said again.

"How do you know?" Evelyn asked.

"Because we were at a twenty-four-hour coffee shop all night last night. We drank coffee and talked until about an hour ago. I just had time to go home and shower."

No one said a word for a moment, and then Shirley started to bustle around again. "Well, if there's no one else…"

Someone else did come to mind, but it seemed so preposterous, Evelyn almost didn't say anything. "There might be one other person."

"Who?" Joy asked. "We don't want to leave any stone unturned."

"She's a temp nurse who's been caring for Jeanne. She's always close at hand whenever I've been to see Jeanne, and I know she's heard us talking about the ring."

"Which temp nurse?" Shirley asked. She usually knew most of the nurses who were in and out of Mercy.

"Her name is Madison Cummings," Evelyn said. "I don't know much about her, except that she's new to Mercy."

"I know who she is," Shirley said. "I gave her a ride home last night when her carpool person didn't wait for her."

"She seems very nice, if a little bit private." Evelyn nibbled her bottom lip as she thought through all the suspects.

"You're telling me," Shirley said. "I could hardly get two words out of her."

"I hate to run," Joy said, "but no one is covering the gift shop right now."

"Don't worry about me," Evelyn said. "Stacia and I can finish cleaning things up in the Vault, and as we get time, we'll try to organize it again. Can we talk through the suspects at dinner?"

Evelyn's friends all nodded their approval. They set a time and place, and then they were off to their various positions within Mercy Hospital.

And it was just Evelyn and Stacia again.

They went into the Vault to start putting things back in place. The break-in was foremost in Evelyn's mind, and as soon as she had a spare minute, she'd make a visit to Jeanne to see if she could get a few more answers from their patient.

It was lunchtime before Evelyn knew it, and she was finally able to take a break to go visit Jeanne.

The hospital was bustling, per usual. It was Friday afternoon. For many of the staff members, it meant just a few more hours before their weekend rest—but for most who worked long, tedious hours at all times of the day and night, it was just another day at work. Nurses, doctors, and the custodial staff didn't often get the luxury of working eight to five, Monday through Friday, like Evelyn.

Clouds marred the vast sky outside the windows on the second floor as Evelyn walked toward Jeanne's room. Madison was settling

Jeanne's lunch tray on her table when Evelyn entered. She glanced up and offered a weak smile before busying herself with helping Jeanne.

"Good afternoon," Evelyn said to them.

Jeanne just nodded once in acknowledgment, but Madison seemed to ignore her—or assume the greeting was for Jeanne alone.

"We had some excitement in the records department this morning." Evelyn took the seat next to Jeanne's bed.

Madison finally met Evelyn's gaze, straight on, but Jeanne didn't seem too interested.

"It appears that someone broke into the Vault trying to get at your ring."

That information brought Jeanne's head up, and she stared at Evelyn. "Seriously?"

Evelyn nodded. "Not only did they try to get into the safe, but they tore apart our historical files and left an ominous note."

Jeanne's mouth slipped open, and she blinked several times before she spoke. "Are you okay?"

"I'm fine." Evelyn shrugged as if it was no big deal, but just thinking about the break-in made her pulse thrum again. "They weren't able to get into the safe."

"I'm really sorry for the trouble," Jeanne said with a scowl. "If my leg would heal, I could get out of here and take the ring so I wouldn't bother you anymore."

"It's no bother." Evelyn leaned forward in her chair. "I have a list of suspects and will be doing some digging to see who tried to break into the safe." She looked at Madison, who turned and lifted a pile of dirty laundry into her arms.

Without even glancing back, Madison left the room.

Evelyn decided not to bother Jeanne with her list of suspects. If she had specific questions about them later on, she'd share their names. For now, she had other things to tell Jeanne.

"I stopped by Sinclair Antique Jewelry yesterday." Evelyn watched Jeanne's face to see if there was any recognition but received none. "Apparently, you made a stop there after picking up the ring on Monday, before you went to lunch with Roy."

"I did?" Jeanne's eyebrows came down in a frown as she appeared to concentrate. "It doesn't sound familiar."

How much should Evelyn share? Should she tell Jeanne that she had been rude to Abigail?

"The jeweler told me that you weren't aware of the ring's history or value until she told you." Evelyn continued to study Jeanne for any spark of memory. "She also made an offer to purchase the ring from you, but you refused her."

"Of course I did." Jeanne reached for the jiggly red Jell-O on her tray. "Why would I sell something I just acquired?"

"You don't remember going to see her?"

Jeanne shook her head. "No."

"She said you were a bit agitated, and it looked like you were texting someone."

Jeanne indicated her phone. "The only person I texted on Monday was Roy. And I can see why that would make me agitated. The man makes my skin crawl."

"Why the animosity between you?" Evelyn asked.

"He's a cheat, a thief, and a scoundrel."

"Well," Evelyn said, a bit taken aback. "Those are pretty serious charges."

"He was stealing from my uncle for years, and when I stood up to him to accuse him, he lied to my uncle about me. Said I was only using him for his money and only came around when it was convenient for me." Jeanne shoved a spoonful of Jell-O into her mouth. She swallowed and went on to say, "Every time I came to visit, Roy made my time with my uncle unbearable. I loved Uncle Tony, and Roy was threatened by that. Thought he was going to get this windfall when our uncle died. Turns out, there was not much money or property left, just the ring and a run-down Ford Taurus."

"Do you think he could have broken into the Vault?" Evelyn asked.

"I wouldn't put it past him."

Evelyn nodded. She would need more evidence than suspicion before she could make an accusation. "Is there anyone else who might think they're entitled to the ring?"

Jeanne thought for a minute but then shook her head. "I can't think of anyone. Until Monday, no one but my uncle even knew about the ring. At least, no one that I know of."

Her uncle and all the people around the world who were familiar with the Lords Proprietors of Carolina and the rings the king had given to them.

"After the will was read, you went to the bank," Evelyn continued. "Do you remember what bank?"

"I don't remember going to the bank," Jeanne confided, "but I do remember Roy mentioning the name of it when he was here."

"That's right." The memory was coming back to Evelyn. "He said North Harbor Trust, correct?"

"I believe so."

"Would you mind if I made a stop there to inquire on your behalf?" Evelyn asked.

"Of course not. I'll call ahead and tell them you're coming and give you all the pertinent information they might need to verify my uncle's accounts. I'll also send a letter to let them know you're representing me, and you should have access to whatever might help us."

"I'll probably ask my friend Joy to come with me. She gets off work at three, so I'll just clock out early and we can go there together."

"I'll let the bank know you'll be there a little after three then." Jeanne took another bite of the Jell-O but frowned and put it down. "I've never been a big fan of wiggling, slimy food."

Evelyn smiled. "I can't say I like it either."

Jeanne looked up at Evelyn, and her face softened. "Thank you for helping me, Evelyn. I appreciate it more than you might know." She became quiet and reflective for a second as she examined her broken leg. "I've had a lot of time to just sit here and think about some things. The accident and memory loss have had a way of making me question my life a little bit—and I'm not too happy with the conclusions I've come to."

Evelyn nodded in understanding.

"See that bouquet over there? The one given to me by Mr. Preston?"

The bouquet had started to wilt a little, and the balloons weren't as full as they had been the day Mr. Preston had brought them. "Yes, I was here when he dropped them off."

"They're the only ones I have—and they were given to me by a man who was obligated to offer them. I didn't even receive anything from my employer. Makes me wonder why I'm investing in certain relationships. They haven't ever been all that important to me—but I'm starting to think more about them as I think about how my uncle died. The only two people who spent any time with him were his niece and nephew, and, I hate to say it, we both thought we'd get some monetary compensation out of it."

"I see."

"Do you have a family?" Jeanne asked unexpectedly. "Friends? I imagine you do. You seem like a nice woman. People probably like to spend time with you."

Evelyn was blessed with friends and family—especially James and the ladies she worked with at Mercy. James loved her and cared for her like no one else. Joy opened her home to her in need. Anne came to her aid at a moment's notice. And Shirley was quickly becoming someone she could depend on. If she ever ended up as a patient in the hospital, she could imagine a whole room full of flowers and balloons sent to her from her friends and family.

"Don't take any of them for granted," Jeanne said. "Not for a minute. If I'm learning anything it's that I need to appreciate the people in my life more and let them know I'm thankful for their friendship." She made a funny little noise. "I suppose I'd have to make some friends first to show them my gratitude."

"I think you're well on your way, Jeanne." Evelyn smiled. "Sometimes a little self-examination is all we need to recognize why the people around us are either caring for us or avoiding us."

Jeanne nodded.

The two ladies sat for a quiet moment, both in thought.

"I should probably let you eat your lunch and give the bank a call," Evelyn said. "I'll head over there as soon as possible and then let you know what we discover."

"Will there be better security for the safe over the weekend?"

"Yes. The security team is installing a temporary camera until they can get a more permanent one in place, and they'll be monitoring the hallway outside the records department a little closer."

"Good." Jeanne nodded. "I'd hate to see more damage done because of the ring."

"No need to worry." Evelyn stood up and went to the door. She turned to say goodbye.

"Thank you, Evelyn." Jeanne's eyes seemed to soften around the edges. "Thank you for being a real friend, just when I needed one. I hope to repay you someday."

"Just get well," Evelyn said. "That's all the repayment I need."

As Evelyn left Jeanne's room, she thanked God that she was in a position to help and that she had the love and support of her friends and family to do what she needed to do.

Next, she would go to the bank. Hopefully she could find another clue to help her uncover who might have broken into the Vault—and stop them before they tried again or did something worse.

Chapter Ten

NORTH HARBOR TRUST WAS LESS than a mile away from Mercy Hospital and within easy walking distance for Evelyn and Joy. Sunshine warmed Evelyn's back and shoulders as they traversed the familiar streets of Charleston. She loved the historic buildings and beautiful architecture. Everywhere she looked, she was reminded of the men and women who came before her to this great city. She had never really thought too much about the eight Lords Proprietors of Carolina, because none had actually stepped foot in Charleston, but she thought about them today.

"If Jeanne's ring really is the long-lost ruby ring of Sir Anthony Ashley Cooper," Evelyn said to Joy as they walked, "I wonder how it came into her uncle's possession."

"I've been wondering the same thing," Joy said. "I wonder why he never mentioned it to her or her cousin. If he didn't tell them about it, how will we ever know how he got it and where it's been all these years?"

"There has to be someone who would know," Evelyn said.

"Maybe the jeweler you talked to has some idea."

"She said she knew about the history of all the rings, but she didn't mention whether or not she knew where the ruby ring has been." Evelyn shrugged. "I could always contact her again to ask her, and it would give me an opportunity to question her to see if she's the one who broke into the Vault."

They crossed George Street and took a left onto Meeting Street. The bank was only a block away, and Evelyn could already see the stone pillars and the roof lines of the Greek Revival architecture.

A gust of hot wind blew down the street and tore at the sheer scarf Evelyn wore at her neck. She held on to it as they entered the bank.

Immediately, they were greeted by cooler air, rich walnut trim, and marble flooring. It was an opulent space, meant to impress wealth and status upon those who entered.

Evelyn and Joy went to a teller behind a marble counter. The young man gave them a practiced smile.

"Hello," he said. "How may I help you?"

"We're here on behalf of a patient at Mercy Hospital." Evelyn motioned to both herself and Joy. "She's called the bank to let someone know we were coming to ask a few questions."

"One moment, please." The teller, whose name tag said MICHAEL P., picked up a phone and pressed a button. "May I have your name?" he asked Evelyn, almost as an afterthought.

"Evelyn Perry. I'm here on behalf of Jeanne Robertson."

Michael nodded and then put up his finger, as if to quiet her. "Hello, Mr. Smythe. I have a lady here by the name of Evelyn Perr—" He paused and then nodded. "Yes, sir, I will send her to you."

Michael put down his phone and motioned toward a hallway to his left. "Kendall Smythe, the bank president, is waiting for you. His office is down the hall to your right. You'll see his name plaque on his door."

"Thank you." Evelyn and Joy walked down the hall until they found the door with Mr. Smythe's name.

Evelyn knocked, and the door was soon opened by a large, balding gentleman. "Mrs. Perry?" he asked.

"Yes. And this is my coworker, Joy Atkins."

"Come in, come in. It's nice to meet you both," Mr. Smythe said. "Please, have a seat and make yourselves at home."

Mr. Smythe's office boasted two large floor-to-ceiling windows that looked out onto a charming courtyard. Bright sunshine poured through the wavy glass and made the otherwise dark interior warm and welcoming. When he seemed satisfied that they were settled on the cold leather chairs across from his desk, he took a seat.

"Ms. Robertson called me a few hours ago and told me you'd be coming," he said. "She explained that she was involved in a car accident and she lost her memory surrounding the day of her accident. I cannot provide any personal information about her uncle's account to you without her here, but I can answer general questions. She said you'd have a letter and some items to verify your identity."

"That's right." Evelyn handed him Jeanne's letter as well as her own driver's license. "We're trying to retrace her steps and see where she went and who she might have interacted with that day. There are several questions we haven't been able to answer. We were hoping you might help us."

"I will gladly do what I can to help." He perused the items Evelyn had presented and then handed them back to her. "Unfortunately, I wasn't the person who assisted Ms. Robertson on Monday, but it will be easy enough to find out who that was and chat with them." He turned in his swivel chair and moved his mouse to wake up his computer screen. "I haven't had a chance to look into this since Ms. Robertson called, but it shouldn't be too difficult."

Evelyn and Joy sat patiently while he clicked his mouse, typed in a few things on his keyboard, and then pulled up what looked like surveillance footage.

"Ms. Robertson told me she came into the bank around nine thirty on Monday morning. She said she came to retrieve an item from a safe-deposit box." He spoke to them but didn't look at them. Instead, his focus was on his computer. "Aha! I think I might have found it."

Evelyn leaned forward to look at the video footage with the time stamp of 9:37, with Monday's date. It was a black-and-white image looking from behind the front counter where they'd just met Michael, to the lobby beyond. Jeanne could be seen leaving a room and entering the lobby.

"Does that look like Ms. Robertson?" Mr. Smythe asked.

"Yes," Evelyn said. "I believe that's her."

"Wonderful." He leaned forward and studied the screen. "And it looks like she's being assisted by our bank manager, Kathleen Erickson."

Another person entered the bank on the video and walked up to the teller. He was a tall man wearing a dark delivery uniform.

Evelyn's pulse picked up speed. "Wait," she said, "can you pause the video?"

Mr. Smythe did as Evelyn requested. It paused with a clear view of Wayne Preston handing a package to the teller.

"What is it?" Joy asked.

"That man." Evelyn pointed to Wayne's image. "I know him."

"You do?" Mr. Smythe leaned closer to the screen, apparently trying to identify the man himself. "Who is he?"

"I believe he's the man who caused Ms. Robertson's accident." Evelyn rose from her chair to try to get a better look. "Is there a way to magnify the image?"

"I can try." Mr. Smythe pressed a few buttons, and Wayne's image grew larger.

"His name is on his coat." Evelyn pointed at the screen. "Can you make out what it says?"

Mr. Smythe got closer and said, "It looks like it says Wayne."

Evelyn slowly lowered herself back into her chair. "Wayne Preston is the name of the man who forced Jeanne off the road." She could barely contain her shock. What would be the odds that Wayne and Jeanne would be in the same place, at the same time, twice in one day, and that the second time would lead to such a horrible accident? "Can you continue playing the video so we see if they interact?"

"Of course." Mr. Smythe's eyes were wide in surprise, and he was quick to assist Evelyn.

The video went back to its original size and continued to play on the screen. When Wayne turned away from the teller, he paused, and it appeared as if Jeanne caught his attention.

At the same moment, Jeanne was admiring something in her hand—possibly the ring? She held it up to look at it while the bank manager came out of the room she had just been in.

Wayne stood in the same spot for another moment, and then he walked out of the bank. His brown truck was barely visible through the front windows. But instead of pulling away, it remained there as

Jeanne concluded her transaction at the bank. It wasn't until Jeanne left the bank that the delivery truck finally pulled away from the front of the building and disappeared.

Mr. Smythe paused the video when both Jeanne and the truck were no longer in view.

None of them said anything for a moment, and then Joy said, "What do you make of that?"

"I don't know." Evelyn shook her head, still flabbergasted that Wayne and Jeanne had crossed paths before the accident.

Or was it an accident?

"I'll call Ms. Erickson in to speak with us," Mr. Smythe offered. "Perhaps she might be able to shed a little light on this situation."

A few minutes later, the bank manager entered Mr. Smythe's office. She was a polished-looking woman in a smart blazer and perfectly manicured nails. Her auburn hair was curled just so, and she wore bright red lipstick. Mr. Smythe quickly explained who Evelyn and Joy were and why they had come to the bank.

"Of course I remember Ms. Robertson," Ms. Erickson said. "I assisted her on Monday. She retrieved her uncle's beautiful ruby ring and an old letter or form of some kind."

"Did she show the letter to you?" Evelyn asked.

Ms. Erickson shook her head. "It was folded, and I didn't bother to look at it. I don't know what it said, but I can tell you it was yellowed and worn with age."

Evelyn glanced at Joy to see if her friend might have any thoughts or questions.

"Do you remember seeing a piece of paper like that in Jeanne's personal belongings?" Joy asked Evelyn.

"I don't." Evelyn nibbled her bottom lip as she thought. "But if it was old and with the ring, it's probably very important."

"Perhaps she put it in her purse," Ms. Erickson suggested.

"If she did, she hasn't mentioned it." Evelyn tried to think through any conversation she might have had with Jeanne about a piece of paper, but nothing came to mind.

"If it's not in her purse, maybe it's still in her car," Joy said. "Where would her car be located?"

Mr. Smythe shook his head. "I'm not sure. It's probably in an impound lot. You'll have to call the police to find out for certain, and you'd need Ms. Robertson's permission to search the car, if that's what you intend to do."

"It might not be a bad idea," Evelyn said. "There could be other clues in the car that could help us."

"Is there anything else you remember about the day Ms. Robertson visited the bank?" Mr. Smythe asked Ms. Erickson.

It took a moment, but Ms. Erickson eventually shook her head. "Nothing helpful, I'm afraid. It was a fairly uneventful transaction. She came in, told me who she was, presented a copy of her uncle's will and instructions to hand over whatever was inside the deposit box. She gave me her key, I retrieved the box and gave it to her. She opened it, found the ring and the paper, and signed all the necessary paperwork. Then she left."

"You didn't see anyone lurking around the bank that day? Perhaps an overly curious delivery driver?"

Ms. Erickson frowned and shook her head. "Nothing that stands out to me."

"Thank you, Ms. Erickson," Mr. Smythe said. "I think that will be all for now."

A few minutes later, Evelyn and Joy said goodbye to Mr. Smythe and left North Harbor Trust.

The heat was especially noticeable after being inside the cool building for so long.

"What are the odds?" Evelyn asked Joy. "I wonder why Wayne didn't mention that he'd run into Jeanne earlier that day."

"Maybe he didn't realize who she was," Joy offered.

"Maybe." Evelyn frowned. "But he did come to the hospital the day after the accident and inquire about the ring. He knew she had it, even though Shirley said she pulled it from Jeanne's pocket—and not her hand." She shook her head. "No, I think Wayne knew exactly who Jeanne was—and he knew about the ring *before* the accident, based on the surveillance video."

"Do you think he followed her all day?" Joy blinked against the bright sunshine and then pulled a pair of sunglasses from her purse. "It was about nine thirty in the morning when he first saw the ring, and it was after one o'clock that afternoon when the accident happened, correct?"

"I believe that's correct."

"That's an awfully long time to follow someone, especially in a big brown truck. If he was going after the ring, don't you think he would have had a better opportunity than pushing her off the road?"

"Maybe he was getting desperate. Maybe he hadn't found a better time to make his move."

Joy shrugged. "It might just be a coincidence. We need more information before we can know for certain."

Evelyn nodded. "But right now I'd like to call Jeanne and find out if she still has the paper from the deposit box. If she doesn't, I'd like to locate her car so we can look through it."

"I agree."

"I'll call her now and see what I can find out."

"Should we start walking back to my house?" Joy asked. "I have a feeling the impound lot isn't within walking distance, and if we want to get to the lot and then over to the Fleet Landing for supper by six, we'll need to hurry."

Evelyn's hand was already on her phone to call Jeanne. Hopefully Jeanne could answer some of Evelyn's questions, because they were piling up fast.

Within an hour, Evelyn and Joy were pulling up to Sam's Autobody Shop in North Charleston in Joy's blue Mini Cooper. Jeanne had said she didn't remember a piece of paper, nor had she found anything like it in her purse. She even double-checked as Evelyn had her on the phone. Then Jeanne called the police, and they'd told her where her vehicle had been towed after the accident. Then Evelyn called Jeanne back to ask her to call the shop to give them permission to show Evelyn and Joy the car.

Now, as Joy parked her car, Evelyn glanced out at the autobody shop, quite impressed with the clean, orderly, retro look of the establishment.

"I feel like we've just walked back in time," Joy mused as she turned off her engine. "I half expect to be asked to a sock hop by one of those young men in white caps."

Evelyn chuckled but couldn't disagree with her friend.

Everything about Sam's echoed from the past. The chrome around the doors and windows, the retro gas pumps out front, and the teenage boys in white uniforms, black bowties, and white caps scurrying about the place. There was even a beautiful 1950s black convertible parked outside.

"Definitely not what I expected," Evelyn said as she got out of Joy's car.

"It's charming." Joy closed her car door and followed Evelyn into the building.

The inside of Sam's Autobody Shop was even more reminiscent of a bygone era than the outside. Black-and-white checkered floors, retro vinyl chairs, a '50s style counter, complete with stools, and an old jukebox playing Elvis Presley's "Hound Dog."

A woman, probably in her late forties, saw them enter. She was wearing a pair of denim coveralls and had her hair in a ponytail with a red bandana tied around her head. Her name was embroidered on a white patch that simply said SAM. "Hello," she said. "How may I help you?"

"Are you Sam?" Evelyn asked, a bit surprised.

The woman grinned. "I am, indeed."

"This place is amazing," Joy said. "I've never been in a cleaner autobody shop in my life."

Sam ran a dustcloth over the counter. "Thanks. It's my pride and joy."

Evelyn had almost forgotten why they had come into the establishment, but she quickly brought her thoughts back to her task. "We're here to look at Jeanne Robertson's car. She said she'd call you to let you know we were coming."

"She did." Sam hung the cloth behind the counter and then grabbed a cardboard box. "Come with me. It's out back."

Evelyn and Joy followed Sam through a side door and around the back of the building. A tall wooden fence kept the less-appealing part of the property from view. Here and there were several old and rusted cars, many banged up from accidents, no doubt.

"I haven't had time to take out Ms. Robertson's personal belongings and send them to her," Sam said. "But she told me you would be able to take them today."

Evelyn nodded. "I hope it's no bother."

Sam shook her head. "You're actually saving me from the chore." She pointed to a white Toyota Corolla. "As you can see, Ms. Robertson's car is totaled. It's only good for parts now."

"This is Jeanne's car?" Evelyn's voice went up an octave.

"That's the one."

Evelyn and Joy just stood and stared at the vehicle.

"It's a miracle she survived," Joy said in awe.

The entire front end of the vehicle was smashed, and the windshield was completely shattered and had fallen into the car.

"Angels were watching over Ms. Robertson," Sam said with deep conviction. "That's for sure."

For the first time, Evelyn wondered if Jeanne's memory loss was a gift from God. How traumatic it would be to live through a crash like this one and then have the horrible memories to relive over and over again.

"Please be careful," Sam said as she brought them to the car. "There is a lot of broken glass and jagged metal. I'll try to recover whatever is within reach."

The driver's door had been removed, no doubt to extract Jeanne from the accident. For the most part, other than the debris from the wreck, the car looked clean and organized.

Sam reached into the front and removed a few miscellaneous items like a pair of sunglasses, a cell phone charging cord, and a travel mug.

"We have reason to believe there might be an old piece of paper in the car," Evelyn said to Sam. "It was in a safe-deposit box at the bank, and Jeanne retrieved it a few hours before her accident."

Sam nodded her understanding. She came out of the car and went around to the passenger side where the door was not as damaged, and she was able to get inside. There, she opened the glove compartment and pulled out a few things that looked promising.

"Here's an owner's manual," she said as she put it into the cardboard box at her side. "Insurance cards and—" She paused as she held a folded, yellowed piece of paper in her hand. "Is this what you're looking for?"

Evelyn took the paper. It was brittle and felt as if it could disintegrate in her hands. "This might be it."

Joy moved close to Evelyn. "That looks really old."

"I'm not an expert on paper," Evelyn said, "but I would have to agree."

The paper was not only yellowed, it was fibrous and thicker than modern paper.

"I'm afraid to unfold it." Evelyn turned it over gently in her hands. "In case it tears."

Sam was still cleaning out the car and didn't seem as interested in the paper as Evelyn and Joy.

"It's not much use to us folded up," Joy said. "Just be careful."

Evelyn gently unfolded the paper. The seam was very delicate, and it cracked as she pried it apart. Pieces of fiber floated away from the paper and caught on the breeze.

But she was able to unfold it, and when she did, she found names with dates written in different colors of faded ink.

"It's a list," Evelyn said, almost to herself.

"And the Earl of Clarendon is the first name on the list," Joy added.

Next to the Earl of Clarendon's name there was a date, 1668.

The first three names on the list all seemed to be written in the same ink, with the same handwriting. But after that, they were all different.

At the very bottom of the list was the name Anthony Ashley Cooper Robertson, 1976.

Evelyn thought for a moment. Could Anthony Ashley Cooper Robertson be Jeanne's Uncle Tony?

"Is this what I think it is?" Joy asked Evelyn in a hushed whisper.

"If I had to guess," Evelyn said, "I would say it's a list of all the people who have owned the ruby ring—but that would mean that the rumors are true and the Earl of Clarendon stole the ring from Sir Anthony Ashley Cooper in 1668."

"At some point, someone started this list." Joy's voice held a hint of awe. "And it has probably traveled with the ring since then."

"How strange that Jeanne's uncle had the same name as the original owner," Evelyn mused. "I wonder why he was named after Sir Anthony Ashley Cooper."

"I have no idea," Joy said.

"Maybe Jeanne could help us." Evelyn folded the paper back into its original position. "She doesn't seem to know anything about the ring, but maybe she can tell us more about her uncle."

Sam picked up the cardboard box and handed it to Evelyn. "I think that's about everything."

"Thank you." Evelyn took the box from Sam. "We found what we came for."

"Excellent. I'm happy to help." Sam put her hands on her hips. "If you need anything else, don't hesitate to ask."

Evelyn and Joy said their goodbyes and went back to Joy's car.

"Well," Joy said, "another piece of the puzzle."

Evelyn buckled her seat belt. "Every time I think I'm going to get an answer, I only get more questions."

"Hopefully all the pieces of the puzzle start to fit into place." Joy started her car. "It's about time to meet the others at the restaurant. Maybe they can help us put some of this together."

Evelyn nodded. She looked forward to sharing what they had found with Shirley and Anne. The four of them worked well together and what one of them didn't think of, the next one did.

Chapter Eleven

THE FLEET LANDING RESTAURANT SAT on a wooden pier near the Waterfront Park with a pristine view of Charleston Bay and Fort Sumter. Behind it stood the majestic, if somewhat imposing, United States Custom House, built in the Roman Corinthian style in the late 1880s. The restaurant boasted some of the finest seafood in the city and was a favorite of Evelyn's.

When Evelyn and Joy arrived, Shirley and Anne had already been seated on the open deck. The late afternoon sunshine sparkled on the bay, but a gentle breeze off the water offered a respite from the heat. Overhead, an umbrella provided more relief from the sun. It might have been more comfortable to sit inside, but the views of the harbor were one of the reasons most people came to the restaurant.

"It's been far too long since I've been here," Evelyn said as she took a seat next to Shirley. "Thanks for agreeing to meet here."

A large pitcher of sweet tea was on the table, as were four tall glasses. Anne poured the dark liquid into their glasses as Evelyn and Joy settled in.

Evelyn took a deep, relaxing breath. It was Friday, she was with her friends, and she was about to enjoy a wonderful meal. A twinge of longing tugged at her heart when she thought about James, home by himself, working on the kitchen project. As soon as they finished eating, she would give him a call to see how things were progressing and to tell him all that had transpired that day. She missed him, though it had only been twenty-four hours since he had dropped her off at Joy's.

"Any leads on who might have broken into the Vault?" Shirley asked as she lifted her glass to take a sip of sweet tea.

"No," Evelyn said, "but Joy and I discovered a couple more clues today."

Anne's eyes lit up with interest. "What sort of clues?"

Evelyn explained the connection they had discovered between Wayne Preston and Jeanne's visit to the bank, and then Joy told them about Sam's Autobody Shop and discovering the list of names.

"I have the list with me." Evelyn had copied the names and dates onto a separate piece of paper and put the original into an acid-free envelope they had purchased at a stationery shop before coming to the Fleet Landing. She took the copied list out of her purse, but the waitress returned at that moment to get their orders.

"I'll have the Low Country Boil," Evelyn said with a smile. It was a large meal, and she and James usually shared it when they ordered together, but what she didn't finish at the restaurant, she would take with her and store in Joy's refrigerator. Tomorrow, when she met up with James, she would give him the leftovers to reheat at home. He often said he liked the leftovers better anyway.

Joy ordered the Carolina Lump Crab Cakes, Shirley ordered fried green tomatoes and a salad, and Anne ordered the Low Country Seafood Gumbo.

As soon as the waitress walked away, Shirley nodded at Evelyn. "Can we see the list?"

Evelyn handed the list to her.

"Interesting," Shirley said as she inspected the names. There were only nine of them, starting with Edward Hyde, 1st Earl of Clarendon and ending with Anthony Ashley Cooper Robertson.

"We think the last person is Jeanne's uncle, but I haven't had a chance to ask her yet." Evelyn refolded the paper and slipped it back into her purse.

"So, presumably, Jeanne's name should go next on the list." Anne put her chin in her hand. "Did anyone else notice that there are only men's names on that list? Jeanne would be the first woman."

"I didn't notice that," Joy said.

"Did Jeanne's cousin know about the ring before the will was read?" Shirley asked Evelyn. "If he did, perhaps he assumed it would rightfully be his as a male heir."

"I don't think so, given his conversation with Jeanne at the hospital." Evelyn shrugged. "Either way, on Monday I plan to present this new information to Jeanne and see if she remembers anything else. I also plan to call Wayne Preston and ask him some questions."

"Are you going to talk to the cousin?" Joy asked. "Maybe he could shed some light. And when you ask him about the ring you could find out if he was anywhere near the hospital last night during the break-in."

"That's a good idea." Evelyn took a sip of the cold sweet tea, savoring the flavor.

"How is Jeanne doing?" Anne asked anyone at the table who might know.

"I had the opportunity to stop by and check on her," Shirley said. "Dr. Tennyson is optimistic that she might be able to go home next week, though he's still observing her leg for infection."

"I'm happy to hear that he's optimistic," Evelyn said. "I hope we can have some answers for her by then."

"I was able to visit today with the nurse you told me about." Shirley crossed her arms and put her elbows on the table. "She was in the room with Jeanne when I checked on her, and she actually talked to me."

"I've never known a more attentive nurse," Evelyn said. "Did you find out anything about her?"

"Nothing that sounded alarming or suspicious." Shirley shrugged. "She told me she's originally from Spokane, Washington, and has been traveling all over the world as a temp nurse for the past five years, including Rome and London."

"Wow." Joy lifted her eyebrows in surprise. "I'm impressed."

"Wouldn't it be fun to travel like that?" Anne said, her gaze drifting off a bit. "As a younger person, of course. Now that Ralph and I are semiretired and caring for Addie, I love that we have a permanent home and community. But, if I could go back, it would have been interesting to travel a little more."

Anne and Ralph had taken on raising their granddaughter while their daughter, Liliana, was deployed. The new responsibility had come at a good time, since Ralph had recently retired from his position as head pastor at St. Michael's Church and taken a less-demanding job as a chaplain for Mercy Hospital.

"And speaking of Ralph," Anne continued, "I hope everyone is still able to join us next Thursday to celebrate our anniversary."

"Of course," Evelyn said, while Shirley and Joy nodded.

"I can hardly believe it's been forty years." Anne shook her head. "What a wonderful journey it's been." She smiled. "If given the chance to go back to the beginning, I wouldn't change anything."

Evelyn, Joy, and Shirley all smiled with their friend, and Evelyn decided that she wouldn't change anything either. She still lived in the house she grew up in and hadn't lived outside of Charleston a day in her life, though she had stayed in the dorms while going to college and had rented a small apartment with James when they were first married, before they bought her parents' home. She'd been so content with Charleston, she hadn't ever had the itch to wander. But she couldn't deny that it would be an exciting and thrilling adventure to be a temp nurse like Madison.

The waitress returned with a breadbasket and to refill their tea.

"Maybe Madison is just attentive," Evelyn said, picking up the conversation again. "She's probably nothing to worry about. She does seem a little curious about the ring, but I can't imagine why she would have tried to break into the safe or claim the ring right-fully belonged to her."

"I agree." Joy took a piece of bread as the basket passed her by. "But we can't pass over a suspect just because they don't fit the profile."

Evelyn nodded. She would continue to keep her eye on Madison, but, in the meantime, she would focus on Wayne and Roy. They seemed to be the most likely suspects.

The next morning, Evelyn was dressed and waiting by Joy's front window, watching for James like a young woman waiting for her first date to arrive. Her bags were packed, and she was ready to go home. Joy had been a wonderful hostess and Evelyn had loved getting away from the mess of their remodeling project for a couple of nights, but she didn't care what she had to put up with if it meant being with her husband again.

Joy walked out of her kitchen with two to-go cups in her hands. Mopsy trotted along beside Joy, her nails tapping on the hardwood floor. "I thought you and James might like some coffee while you're shopping."

"Thank you," Evelyn said. "For everything. I appreciate the warm bed and the wonderful hospitality these past couple of days."

"It's my pleasure." Joy handed Evelyn one of the coffee cups and set the second one on a small table near the door. "I enjoy having company, so you're always welcome."

"When I talked to James last night, he said he was staying up late to get the house clean for me. I'm looking forward to sleeping in my own bed again tonight."

"I don't blame you." Joy smiled.

A car slowed outside Joy's house, and Evelyn's heart skipped a beat, but it wasn't James. She tried not to sigh in disappointment, and instead, turned back to Joy. "What do you have planned for today?"

"I'm taking Mallory and Eloise back-to-school shopping." Joy's grin made it clear that she was thrilled to spend the day with her granddaughters. They were, after all, the main reason she'd moved from Houston to Charleston after her husband passed away. "Sabrina will meet us for supper later on, and then Mopsy will be heading home with them."

Joy's daughter, Sabrina, had been a key player in getting Joy the job at Mercy. Her best friend worked at the hospital and had put in a good word for Joy when the administration was looking for a gift shop manager. The work had not only given Joy a purpose in Charleston, but it had brought her into Evelyn's life.

Another car slowed outside, and this time it was James. "He's here," Evelyn said, a bit breathless. "Thanks again for your hospitality." She picked up her overnight bag and put it on her shoulder, then she picked up the takeout bag full of leftovers and the to-go cups of coffee. There was no place for James to park, so he couldn't come and get her. Evelyn didn't mind—she was ready to go.

"Goodbye," Joy said as she opened the door and held Mopsy back from bounding out to the street. "See you on Monday at work."

Evelyn's hands were full, so she couldn't wave or give Joy a hug. Instead, she simply smiled. "Goodbye!"

Despite the lack of parking spaces on the street, James put the Toyota in park and jumped out to open the passenger door for her.

"Hi," he said.

"Hi, yourself." Evelyn leaned in for a quick kiss and allowed him to take the coffee and her overnight bag.

He waved at Joy and closed the car door after Evelyn got in.

Soon they were on the James Island Expressway, heading west off the peninsula, toward a large home improvement store.

"How are you?" They both asked the question at the same time—and then promptly laughed.

"I'm good," Evelyn said. "But I missed you."

James took her hand in his. "I missed you too. I'm sorry about the mess."

"No, I'm sorry." She shook her head. "The new kitchen is a gift and a blessing. I've behaved poorly."

"You were overwhelmed."

"That doesn't excuse my behavior."

"No." He brought her hand up and kissed it. "But it does explain it."

She smiled at him. "I promise to be more patient."

"You won't need to worry about the mess. I stayed up until after midnight last night cleaning every surface in the house." He grinned. "Other than the fact that we don't have a counter or appliances, or that all of our kitchen items are stacked in the living room, you'd never guess we were in the middle of a remodeling project."

"You stayed up until midnight cleaning?"

"Of course I did. I knew you'd be coming home today, and I wanted to make sure you didn't need to worry about that."

"James." She squeezed his hand. "You're amazing."

He laughed. "I'm desperate to get my wife home is what I am."

Evelyn joined in his laughter. "Well, I'm just as anxious to be home as you are to have me there."

It took them about fifteen minutes to get to the home improvement store. James had a list of miscellaneous items he needed to purchase after they shopped for appliances. Over the years, they had replaced the olive-green appliances her parents had installed in the house during the 1960s, but the off-white ones James had removed during this remodel were well-used and in need of replacement.

"What do you think about going with all white appliances?" Evelyn asked.

"Aren't the cabinets going to be white?"

Evelyn nodded. "It would look so fresh and bright in there. And with the black-and-white granite countertops, I think there'll be enough contrast to break up all the white. We could hang a pot rack in the center with brass pots and pans to help tie in the wood floor."

"What about the sink and cooktop? Do you want those to be white too?"

Evelyn thought about them against the black-and-white countertop and shook her head. "Perhaps those could be stainless steel, so they blend in with the granite."

James stood for a moment as he looked at the appliances and seemed to be imagining it in his mind. "I think it would look nice." He nodded. "Really nice."

"So do I." Evelyn smiled. "What about light fixtures?"

"Maybe we could bring in a splash of color with our lights. I saw some that caught my eye."

Evelyn put her hand on his forearm. "How about you surprise me with the lights?"

"Are you serious?" He studied her face. "You said you don't like surprises."

"I don't like change—which is quite different." She laughed. "But since the kitchen is already changing, what's a little surprise here and there?"

James pulled her into his arms, right there in the middle of the appliance department at the home improvement store. "How about you surprise me with the counter stools, then?"

"It's a deal," she said as she wrapped her arms around his midsection, not caring if anyone saw them embracing.

It felt good to be back with James, doing life together. She had no wish to ever leave his side again.

Chapter Twelve

THERE WAS A BOUNCE IN Evelyn's step on Monday morning. She couldn't stop herself from smiling. Not only was the house clean, the appliances were ordered, and the majority of the demolition in the kitchen was done. Then, after church on Sunday, she and James had spent the afternoon on a picnic in Colonial Lake Park, not too far from their home and near Charleston Harbor. Both of them needed a little respite and they had enjoyed every minute of it together. It had given Evelyn time to look over the article about the ring in the *Charleston Times*, written by Hunter O'Reilly. He hadn't shared anything she didn't already know, but it was still interesting to see it in the paper.

Now, as she walked toward the grand staircase in Mercy Hospital to pay a visit to Jeanne and to share the information they had uncovered on Friday, she hummed to herself. She held the acid-free envelope with the list in her hands. Hopefully Jeanne might remember more about the ring than the last time they spoke.

A familiar figure stepped out of the elevators, causing Evelyn to pause.

"Mrs. Perry?" Jeanne's cousin asked when he met her gaze. He had bags under his eyes, and his clothes were wrinkled. He also looked like he hadn't shaved in a few days.

Evelyn nodded. "Yes. And you're Mister...? Jeanne didn't tell me your last name."

"I'm also a Robertson. Our fathers were brothers. I'm sorry I wasn't friendlier when we were introduced." The elevator doors closed behind him, but he didn't make any move to walk away.

"Are you here to see your cousin?" Evelyn asked.

Roy glanced up the stairs and shook his head. "I'm actually here for my daughter."

"Oh?" Evelyn frowned. "Is she a patient here?"

"Yes, since Thursday evening." He shoved his hands in his pockets. "I was just headed to the coffee shop to get some caffeine. It's been a long weekend, and we're not out of the woods yet. I feel like I haven't slept since Wednesday night."

Genuine concern filled Evelyn's chest. "I'm so sorry to hear that. How old is she?"

"Ten." He sighed. "We just thought it was the stomach flu, but when we brought her into the clinic on Thursday morning, we learned it was appendicitis. By the time they sent her in for emergency surgery, it was too late. Her appendix burst. We've been told we'll probably be here for another day or two. She's on a strong antibiotic, and they need to keep monitoring her." Guilt shone from his eyes. "We feel horrible that we didn't realize what it was sooner. Thankfully, she hasn't had any more complications."

"Again," Evelyn said. "I'm very sorry to hear it. I'll put her on my prayer list for a speedy recovery."

"I appreciate that. I'm getting tired of this place. I haven't left this building since Thursday."

Evelyn nodded in understanding. "I don't want to keep you from your coffee." She smiled. "I was just on my way to see Jeanne. Would you like me to give her an update on your daughter's progress?"

Roy snorted. "I haven't even bothered to tell her we're here. I doubt she'd care."

"I'm sure she'll be very concerned."

His laugh was filled with derision. "I don't even think she knows Kaley's name. Go ahead and ask her. Maybe you'll see for yourself that meddling in her affairs isn't worth your time."

Meddling in her affairs?

The note they had found in the Vault was seared into Evelyn's mind, because it had been so threatening, especially to her. *Next time, I'll get into the safe and take what's rightfully mine. Don't try to stop me from getting the ring or the destruction will be worse. You'll regret meddling, Mrs. Perry.*

Had Roy written the note and left it in the Vault on Thursday evening? Perhaps while his daughter had been recovering?

Evelyn hated to think he would have used his daughter's stay in the hospital as a cover for such a nefarious act.

"I should probably get my coffee and head back to Kaley." Roy nodded at Evelyn. "Good day, Mrs. Perry."

"Goodbye, Mr. Robertson."

He walked away and headed toward the coffee shop. His shoulders were slouched, and if she wasn't mistaken, he glanced toward the records department, and his gaze stayed there longer than necessary.

A group of people walked down the staircase, and Evelyn had to move aside for them. She didn't feel like humming anymore, but she wouldn't let Roy, or anyone else, dictate her mood today.

When she arrived at Jeanne's room a couple of minutes later, Madison was standing near the door, writing something on a chart.

"Good morning," Evelyn said to her, hoping she wouldn't startle the nurse.

Madison looked up and smiled. "Hello."

"How is our patient today?"

Concern wedged between her eyes. "It sounds like she might not be going home this week, after all."

"Oh, really?" Evelyn frowned. "Is she all right?"

"You might want to talk to her about it." Madison slipped the chart back into the holder near Jeanne's door and nodded goodbye as she turned and walked away.

Evelyn stepped into Jeanne's room. The shades were drawn. At first, Evelyn thought she was sleeping, but Jeanne turned to see who had come into the room.

"Good morning," Evelyn said.

Jeanne didn't respond but looked away again.

"How are you doing?"

"What does it matter?"

Evelyn took the seat next to Jeanne's bed. "It matters a lot. We're in the business of healing people in this hospital."

"Tell that to Dr. Tennyson. He seems to think I need more surgery."

"Why?" Evelyn wished that Jeanne would look at her. "What's going on?"

"It's my leg. Apparently, it's not healing like they had hoped. It looks like there might be an infection. He said there's no way of knowing without an MRI. If there is an infection, he might have to do more surgery, and I'll be forced to stay longer."

"I'm sorry to hear that. If there's anything I can do—"

"Tell them to let me go home." Jeanne finally looked at her. "I feel like I'm being held here against my will."

"Of course you're not. The doctors just want to make sure you're as healthy as possible when you leave. If there is an infection, and they don't deal with it, you could lose your leg. Dr. Tennyson is an amazing physician. I've known him for years. He has your best interest at heart."

Jeanne snorted.

Evelyn wanted to change the subject. "I ran into your cousin Roy downstairs. Apparently, his daughter was brought in on Thursday morning with appendicitis, and they've been here ever since."

"Kaley?" Jeanne's eyes filled with alarm. "Is she going to be okay?"

"She's on antibiotics and she's staying to be monitored, but she'll probably be discharged in the next couple of days."

"They've been here since Thursday and didn't bother to let me know all weekend?" Jeanne's voice was full of hurt.

"I told him I would give you an update. Maybe you could call and tell them you're thinking of them." Maybe, just maybe, their relationship wasn't beyond repair. Bigger miracles had happened at Mercy Hospital over the years.

"Hmm." Jeanne didn't commit one way or the other. But then her eyes narrowed. "Thursday, you said?"

"Yes."

"Wasn't that the day someone tried to break into the safe?"

Evelyn nodded. Even though she had suspected Roy's involvement, she wasn't going to encourage Jeanne's suspicion. They needed more proof.

"That's convenient," Jeanne said.

"I know what you're thinking, but I haven't received the report yet from security." Evelyn was hoping that Seamus would be able to review the hallway security footage to see if they could get a glimpse of the perpetrator. "Until we have more proof, we can't accuse anyone."

"Even if he showed up on video footage, he'd probably use the excuse that he was in the hospital for his daughter, and that's why he's on camera."

It was time to change the subject again. "I wanted to talk to you about what we learned at the bank and the autobody shop."

Jeanne raised her eyebrows. "Did you find the paper you were looking for?"

"We did." Evelyn opened the envelope and gently pulled out the list, conscious that every time it was handled, it was compromising the integrity of the paper. "It looks like a list of the owners of the ring."

"Really?" Jeanne pushed the button to raise the head of her bed up so she was in a sitting position. The bruises on her face were healing nicely but were still a garish color.

"You don't remember anything at all about the ring?" Evelyn asked.

"No." Jeanne took the list from Evelyn, her hands shaking a little. She hit another button on her bed railing and a light turned on over her head. "My uncle never mentioned it to me. I didn't know it existed until they read his will."

"Do you think he mentioned it to Roy?"

"You were here when Roy said he didn't know about it either. But if he's lying, and Uncle Tony told him about it, that might be one reason why he thinks it should be his."

Jeanne looked over the list.

"We were wondering if your uncle's name was Anthony Ashley Cooper Robertson." Evelyn pointed to the last name on the list.

"His name was Anthony, but I didn't know his middle name." She shrugged. "It could be him—probably is, because the name before his on the list is his father's. Thomas Merrick Robertson."

"Do you know if you have any family connection to the first Sir Anthony Ashley Cooper, or Edward Hyde, the first Earl of Clarendon?"

Jeanne shook her head. "I have no idea. I'm not much for family genealogy. Didn't seem to matter too much to me before now."

"Do you recognize any of the other names on the list?"

After a couple of seconds, Jeanne shook her head again. "No, but then again, I don't know any of my ancestor's names beyond my grandfather." She pointed to the man above Thomas Merrick Robertson. "Cedric Prior." She frowned. "Prior sounds familiar. I'm pretty sure it was my grandmother's maiden name. She married Thomas Merrick Robertson."

"Do you know of anyone in your family who might be able to help with your genealogy?"

"I have a cousin on my mother's side of the family who might know." Jeanne reached for her cell phone. "Let me take a picture of this list and text it to her. See if she recognizes any of these names."

Evelyn held the list while Jeanne snapped a picture, and then she put it back into the envelope. "Would you like me to leave this with you, or put it in the safe?"

"The safe, please. It looks like it's pretty fragile."

"There's one more thing I'd like to discuss with you." Evelyn held the envelope in her hands and studied Jeanne as she spoke. "When I was at the bank, I saw security footage from last Monday. It appears that Wayne Preston was also at the bank delivering a package when you were there picking up the ring."

Jeanne's eyes narrowed.

"Do you remember seeing him at all that day?"

She shook her head. "No."

"It seems too coincidental that you would both be at the bank at the same time and then he would force you off the road later that day."

"That's what I'm thinking," Jeanne said.

"I'm going to call him and ask him some questions, if you don't mind."

"Not at all." Jeanne pursed her lips.

"Do you think he might be after the ring?"

"Who's to say?"

Evelyn nodded. "I'll head back to the records department and let you rest. Maybe I'll call Mr. Preston and ask him to come by so I can speak to him in person. Sometimes people are more likely to tell the truth when they're looking you in the face."

"Be my guest—and let me know what he says."

"I will." Evelyn stood, eager to put the list in the safe. "I'm sure I'll be talking to you again soon. I'll be praying your MRI comes out well."

As Evelyn left Jeanne's room, she pulled her cell phone from her pocket to look up Wayne Preston's number. Hopefully she could locate him.

It was easier to find Wayne Preston than Evelyn anticipated. There were only five men with his name in South Carolina and only one in Charleston. As she stood next to the window overlooking the Grove, she called the number off the internet and he picked up after the second ring.

"Hello, this is Evelyn Perry from Mercy Hospital. Is this Mr. Wayne Preston?"

"Yes, ma'am." He hesitated. "Is there a problem?"

"No." She tried to make her voice sound as light and neutral as possible. "I met you last week while I was visiting Jeanne Robertson."

"I remember."

"I'm wondering if you'd be willing to come to Mercy to chat with me. I have a couple of questions, and I'm hoping you can answer them."

There was silence on the other end of the phone.

"Mr. Preston?"

"What sort of questions?"

"Since Jeanne has memory loss, there are a few things about last Monday that she's struggling to remember. I was hoping you might be able to shed some light for her."

"Her memory still hasn't come back?" His voice was filled with deep remorse.

"Only little snippets of the day, but the majority of it is still lost to her."

"I'm really sorry to hear that." He sighed. "I suppose I owe it to her to fill in whatever details I can, though my lawyer warned me not to talk about the case."

Evelyn briefly closed her eyes in relief. She had thought it might be harder to get him to agree. "Are you available today?"

"I'm actually taking a break not too far away. I can be there in the next ten minutes or so."

"Perfect!" Evelyn smiled. "Please come to the records department."

"Doesn't Ms. Robertson want to speak to me herself?"

"I think it will be better for her if I talk to you and fill her in. She's given me permission to discuss her case with you."

"I'll see you soon, Mrs. Perry."

Evelyn ended the call and put her phone back in her pocket. She took the stairs down to the main floor and walked into the records department. Stacia was not at the front desk, which surprised her. A quick look around told her that no one was in the office—yet the door was unlocked and the lights were on. Pam and Rick wouldn't be in until later that morning.

A sound from the Vault snagged Evelyn's attention. The door handle had not been fixed yet—and someone was clearly inside.

"Stacia?" Evelyn called, hoping her assistant was in the Vault, though she'd never had reason to be in there without Evelyn's permission before.

The noise ceased.

"Is that you?" Evelyn stood near her desk, unable and unwilling to move. What if it wasn't Stacia? What if the perpetrator was back and he or she meant to harm her?

With shaking hands, Evelyn lifted the receiver on her desk phone and was about to press the SECURITY button when the Vault's door opened and Madison appeared.

Evelyn's mouth slipped open. "Madison?"

The temp nurse smiled. "There you are. I came looking for you, but you weren't here."

Confusion warred within Evelyn's mind. "What are you doing here?"

"No one was here, so I let myself in. I hope that's okay."

"It's not okay." Evelyn shook her head as she set the receiver back in its cradle. "You don't have clearance to be in the records department without a supervisor present."

"I'm not here looking for a current record." She put her hands up. "Honest. I was curious about the history of Mercy Hospital, and I heard someone say there are excellent historical records on file here in the Vault—is that what you call this room?"

Evelyn nodded, still confused and suspicious. "Even if that's true—"

"It is true."

"You should know better than to rummage around in there by yourself." She looked around. "Where is my assistant? Was she in here when you came in?"

Madison shook her head. "No one was here, and I saw that the door was open, so I thought I could help myself. I was told the Vault was more like a museum than anything else."

"A museum?"

"Yes—and I was under the impression that the files are available to the public. They're not protected by HIPAA or anything, are they?"

"Of course not."

It was Madison's turn to look confused. "Then why can't I be in here?"

Evelyn opened her mouth to respond but couldn't think of a reason. The historical records *were* for public use and had no restrictions. "It's against policy."

"I'm sorry." Madison's eyes filled with remorse. "I've been to several hospitals, and many of them have historical records on file, which I've had access to. I love history, and I've made a scrapbook for each one I've worked at."

Was she telling the truth? She hadn't really done anything wrong—yet. But Evelyn didn't like the idea of anyone coming into the records department unsupervised. Granted, as a nurse, Madison could gain access to almost any record she wanted on the computer system, and there was very little within the actual records department she could tamper with that would cause trouble—but it still didn't sit right with Evelyn.

"Again," Madison said, "I'm very sorry. If you or your assistant had been here when I stopped in, I would have asked permission to go into the Vault, but I really didn't think it would be a problem."

Evelyn walked toward the Vault, and Madison moved aside. Evelyn peeked into the room. Nothing looked out of the ordinary.

"Was there something in particular you were looking for?"

"I was just curious about the origins of the hospital—but I was having a hard time figuring out your filing system."

At present, their filing system had been compromised by the break-in and there hadn't been time to fix it.

"I'm happy to tell you about the origins," Evelyn said. "And to look for some of the documents that tell the story." She turned to face Madison, who had moved away from the Vault door. "But you'll have to give me a little time. I have an appointment in a couple of minutes."

"Of course." Madison smiled again. "I'm not going anywhere for a while. Just let me know when you find it, and I'll gladly come back."

Evelyn nodded.

"I won't bother you anymore." Madison gave a little wave. "I'm heading home now. I hope you have a good day."

Madison took her leave, and Evelyn just stood there for a few moments, collecting her thoughts. She had run into Madison when she'd entered Jeanne's room earlier. Clearly Madison knew Evelyn wouldn't be in the records department, so why did she say she'd come looking for Evelyn? And where was Stacia? She should have been there.

Was Madison telling the truth?

The door opened, and Stacia walked in.

"Where have you been?" Evelyn's voice was a little sharper than intended.

Stacia frowned. "I'm sorry. I had to run to the ladies' room. Is that a problem?"

Evelyn shook her head. "Of course not. But why didn't you lock the door when you left? I just walked in to find a temp nurse in the Vault."

"Really?" Stacia's frown deepened. "I was only gone for about five minutes, at the most. I didn't think it would be a problem, so I didn't bother to lock the door. She must have come in right after I left."

"Please lock the door anytime you leave this room unattended, no matter how long you plan to be gone."

Stacia nodded, her face serious. "Of course."

Evelyn was still holding the envelope with the list of names, so she went into the Vault and surveyed the room a little closer as she walked to the safe.

Nothing looked out of the ordinary—other than the random piles of paper still stacked on the surfaces of the room.

When she opened the safe, everything looked untouched in there as well. After slipping the piece of paper under the ring, Evelyn closed the safe and turned the knob to make sure it was secure.

She left the Vault and went to her desk. She was about to pick up the phone to check on the maintenance request she'd put in last Friday about fixing the Vault door when Wayne Preston walked into the records department.

He was wearing his brown uniform and holding his hat in his hands.

"Hello, Mr. Preston."

"Hello." He gave a nervous smile.

Stacia glanced up and nodded a greeting and then went back to her work.

"Won't you come in?" Evelyn pointed at the chair in front of her desk. "Would you like to sit down?"

Wayne glanced at Stacia, but she had taken a phone call and was distracted. He took a seat.

Evelyn also sat down. "Thank you so much for coming in to speak to me."

"I feel horrible about what happened to Ms. Robertson. I just hope I can help."

"I'm sure you do." Evelyn smiled, hoping to put him at ease. "I'd like to get right to the point of this meeting. When I was at North Harbor Trust on Friday, I saw some video surveillance from when Jeanne was in the bank retrieving her family ring."

Wayne visibly swallowed, and his knuckles turned white as he clenched his hat.

"I was surprised to see someone who looked just like you show up on the video."

"I can explain." He leaned forward. "I—I was there delivering a package."

"Yes, I could see that." Evelyn folded her hands on her desk. "But I find it very strange and too coincidental that you crossed Jeanne's path twice that day—don't you?"

Sweat gathered on Wayne's brow as he glanced toward Stacia again, and then back to Evelyn.

"Did you know who Jeanne was when the accident occurred?" Evelyn asked. "Had you recognized her from the bank?"

Wayne licked his lips, and his breathing was shallow. "I can explain," he said again.

Evelyn frowned. "Please do."

"I saw Ms. Robertson at the bank—or more accurately, I saw the ring. I didn't even really notice who was holding it, but I did hear her say 'LPOC' when she looked at it. Later, when I looked up LPOC, I realized the ring's value. But—" He swallowed again and seemed to be struggling with how to share his story. "None of that matters. I got myself into a lot of debt—more than I can handle. My wife's been working two jobs to try to help pay for it, but we can't seem to make a dent. It's put a strain on our marriage and on our family life. When I saw that ring, all I could think about was how much money it was worth." He licked his lips again and looked down at his hands. "I waited to see where Ms. Robertson was going—thinking that if I could get my hands on the ring, I'd be set. All my problems would go away." He shook his head. "I'm ashamed to admit that was where my thoughts were—but I was desperate."

Evelyn listened quietly and patiently as he told his story. She could tell he was embarrassed to admit the truth—but she also knew he was courageous to tell a complete stranger his troubles.

"I followed Ms. Robertson for a while, but I told myself it was a fool's errand I was on. I couldn't take that ring, even if I wanted to. How could I face my wife and children if I did something so despicable?"

"Where did you follow her to?"

"She left the bank and went right to a jeweler. After that, she went to a restaurant. It was while she was eating lunch that I talked some sense into myself." He lifted his gaze and looked directly at Evelyn. "I wouldn't have taken it. I promise you that."

Evelyn nodded, wanting to believe him.

"So I left. Returned to my route." He bit the inside of his mouth for a moment. "But later that day, right before the accident, I saw her car again. I was surprised to see it. So surprised, in fact, that I didn't notice a car stop in front of me. On instinct, I swerved, but it pushed Ms. Robertson off the road." He closed his eyes, pain and guilt tightening his mouth. "I'm certain this shame I'm living with is my punishment for considering stealing the ring in the first place."

"I don't know about that." Evelyn crossed her arms as she leaned back in her chair. "Why did you come to the records department the next day, asking about the ring?"

Wayne didn't look her in the eyes. "I don't know. I couldn't get the ring out of my head. I—" He stopped talking and twisted his hat once again.

"You could take it and she wouldn't even know?"

He didn't respond. His silence was answer enough.

"I'm not proud of myself, Mrs. Perry."

Evelyn let out a sigh. No crime had been committed. He hadn't actually attempted to steal the ring—at least, according to his story.

"Why should I be certain you won't try to steal it?" Or that he hadn't been the one to break in last Thursday evening and attempt to steal it?

He met her gaze again. "After I saw Ms. Robertson lying in that bed, all banged up so bad, I've never felt worse in my life. Even if she doesn't remember what happened, I remember—and I couldn't live with myself if I made things worse." He studied Evelyn for a couple of seconds. "Will you call the police?"

"I don't think a crime has been committed, Mr. Preston." Evelyn considered him for a moment. "But someone did try to break into the safe last Thursday. Can you tell me where you were then?"

"Last Thursday?" He nodded. "It was my wife's birthday. We stayed home all evening watching movies. You can ask her—though I'd hate for her to hear about what I considered doing."

Evelyn had no wish to pull Wayne's wife into this trouble. She sighed. "I'm choosing to believe you. But if I see you anywhere near this department again, or if I learn anything that doesn't align with your story, I will be forced to alert the police."

He nodded. "Of course."

"Thank you for meeting with me," Evelyn said as she stood and extended her hand to shake Wayne's. "I'm sure you've got more than your fair share of troubles just dealing with the accident."

"I do." He clasped her hand and looked her in the eyes. "Thank you, Mrs. Perry."

"Thank you, Mr. Preston."

He left, and Evelyn took a seat at her desk once again.

Stacia turned, her eyebrows raised. "Wow."

"I know."

Evelyn had a pile of work she needed to attend to, but she couldn't stop thinking about Jeanne and the ring. Between Roy, Madison, and Wayne, she wondered who was telling her the truth and who was lying.

Chapter Thirteen

IT WASN'T UNTIL THE FOLLOWING afternoon that Evelyn had a chance to make another visit to Jeanne. Work had prevented her from checking in to see how the MRI had gone, but with a cup of coffee from Joy and the knowledge that the Vault's lock was finally being fixed, Evelyn entered Jeanne's room.

For the first time, Madison was nowhere to be seen.

"How are you today?" Evelyn asked as she gave Jeanne a smile.

Jeanne frowned. "Tired, crabby, and in pain. Dr. Tennyson just came in with the MRI results, and he's putting me on a stronger antibiotic and plans to take me into surgery bright and early tomorrow morning. Apparently, there is an infection in there."

"Oh, I'm sorry to hear that, Jeanne." Evelyn shook her head. "Is there anything I can do for you or get for you?"

"Help sneak me out of here?" Jeanne gave her a hopeful, if facetious, smile.

"You're exactly where you need to be. Mercy Hospital is one of the best."

Jeanne sighed. "That's what everyone keeps telling me. And, to be honest, this pain is so bad, I wouldn't want to leave here, even if I could right now."

A light knock sounded at the door. "Hello?" a female voice said.

"Who is it?" Jeanne's voice was a bit harsh.

"It's me, Abigail Sinclair, from Sinclair Jewelry." Abigail walked into the room. She was wearing a black pantsuit with a pretty pink blouse. "Is this a good time?"

"What else do I have to do?" Jeanne frowned. "Are you the jeweler that Evelyn met last week?"

Abigail nodded. "Yes. I also spoke to you, though I've heard you don't remember."

Jeanne crossed her arms and narrowed her gaze. "You look familiar."

"Do you remember Ms. Sinclair?" Evelyn asked, hopefully. Was more of her memory coming back?

After a moment, Jeanne shook her head. "No."

Abigail pressed her lips together in a disappointed look. "I'm sorry to hear that."

"What can we do for you?" Evelyn asked Abigail.

Abigail stood very straight and uncomfortably near the foot of Jeanne's bed. She did not look around the room, or even at Jeanne's broken leg. Her face was a bit ashen. "I learned more about the ring and thought, perhaps, you'd like to know."

Excited energy rushed through Evelyn. "Yes?"

"Upon doing a little research—" She closed her eyes briefly and swallowed. "I learned that the ring did show up in a public record, sometime around 1890."

Evelyn wondered if Abigail was about to pass out.

"Do you need a chair?" Evelyn pointed at the vinyl chair she usually occupied when she was in the room.

Abigail nodded and slowly sat down. "I'm sorry," she said. "I don't do well in hospitals. I'm trying to hold it together, but everything about this place makes me feel panicky."

"Is there anything I can do to help?" Evelyn tried not to hover over the young woman, but she didn't look well.

"No, thank you. I usually avoid these places at all costs. It's really the only solution to my anxieties."

"Then this must be an important visit for you to put yourself through such discomfort." Evelyn smiled, hoping to ease her worries. It also made her wonder if Abigail could have broken into the Vault if she hated hospitals as much as she said.

Abigail took a steadying breath. "I do have some interesting news to share. When I was going through one of my research books, I found a very obscure article originally published in the *New York Times* in 1890. It mentions an acquisition of a seventeenth-century ruby and diamond ring with the letters *LPOC* inscribed in it, but there is nothing else about the history of the ring in the book."

"Does it say who acquired the ring?" Evelyn asked.

"A man by the name of Cedric Prior."

Evelyn turned her wide eyes to Jeanne. "His name is on the list. Didn't you say Prior was your grandmother's maiden name?"

Jeanne nodded. "Yes. And I heard back from my cousin. She confirmed my suspicions. Her father was Cedric."

"I dug a little into Mr. Cedric Prior's history," Abigail said. "He owned a modest shipping company in New York during the Gilded Age. He was wealthy, but he was never part of the upper crust, so to speak. He and his wife were new money and didn't fit in with the Knickerbockers or Mrs. Astor's Four Hundred."

Evelyn had heard of Mrs. Astor's Four Hundred. It was rumored that only four hundred people could fit into her ballroom, and if you made the list to one of her parties, you were considered the crème de la crème of society. The famed Four Hundred. But Mrs. Astor had strong feelings about new money versus old money, and new money was often shunned.

"From what I could discover," Abigail continued, "Mr. Prior and his wife tried to fit into society, spending extravagantly. They purchased the ring, though the newspaper article never listed the seller. I'm not sure if anyone knew the significance of the ring."

"I believe the owner of the ring, before Cedric," Evelyn said, "was a Reginald Peabody." She had memorized almost the entire list, and a name like Reginald Peabody was one she wouldn't soon forget.

"List?" Abigail asked.

Evelyn quickly explained the piece of paper that came with the ring.

"That only increases the value," Abigail said with excitement. "It's remarkable to have such a list. It gives us the history of the ring. We could easily trace the ring and where it's been since 1668."

"What happened to the ring after Cedric Prior purchased it?" Jeanne asked. "Did he buy it and then hide it away? What would be the purpose of that?"

Abigail shook her head. "From what I could determine, Mr. Prior bought the ring to flaunt it—but soon after, he was ruined financially, probably because of his extravagant living, and left New York with his wife and only child, a daughter. He seemed to vanish from all records after that."

"He would have been my great-grandfather," Jeanne said.

"I'm shocked he didn't sell the ring to make ends meet," Evelyn mused.

"I would have thought the same," Abigail agreed. "But, for whatever reason, he must have kept it."

"And given it to my grandfather, Thomas Merrick Robertson, who married Cedric's daughter, Penelope Prior," Jeanne said. "And, if the list is correct, Thomas gave it to Tony Robertson, my uncle, in 1976."

"Do you think your uncle's name, Anthony Ashley Cooper Robertson, has anything to do with the ring?" Evelyn asked Jeanne.

"I have no idea." Jeanne shrugged. "Maybe he was named in honor of one of the Lords Proprietors. His brother, my father, was named Charles, in honor of King Charles II—at least that's what my cousin just told me. My grandparents on my father's side were very proud of their Charleston roots."

"Now we know how the ring came into your family's possession," Evelyn said with a smile. One mystery solved.

Abigail sat up straight, her hands clasped in her lap. "I'm happy I could provide some answers for you."

"Thank you." Jeanne's voice was solemn. "I have a feeling I wasn't very kind to you when I went into your store." It was apparent that Jeanne was analyzing her behavior—and Evelyn was quite proud of her.

"No lasting harm done, Ms. Robertson." Abigail clasped and unclasped her hands. "I do have a question for you, though."

"I'll answer it to the best of my ability." Jeanne's face softened, though she didn't smile.

"I made an offer to purchase the ring from you last Monday—and I want you to know that I'm willing to increase the offer, if you'd like to sell it."

Jeanne didn't speak for a moment as she studied Abigail. Finally, she said, "The ring is not for sale."

"Is it more money you want?" Abigail swallowed. "Because I'm willing to pay more."

"Is that why you came here?" Jeanne asked. "To butter me up with all your 'help,' just so you could try to swindle me?"

Abigail pressed her lips together and rose. She was still a little unsteady on her feet. "You do me a disservice when you say things like that, Ms. Robertson. I'm a professional. I would not try to 'swindle' anyone."

Evelyn bit her lip and stepped forward to intervene.

But Abigail was done. She tugged on the bottom of her suit coat and walked to the door. "Goodbye, Ms. Robertson."

And, with that, she was gone.

Jeanne crossed her arms and scowled. "I hate dealing with people like her. Always out to get something for nothing."

"It was very kind of her to bring us that information. She didn't have to do that."

"She thought she would get something for it." Jeanne pressed the button to lower her bed back into a sleeping position. "I'm tired."

Evelyn sighed. She had hoped Jeanne was making progress but saw she still had quite a way to go. "I'll leave and let you sleep."

She walked out of Jeanne's room and saw Abigail standing by the elevator, leaning against the wall, her eyes closed.

"Are you okay?" Evelyn asked, concern tightening her stomach.

The elevator dinged, and the door opened. Evelyn didn't usually use the elevator unless she was going up several floors, but she followed Abigail onto it now.

"I'm fine," Abigail said.

Her face was white, and sweat had beaded on her brow. She didn't look fine.

"Ground floor?" Evelyn asked as her hand hovered over the buttons.

"Yes, please." Abigail leaned up against the wall of the elevator and placed her hand on the handrail.

"Do you need assistance?"

Abigail shook her head. "It's just that hospitals bring back really bad memories for me." She looked down. "My mother was in the hospital for several months before she died."

Heaviness settled over Evelyn's heart. "I'm so very sorry."

The elevator lowered and within seconds, the doors opened. Abigail took an unsteady step into the hall. But as soon as Evelyn joined her, she turned. "I don't know why I even tried with Ms. Robertson. She treated me the same way the last time I made an offer for the ring. I can't handle being accused of swindling people." She put her hand on Evelyn's forearm. "I would never do something like that. I wouldn't have even come to this hospital if I wasn't very serious about acquiring the ring and paying whatever Ms. Robertson asked."

"I believe you."

She seemed to become aware of the fact that she was touching Evelyn's arm, and pulled back suddenly. "She doesn't have to worry about me anymore. I won't ever seek her out again. I have better things to do with my time and money."

Evelyn wanted to ask Abigail if she had been the one to break into the Vault last Thursday but didn't want to upset her more. Now was clearly not the time to ask. "For whatever it's worth, I appreciate that you shared information with us about the ring."

Abigail nodded and then walked toward the main entrance.

In all the commotion, Evelyn realized she had forgotten her coffee in Jeanne's room.

At least it gave her another excuse to drop by the gift shop and chat with Joy.

The sky was overcast when Evelyn walked home from Mercy that afternoon. James had told her there would be a surprise waiting for her when she got off work, and given his history of surprises, she was a little leery.

But she had promised him to be more patient, so no matter what he planned to surprise her with, she'd love it.

"Hello," she called as she walked into the house. A light drizzle of rain began to fall, and droplets of water speckled the windows lining the long hall. "James, I'm home."

"Wait right there, Evie." James stepped out of the kitchen, his ever-present blue jeans and faded T-shirt in place. In less than two weeks, he would be heading back to school in his suit and tie again. But whether he was dressed in business attire or remodeling dust, she'd never known a more handsome man.

She did as he instructed and waited by the front door.

"Hi," he said with a grin and a kiss when he was close. He took her purse and hung it on the coat-tree. "How was your day?"

Evelyn smiled at him and tickled his ribs. "Are you trying to stall? I've been waiting all day for this surprise."

He playfully grabbed at her hand and then wrapped her arms around him. "What if it didn't get installed like I had hoped? What if you have to wait?"

"I can tell from the grin on your face that it's ready, James Robert Perry."

James hugged her tight. "All right, if you insist upon seeing it."

She started to pull away from him to go and see whatever it was for herself, but he held her back.

"Cover your eyes," he said.

Evelyn giggled, willing to play along. She covered her eyes with her hands and allowed him to lead her down the hall. When they stopped, he said, "Open them."

Pulling her hands away, Evelyn opened her eyes and blinked several times. "Oh, James! I love it."

The new cabinet doors had been installed. Everything was bright, fresh, and clean. Even the floor had been mopped.

"All we need is the counter, the appliances, the sink, and the light fixtures." James crossed his arms as he looked at her, pleased as could be.

"Don't forget the stools." She smiled back at him. "I ordered them today. They should get here by Saturday."

"I can't wait."

"And I can't wait to get everything out of the living room and back into the kitchen."

"We'll have to wait until the countertop is installed." James walked over to the new window and turned around to lean against the cabinets. "The countertop installers are supposed to come on Saturday morning. I hope to get the trim up around the window that day."

"Isn't the plumber coming Saturday?"

James nodded. "And the electrician."

Evelyn lifted her eyebrows. "It's going to be busy in here."

"I'm trying to space everyone out, so they come at different times. The plumber can't come until the countertop is installed, since the sink goes in after that. And the electrician also has to wait for the countertop so he can install the cooktop."

"And the light fixtures." Evelyn walked up to James and offered him a smile. "Have you picked them out?"

He wiggled his eyebrows. "Wouldn't you like to know?"

"Where did you order them from?"

James shook his head, chuckling. "I'm not saying a word. You'll have to wait and see."

Evelyn winked at him. "I guess I have to wait until Saturday, hmm?"

Wrapping his arms around her, James pulled her close again. "I have an idea."

"What's that?"

"It's going to be crazy here on Saturday. Why don't you call your friends and see if they're available to do something with you that day? When you get home in the evening, everything will be done."

Evelyn pulled back to look at him. "Are you serious?"

"You said you hoped that when we did this project we could go on vacation and come back to have it all done. Why don't you take a mini-vacation and have fun Saturday? You said you've been meaning to go antiquing for a while. Maybe your friends would like to join you. Make a day of it. Stay out for lunch and supper. Be a tourist in your own hometown."

It sounded like a lovely idea. Just like something James would suggest.

"You won't mind if I'm out having fun while you're here working on the kitchen?"

"I made the decision to start this project, so I plan to see it through. As soon as it's done, you and I will celebrate. Until then, it'll be a little chaotic and crowded here. Go have fun."

"Only if you're sure."

"I wouldn't have suggested it unless I was sure." He kissed her. "Maybe you can go shopping for some new accessories to decorate the kitchen."

"That's a great idea." She brushed some dust off his shoulder. "If you let me know what color the light fixtures will be, it would help me in choosing some accent pieces."

"Ha!" James laughed. "Nice try, Evie."

Evelyn hugged James close.

"How was work?" he asked again. "Any leads on the break-in?"

"Not really, but I did learn something new about the ring." She told him about Abigail Sinclair's visit and the history she shared. "The lock was finally fixed on the Vault door," she added.

"I'll feel a lot better when that ring is out of the hospital." James shook his head. "You don't know how hard it is for me to know someone has threatened you."

"We're doing our best to find out who it was."

"Did security go through the surveillance footage?"

Evelyn sighed. "They did, but there's only one camera in that section of hallway, and Seamus didn't see any suspicious activity on Thursday evening."

"There's a camera in the Vault now, isn't there?"

She nodded. "Yes."

"Good. And what about the four suspects you've been considering?"

"I haven't ruled any of them out. I asked Shirley to see if she could locate the nurse who was on duty Thursday evening with Kaley Robertson and see if she noticed Roy leaving his daughter's bedside for any length of time."

"Whoever did it would have needed a good fifteen or twenty minutes, at least, don't you think?"

"I do." She had already told him about her conversation with Wayne Preston. "I'm still uncertain about Wayne's honesty. If he considered stealing the ring, more than once, what's to say he didn't consider it again?"

"And what about the temp nurse?"

"I didn't see her at all today. I find it odd that she was in the Vault on her own yesterday. Just to be safe, I went to the security office and asked to see the video surveillance when she was in there. She didn't even go near the safe but was riffling through some of the files. She's so evasive when I ask her personal questions, but that doesn't mean she would attempt to steal the ring."

"Didn't you say Shirley is looking into information about her too?"

"Shirley said she'd ask around about her. I'm hoping we can learn something helpful."

"And what about the jeweler? Do you think she could have done it?"

Evelyn lifted her hands in uncertainty. "I don't know. The way she acted when she was in the hospital today suggests that she doesn't go to hospitals very often—but that doesn't mean she wouldn't have done it if she was desperate enough. I couldn't bring myself to ask her about it today. She was already so upset."

"You know where Roy and Wayne were the night of the break-in. Maybe you need to try to figure out where Madison and Abigail were."

"That might be easier said than done."

James shrugged. "But it could help you narrow down your suspects."

"True." Evelyn nuzzled into James a little closer. "But, right now, I'm home, and I want to put work aside."

"Sounds like a great idea."

But as the evening progressed, putting work out of mind was also easier said than done.

Evelyn needed to get to the bottom of this mystery before Jeanne left Mercy—not only for her own peace of mind, but to ensure that no one would go after Jeanne once the ring was no longer in the safe.

Chapter Fourteen

On Thursday evening Evelyn and James were greeted at the Mabrys' front door by both Anne and Ralph. The weather was as close to perfect as Charleston could boast, with a cool breeze and a beautiful sunset in progress.

"Welcome," Anne said as she gave Evelyn a hug. "Thank you both for coming."

"Congratulations on forty years of marriage," James said as he shook Ralph's hand and then gave Anne a quick hug. "It's quite an accomplishment."

Anne smiled up at her husband, her blond shoulder-length hair bobbing as she tilted her head. "I couldn't have done it without Ralph."

"No," Evelyn said with a laugh, "you couldn't."

"That's her joke for the evening." Ralph chuckled and gave his wife a side hug.

Anne grinned. "Everyone is gathering in the backyard. Please grab a plate of food and something to drink. We'll be out shortly."

The Mabrys' home was in North Charleston, in a lovely, new neighborhood. Their one-story house was yellow with black shutters and had a nicely landscaped lawn. It was the perfect place for them to raise Addie while Liliana was deployed.

"Is Addie here?" Evelyn asked as they were walking through the Mabrys' living room toward the backyard.

"No." Anne shook her head as the doorbell rang with the arrival of more guests. "She decided to stay over at a friend's house tonight, since there wouldn't be other children here."

Evelyn nodded and followed James out the back door.

The yard was transformed. Large outdoor lights hung from tree to tree, swaying gently in the breeze. Soft music was playing from a stereo system on the patio where several tables had been set up with food and drinks. Adirondack chairs were grouped around a firepit, where several people had already gathered to visit, while the majority of the other guests stood or sat at picnic tables in little clusters, visiting, laughing, and sharing stories about the Mabrys. Evelyn knew almost everyone in attendance who worked at Mercy Hospital, but there were many others she didn't know, no doubt friends and parishioners from St. Michael's Church where the Mabrys had served for almost twenty years.

"Evelyn!" Joy called out to her the moment they stepped onto the back patio.

Evelyn waved and smiled and then pointed to the food. "We'll join you as soon as we get something to eat."

Joy was sitting at a picnic table eating with Shirley and also Garrison Baker, Mercy Hospital's administrator. He and Shirley had met when Shirley moved to Charleston and started working at Mercy. Garrison's tough exterior was no match for Shirley's no-nonsense personality, and, more than once, Evelyn had seen Garrison light up when Shirley came into a room.

"The food looks amazing," James said to Evelyn as he took a plate and eyed the options. "Takeout is fun for a while, but I miss eating homecooked meals."

"When the kitchen is finished," Evelyn promised, "I'll make your favorite lasagna."

"The one that takes you almost all day?" James's expression was hopeful.

Evelyn nodded. It took her almost all day because she made the sauce and noodles from scratch.

James placed his empty plate over his chest and said, "Be still my heart."

They chuckled as they filled their plates with barbecue pulled pork sandwiches, coleslaw, corn bread, baked beans, and cucumber-dill salad.

"Where will we put it all?" James asked as Evelyn handed him a tall glass of sweet tea. "My stomach hasn't seen this much food since the last time we were here for a barbecue."

"We saved you a spot," Shirley called out to them as she motioned to the opposite side of the picnic table where her mother, Regina, was sitting.

James and Evelyn took their seats.

"Thank you," Evelyn said. "My plate is so heavy I was afraid I wouldn't be able to hold it up much longer."

Joy laughed. "Anne and Ralph sure know how to celebrate a wonderful achievement. Anne must have been cooking for days."

"Ralph's pretty adept at the grill," James said. "If I had to guess, I'd say he's responsible for this amazing barbecue."

The others nodded in agreement as the conversation drifted around aimlessly for a few minutes. They commented on the beautiful lawn, the amazing weather, and the delicious food.

When Garrison rose to refill his plate, Shirley wiped her mouth and said to Evelyn, "I learned a little more about Madison Cummings."

Evelyn noticed James lean forward, just as eager to hear about the temp nurse.

"What did you learn?" she asked.

Shirley's brown eyes sparkled under the outdoor lighting, and her face became animated as everyone turned to look at her. "Apparently, Madison has become friends with Loretta, one of the nurses I work with. She's been a lot more open with Loretta than she was with me."

Evelyn set her fork aside, more interested in hearing what Shirley had to say than in eating at the moment.

"Madison told Loretta that she's lived all over the world, which we already knew, but most recently she was at North Middlesex Hospital in London."

Evelyn nodded. "I remember your saying she lived in London."

"Apparently," Shirley said, "she was there for over a year before she came to Charleston, and that's the longest she's stayed anywhere."

"I wonder why she stayed there so long," James said.

"Loretta mentioned that Madison was engaged to a man she met in London, but things didn't work out. And, if what Loretta says is true, Madison was not the one to break off the engagement. She's still very upset about the whole thing." Shirley shrugged. "I'm assuming that's why she left."

"I'm sorry for her," Evelyn said. "It must be very difficult for her right now. I'm happy she's found a friend in Loretta."

"What kind of a friend shares all your secrets with a coworker?" James asked with a raised brow.

"Loretta didn't act as though Madison had confided in her." Shirley shrugged again. "I think Loretta is very concerned and even asked me if I'd reach out to Madison. I told her I'd already tried, but she didn't seem to want my company."

"Loretta is closer in age to Madison," Evelyn suggested. "Maybe she thinks we're too old to be her friends."

Shirley made a funny face and shook her head. "Ouch."

"If you're too old," Joy said, "that means the rest of us are too old."

"And I, for one, am not," James said while he licked barbecue sauce off his thumb.

Everyone laughed.

"If you get a chance," Shirley said to Evelyn, "perhaps you could try reaching out to Madison again. Maybe she'll warm up to you after all."

"That's a good plan," James said, teasing. "Just wear her down. Eventually, she'll confide all of her secrets to you."

Shirley shook her head, laughter in her voice. "That's not what I meant, and you know it."

Evelyn and James smiled at one another, and then Evelyn said to Shirley, "Did you ever find out who was on duty with Roy Robertson's daughter last Thursday?"

"I did," Shirley said. "Her name is Audrey Heffron. She works swing shift on the pediatric floor but has been working nights lately.

I haven't had a chance to question her since I've been working days this week."

"I'll have to find out when she's working next and ask her about the Robertsons," Evelyn said.

The Mabrys entered the backyard at that moment, and Garrison returned to the table. Everyone began to clap for the couple. There had to be at least seventy people in attendance, and the smiles shining on Anne and Ralph were a great testament to their friendships.

"Thank you," Ralph said as everyone quieted down. "Anne and I are so happy you've come to celebrate our anniversary." He looked down at Anne, a warm smile on his face. "It's hard to believe that forty years ago today I was a nervous young man, waiting at the church altar for my equally nervous young bride."

"Aww," several people in the crowd said.

Evelyn smiled at James, who reached for her hand and gave it a gentle squeeze.

"I thought I knew my bride that day as well as anyone could know the woman he was about to marry," Ralph continued, "but I had only glimpsed a small part of her. It's been over the course of the past forty years, through the good days and bad—" He paused, a little choked up. Anne took his hand and moved close to his side. No doubt he was thinking about the daughter they lost to leukemia five years after they were married. After a moment, he went on. "It was Anne's love and devotion, through both the good and the bad, that taught me about the woman I had married. Anne is exactly the same, whether in public or in private. She's kind, generous, and deeply faithful. She's the sort of person you want at your side, no matter the day, the occasion, or the reason, and I'm so thankful God chose her to be mine." He took a glass of sweet tea off the drink table and raised it in the air. "Here's to my bride of forty wonderful years, Anne Mabry."

"Here, here," everyone called out as they raised their own glasses to toast Anne.

Anne's cheeks blossomed into a delightful shade of pink and she smiled at her husband and then at the crowd.

"Thank you," she said, her gentle voice barely heard over the sounds of their friends. "Ralph is so good to me."

A few people clapped in agreement, and it was Ralph's turn to look a little embarrassed.

"For years," Anne said as the group noise died down, "I've watched my husband serve the people of Charleston, first as a pastor and now as a hospital chaplain. And each time someone tells me what an amazing man I'm married to, I feel like telling them they have no idea! Years ago, when I was preparing to marry Ralph, a pastor's wife came alongside me to mentor me. She taught me many wonderful and valuable things, but there was one thing she told me that I have never found to be true. She said, 'Try not to become bitter about sharing your husband with his community. Everyone will seek out his time, energy, and wisdom. It's easy to get envious.'" Anne looked at Ralph, her eyes shining. "I've never grown bitter about sharing my husband with the community. If anything, I've felt blessed that God has shared him with me. Ralph has always, always put his family first, and for that, I'm deeply grateful." She lifted her glass. "To my husband, Pastor Ralph Mabry."

Everyone raised their glasses to toast Ralph as well, and when they were done, there was another round of applause for the happy couple.

Conversation picked up again while Anne and Ralph made the rounds of all their friends. Eventually, they came over to the picnic table, where they were greeted with more good wishes and congratulations.

"Thank you for this wonderful evening," Evelyn said to her friend as she gave her a hug.

"It wouldn't be the same without all of you here to celebrate with us." Anne gave Shirley, Regina, and Joy hugs as well.

They visited for a few moments about the party before Evelyn remembered to ask them about Saturday. "I was wondering if any of you would be available to spend Saturday with me. The kitchen will be undergoing its final renovations, and James suggested I take myself out for some fun."

Joy's face lit up at the idea. "I'd love to join you. What do you have in mind?"

"I thought we could do some shopping," Evelyn said. "There are a few antique shops I'd love to explore."

"I could join you for part of the day," Anne said. "We have plans for the evening, but that wouldn't be until suppertime."

"What about you, Shirley?" Evelyn asked.

"Mama and I have plans on Saturday," she said. "But maybe I could join you for supper."

"How about we meet at ten?" Evelyn suggested. "There's an antique shop in the French Quarter I saw when I went down to Sinclair Antique Jewelry." She looked it up on her phone and gave them the address and they all agreed to meet in the area, except Shirley, who would text them when she was free to see where she might meet up with them.

Evelyn couldn't wait to spend a day with her friends, and perhaps she could stop by and talk to Abigail Sinclair again. She still wasn't convinced that the antique jeweler hadn't tried to break into the safe—and that there wasn't more to the ring's story than she was letting on.

On Friday afternoon, Evelyn had to run a file up to administration on the fifth floor. Instead of heading right back to the records department, she pressed the button in the elevator to stop on the third floor. She would see when Audrey Heffron might be working next so she could interview her about Roy Robertson.

The pediatric floor of Mercy Hospital was one of Evelyn's favorite places in the building. Immediately upon exiting the elevator, she was greeted with the sights and sounds of a jungle. Not only were the walls painted with murals of trees, monkeys, and all manner of jungle animals, but 3D branches and vines hung from the ceiling with stuffed animals draped in various places. Down the hall, as she progressed to the nurses' station, the jungle slowly changed to become more of a prehistoric scene with large leaves and dinosaurs painted on the walls. But it was the sounds of the jungle, playing gently overhead, that made the whole experience come to life.

Evelyn visited this floor often. She loved the children who were treated with top-notch care at Mercy. Sometimes when she had a spare moment, she came to visit them—especially those children in long-term treatments who were living on the fifth floor with their families in the hospitality facility called the Mercy House. Their courage, fortitude, and strength never ceased to amaze her. Children were truly a gift from God.

But today, it was the nurses' station that garnered her attention. After she had a chance to ask about Audrey, she would see if any of the kiddos were up for a visit.

"Hello, Evelyn." Paige Peterson, the head nurse on the pediatrics floor, greeted Evelyn. "Are you here to visit?"

"In a little while," Evelyn said. "First, I have a question about one of your nurses."

Paige set aside a chart she was working on and gave her full attention to Evelyn. Her strawberry-blond hair was pulled back in a ponytail, and her green eyes shone with interest. "Ask away."

"Last week, there was a patient here named Kaley Robertson."

"A sweet girl." Paige smiled. "She was discharged yesterday."

"I heard that Audrey Heffron was a nurse on duty the night Kaley had surgery, and I was wondering when she's working next so I can ask her a few questions about Kaley's dad."

Paige frowned. "Is there a problem?"

Evelyn didn't want to cast a shadow over Roy's character. "I just have some questions for her."

"She's working now." Paige nodded down the hall. "She picked up a shift this afternoon, but she's with a patient. If you can wait a couple of minutes, I'm sure she'll be available to talk to you."

"Of course." Evelyn would happily wait if it meant she could question Audrey. She hadn't anticipated getting the opportunity for a few days.

"If you want to wait in the playroom, there are some families in there now. I'll send Audrey in as soon as she's finished with her patient."

Evelyn nodded, thrilled to get a chance to visit with the kids.

She left Paige at the nurses' station and walked the short distance to the playroom. It was a large space with padded floors, several climbing toys, a child-sized basketball hoop, and various other activities to keep the kids occupied. A half dozen children were playing there with their parents. Not all the children were patients. Some were siblings who were visiting, and it was fairly easy to distinguish between the healthy and ill children. One of them had lost all his hair and was in a wheelchair, hooked up to an oxygen tank. A second child, a little girl, had a large cast on her arm. She was probably there for a shorter stay.

"Hello, Mrs. Perry," a third child called out to Evelyn. He smiled, his swollen face lighting up with joy. Evelyn had met him two weeks ago and learned his name was Trevin. He was staying in Mercy awaiting a kidney transplant, but they had not found a matching donor yet. He had been on Evelyn's prayer list since she'd met him.

"Hello, Trevin." Evelyn smiled at him and waved hello to his mother and sister, who were sitting at a table putting together a puzzle. "How are you today?"

Trevin shrugged. "Bored. My mom took away my phone again."

"I told him he could have it back as soon as he finished his math homework." Trevin's mom shook her head. "So don't make me out to be the villain here, Trev."

"I'd finish it," Trevin said, "if I knew how to do it. It's so confusing."

"It's been so long since I was in sixth grade," his mom said with embarrassment. "I'm no help at all."

"Would you like me to see if I can help?" Evelyn asked him while looking to his mom to see if she would be open to some tutoring.

"He could use some," Trevin's mom said. "If you don't mind."

"I'd be happy to," Evelyn said. "I love math."

Trevin lifted his eyebrows. "You actually like it?"

"I do." Evelyn laughed at the look on his face.

"We wouldn't want to bother you," Trevin's mom said. "If you're too busy…"

"I have a few minutes to spare." Evelyn was always willing to take time out of her busy schedule for the children at Mercy. Nothing else gave her as much satisfaction.

"Go get your backpack." Trevin's mom nodded toward a hook near the door.

Trevin retrieved his bag and met Evelyn at a table. They went over his homework, and Evelyn helped him understand the problem he was stuck on.

They were sitting there, working, when Audrey entered the room. Though Evelyn had never been introduced to her, she recognized her immediately.

"Hello, Mrs. Perry," Audrey said. "Paige said you'd like to talk to me."

"Yes." Evelyn held up her hand. "If you can give me another second so Trevin and I can finish up this problem."

Audrey smiled and nodded.

Evelyn wrapped up the problem with Trevin and then said goodbye to him and his mom and sister before leaving the room with Audrey.

When they were in the hall, away from curious ears, Evelyn smiled. "Thank you for meeting with me."

"Paige said this has something to do with the Robertson family." She studied Evelyn's face. "Is there a problem?"

"No." Evelyn shook her head. "I just have a couple of questions."

"What would you like to know?"

"Were you on duty last Thursday night into Friday morning? Somewhere between ten and five?" Based on the surveillance footage Seamus had looked over, and the reports of the night custodian, they had narrowed down the break-in to those hours.

"Yes. I was."

"How often were you in Kaley's room?"

Audrey pressed her lips together in thought. "Every hour, at least. She was in a lot of pain and discomfort. She didn't sleep much at all that night, and I was doing everything I could to ease her pain."

"Did Roy leave her room at any time?"

"Not that I know of. Neither of her parents did. They spent the entire night trying to keep Kaley occupied and distracted."

"Are you certain?"

"Completely. I was so impressed with how calm and steadfast they both were. I even commented on it to Paige that morning when she came on duty. I told her Kaley was a very fortunate little girl to have such dedicated parents."

"When you were not in the room, where were you?" Evelyn asked. "Were you seeing to other patients?"

Audrey shook her head. "It was an unusually quiet night on the floor. I had three other patients under my care, but all of them were sleeping and I only checked on them once in the night, for a minute or two. Other than that, I was at the nurses' station all night."

"And what about your break? Did you leave for an extended period of time for that?"

Again, Audrey shook her head. "I didn't take a break. I just ate my lunch at the nurses' station."

"So you're confident Roy didn't leave Kaley's room?"

"Very confident." Audrey nodded.

"Okay." Evelyn thought through everything she'd learned about Roy, and though he had a motive, she couldn't discount Audrey's word. If Roy hadn't left his daughter's room, he couldn't have broken into the Vault. "Thank you for answering my questions. If you think of anything else that might be helpful, please let me know."

"I'm happy to help. I'll gladly contact you if I think of something else."

"Thank you. I'll let you get back to your work."

"Anytime." Audrey turned and walked away.

As disappointed as Evelyn felt that she wasn't any closer to knowing who had broken into the Vault and left the nefarious note, she was happy it wasn't Roy. She had no wish to see him criminalized.

But that still left her with a lot of questions. Who had tried breaking into the safe? And would they make her regret being involved in this mystery? If she could find the culprit before he or she struck again, Evelyn would be relieved.

Chapter Fifteen

A LIGHT DRIZZLE FELL FROM the sky as Evelyn, Anne, and Joy stepped out of an antique store on Saturday morning in the French Quarter. Evelyn put up her black umbrella as she moved away from the awning and onto the sidewalk.

"Where should we go next?" Joy asked as she too put up an umbrella.

"Just enough rain to make an umbrella necessary," Anne commented to herself as she struggled to get hers open.

"How about the jewelry store?" Evelyn asked. "It's not too far from here, and it's really a beautiful store."

"Didn't you mention you wanted to chat with the owner again?" Joy asked.

"I do. I haven't been able to rule her out as a suspect yet."

"Who have you ruled out?" Anne asked as she finally got her umbrella to cooperate and joined Joy and Evelyn on the sidewalk.

Evelyn began to lead them down the street, toward the jewelry shop. "Based on my investigations, I've ruled out Roy Robertson. According to his daughter's nurse, he never left her room that night."

"That's good to know." Joy motioned to a small coffee shop and put her eyebrows up in question.

Evelyn nodded, and she and Anne followed Joy into the building. The scent of freshly ground coffee wafted up to Evelyn's nose and she inhaled a deep breath.

After they placed their orders to go, they stood near the counter to wait for their coffee.

"Sorry," Joy said to Evelyn, putting her hand on Evelyn's forearm. "I didn't mean to interrupt you. But whenever I see a coffee shop I've never tried before, I like to get a sample."

"I completely understand." Evelyn smiled, knowing how much her friend loved coffee. Joy hadn't yet found a roaster in Charleston that she liked as much as the one in her native Houston.

"What were you saying?" Anne asked Evelyn. "About your suspects."

"I don't think it was Roy Robertson, and I'd like to think it wasn't Wayne Preston either—though I can't prove his alibi without involving his wife. And, by his own admission, he was tempted to take the ring on a couple of occasions. Who's to say he wasn't tempted enough to break into the safe?"

"And the other two?" Anne asked. "Abigail and Madison, correct?"

Evelyn nodded. "They're the only other people who knew about the ring being in the safe—except Stacia's new boyfriend, Hunter O'Reilly, but Stacia gave him an alibi right away."

Joy pressed her lips together as she studied Evelyn, and then said, "Did it ever occur to you that Stacia could be lying for Hunter? She's a nice girl," she added quickly, "but perhaps he conned her into letting him into the records department, or even to lie about where he was that night."

Evelyn shook her head. It wasn't that she hadn't considered the possibility but that she had been trying to avoid even going down that line of questioning. She liked Stacia, and Stacia was a great employee. But she had given information away to Hunter right after they had met—what would have stopped her from trying to impress him with giving him more?

"Maybe it's time to have a chat with her," Anne said gently. "If we don't figure this out by Monday, you might want to sit her down and see what she knows."

"You're right." Evelyn sighed.

Their orders were called, and they collected their drinks.

Evelyn was usually happiest with regular black coffee and a little sweetened creamer. But today she had decided to splurge and get a café mocha with milk chocolate. She took a sip and briefly closed her eyes. It was sweet but very good.

"Hmm," Joy said as she sampled the house blend coffee. "It's not too bad."

"But is it good?" Anne asked with a laugh.

Joy smiled as they walked back out into the rain, their umbrellas up once again. "Let's just say I won't be canceling my order with Raphael's Coffee Shop anytime soon."

Evelyn turned down the street to resume their trek to Sinclair Antique Jewelry.

"What about Abigail and Madison?" Anne asked again. "Do you have a gut feeling about either of them?"

"No." Evelyn shook her head. "That's one of the reasons I want to speak to Abigail again. She was so anxious the last time I saw her, I couldn't get a good read."

"She wanted to buy the ring, right?" Joy asked.

"I believe so. Apparently, she made an offer the first time she saw it, but Jeanne refused." Evelyn led them across North Market Street. The jeweler was at the end of the block. "The second time, in the hospital, she mentioned that the ring was worth more with the list of people who had owned it. She increased her offering price, but Jeanne became angry. Abigail left just as upset."

"What if she isn't willing to answer your questions?" Joy asked.

"That's a possibility, but I have to try."

When they finally arrived at Sinclair Antique Jewelry, Joy and Anne looked up at the beautiful, impressive building with appreciation in their gazes. The stone facade was dark with the spray of rain, but the overcast skies made the jewelry under the lights in the front window shine all the more.

"Look at that piece," Joy commented as she pointed to a beautiful diamond bracelet. "Wilson was always trying to buy me jewelry when he was alive. He would have bugged me to get that bracelet. His favorite gemstones were diamonds."

"Why didn't you let him buy you something?" Evelyn asked.

Joy shrugged as she continued to look at the piece. "It made me feel ostentatious. Like I was trying to impress people."

"From some of the stories you've told me," Anne said, "you would have had plenty of places to wear fine jewelry."

Joy's husband had been in the oil business in Texas and the two had traveled extensively, attending oil conventions all over the world. Surely there had been opportunity to dress formally.

"Why don't you try it on?" Evelyn asked Joy. "Wouldn't it be fun to own a piece of jewelry that makes you think of Wilson when you wear it?"

Joy shook her head and laughed. "Where would I wear it in Charleston? My life consists of the gift shop, church, and my garden club."

"You never know," Anne said with a smile. "I'm a firm believer in making things happen. If you want somewhere to wear the bracelet, you need to find somewhere."

"Come on," Joy said, still laughing, as she nodded toward the door. "Let's go inside and talk to Abigail."

"I think you should try on the bracelet," Evelyn said. "It will give us a good excuse to enter the store, and maybe Abigail won't be so defensive."

It didn't take much to convince Joy. Five minutes later, after the introductions were made with Abigail, Joy was trying on the gorgeous diamond bracelet.

"It was designed and created in the 1920s," Abigail said to Joy. "Can't you just imagine a wealthy flapper wearing that bracelet to a speakeasy?"

Evelyn smiled to herself. If Abigail wanted to make a sale, perhaps associating the bracelet to a speakeasy wouldn't sway Joy's opinion.

"It is beautiful," Joy said, a hitch in her voice.

"Keep it on as you browse," Abigail said with a gentle nod. "You'll find yourself admiring it more and more."

Anne leaned close to Joy to look at the bracelet. "And it will make you think about Wilson."

As Joy and Anne looked around the store, Evelyn stayed by Abigail's side.

"I want to apologize for the way Jeanne treated you," Evelyn said to Abigail. "I know you came to the hospital to be helpful. If it's any consolation, your information was very useful in my investigation."

"Investigation?" Abigail frowned. "What are you investigating? I thought you were just trying to help Ms. Robertson piece together the day of the accident."

"I'm actually investigating a break-in at the hospital." Evelyn watched Abigail closely to see if there was a flicker of recognition or guilt in her eyes. "Someone tried breaking into the safe where the ring is being stored."

"How awful." Abigail frowned. "I'm sorry to hear that. Have you found the culprit?"

Evelyn shook her head. "There are only a handful of people who know it's being held there."

Understanding dawned in Abigail's expression, and she stiffened. "Are you here to question me about the break-in?"

A part of Evelyn wanted to ease Abigail's defensiveness, but the other part knew she had to be honest. "I'm not accusing you. I'm just trying to be thorough. I don't like the idea of anyone breaking into my office at Mercy Hospital, and I imagine you would do everything you could to locate a perpetrator if someone tried to break into your store. You can see why I can't leave any stone unturned."

Abigail studied Evelyn for a moment and then finally nodded. "I appreciate your honesty. What night was the break-in?"

"A week ago Thursday."

"The Thursday after the accident?" Abigail's eyebrows came together as she looked off for a moment, no doubt searching her memory for that day. "Just a minute." She left Evelyn and went to the cash register counter where she picked up her cell phone. "I remember exactly where I was that Thursday." She tapped her phone a few times, waited, and then tapped it again. Finally, she brought it back to Evelyn and showed her the screen.

She had opened her Facebook app and was showing Evelyn her post from that Thursday. "I was at a concert with some of my friends." She mentioned the name of the performer and showed Evelyn some of the pictures she'd taken and posted that night. Evelyn recalled hearing that the performer was in town.

"You can see we were up almost all night." Abigail showed her other pictures of her and her friends at a club later that evening.

So it hadn't been Abigail who broke into the Vault.

"Thank you," Evelyn said. "I appreciate your willingness to help."

Abigail set her phone down and then glanced at Joy and Anne, who were oohing and aahing over some jewelry. Abigail bent her head and said in a quieter voice. "I was actually going to call you today and tell you about an interesting conversation I had early this morning."

"Really?" Evelyn frowned as she waited for Abigail to continue.

"Have you ever heard of a man named Lord Marshton?"

"Isn't he trying to purchase all of the Lords Proprietors' rings?"

Abigail nodded with excitement. "He claims to be descended from King Charles II and is trying to gather all of the rings. He hopes to use them to help restore his ancestral home."

"He called you?" Evelyn hadn't given Lord Marshton much thought since hearing about him from Hunter O'Reilly.

"He must have heard about the ruby and diamond ring—"

"Probably thanks to the article in the *Charleston Times*."

"Lord Marshton—his name is actually Randall Hanover, 13th Earl of Marshton—called to inquire about it."

"Why would he call you, of all people?"

"Apparently, Mr. O'Reilly called Ms. Robertson for a follow-up interview after he learned about her being in my store for an appraisal. He wanted to see what I knew about the history of the ring. He mentioned me in the article."

"Oh, that's right." Evelyn remembered now that she'd seen Abigail's name in the article.

"Lord Marshton and I had a long chat about the ring because he wanted to ascertain whether or not it was the real deal."

"And you told him it was?"

"Yes. I am convinced it's the missing one he's been after."

"Did he tell you anything else about the ring?" No doubt Lord Marshton knew more than they did, if he'd been looking for it all this time.

"Actually"—Abigail's face revealed her surprise—"he told me something very interesting. He claims that he is also a descendant of Sir Anthony Ashley Cooper, 1st Earl of Shaftesbury."

"Really?"

"And that he is the rightful heir to the ruby and diamond ring through both the king and Lord Shaftesbury. He claims it was stolen from his ancestor and that it should be returned to his family. But he said that wasn't the last time the ring was stolen. Lord Marshton told me that it was stolen sometime in the 1880s from a man named Reginald Peabody and that whoever stole it sold it to Cedric Prior—but that after Cedric Prior left New York, Lord Marshton lost track of him and the ring, until now."

"He told you all this?"

"Yes."

"Does he expect Jeanne to turn the ring over to him?"

Abigail shook her head. "He understands her family paid for it, and he's willing to buy it back from her. He actually asked if I'd be willing to broker a deal, but I told him I refused to be involved." She crossed her arms. "I will never seek out Jeanne Robertson again."

"Understandable."

"I hope this is helpful," Abigail said. "I wouldn't be surprised if Lord Marshton tries to contact Ms. Robertson, whether through a solicitor, or directly."

"I should probably prepare her for that phone call." Evelyn smiled. "Thank you for all your help."

"You're most welcome." Abigail looked around Evelyn and caught Joy's gaze, a smile on her face. "And what about the bracelet? It looks amazing on you."

Joy glanced at the bracelet again, but she shook her head, sadness in her face. "I'm sorry, but I don't think I could justify the purchase today."

"Okay." Abigail's voice held a hint of disappointment. "But if you change your mind it will be here waiting for you."

The ladies thanked Abigail for her help and left the store.

As they made their way to their next stop, all Evelyn could think about was warning Jeanne about Lord Marshton. No doubt he'd be contacting her about selling the ring. Maybe it would help if they knew more about him beforehand.

Later that day, after Anne had left to join Ralph for a dinner party, Shirley met Evelyn and Joy at Magnolias, an upscale Southern cuisine restaurant in the heart of the historic district. Evelyn had been wanting to try the restaurant for quite some time and was not disappointed with the charm of the interior. Long and narrow, the restaurant boasted hardwood floors, white tablecloths, and unique, oversized wire magnolias climbing the pillars.

"What a great suggestion," Shirley said as she joined Evelyn and Joy at their table. "A bit pricey, but I don't mind splurging once in a while. Thank you for waiting for me."

"Of course." Evelyn and Joy had arrived at the restaurant twenty minutes earlier but had only ordered their beverages as they waited for Shirley to arrive.

After the waitress came and took their orders, and Evelyn chose the grilled salmon with summer beans and fingerling potatoes covered in lemon egg dressing and balsamic glaze. The waitress had barely turned to leave when Shirley burst out with, "Okay, spill. What did you all find out today at the jewelry store?"

Evelyn had briefly mentioned their encounter in her text to Shirley earlier. She quickly filled her in on the rest of what she knew.

"Why don't you do a quick internet search for Lord Marshton?" Shirley asked.

"I plan to."

"How about now?"

"Here? At the restaurant?"

"No time like the present." Shirley nodded at Evelyn's purse. "Use your phone."

"Isn't that rude?" Evelyn glanced around the restaurant and saw no one else on their phones.

"Not when your tablemates are encouraging you." Shirley leaned forward. "I'd be curious to see what we can find on him."

Evelyn pulled her phone out of her purse. She tapped the internet browser icon and then typed in RANDALL HANOVER, LORD MARSHTON. Immediately, several links showed up.

"It looks like our Lord Marshton is a bit of a ladies' man," Evelyn said as she showed Joy and Shirley the gossip magazines his name appeared in.

According to the tabloids, he was in his early thirties and his name was connected to several different women each year. The magazines were full of scandalous rumors about the young earl.

"According to this website," Evelyn said as she touched a link and waited for the page to come up, "it looks like the current Lord Marshton is quite well-off. His official career is 'philanthropist.'"

"Wouldn't that be something?" Shirley chuckled. "To have so much money your job is to give it away."

"I wonder why he's collecting the rings from the Lords Proprietors," Joy mused. "It doesn't look like he needs the money."

"Didn't I tell you?" Evelyn asked. "Apparently, Lord Marshton inherited his ancestral home with his title and hopes to use the rings to generate money to renovate the old house."

"That makes sense." Joy took a sip of her tea and tilted her head. "I wonder how serious he is about acquiring the ruby ring from Jeanne. I wonder how much he'll offer to pay her. It's the last ring of the set, after all."

"And, according to my research," Evelyn added, "the most important."

"But none of this tells us anything about who broke into the Vault," Shirley said. "If it's not Roy and it's not Abigail, then that only leaves Wayne and Madison."

"And Hunter O'Reilly," Evelyn said.

"The newspaper reporter?" Shirley frowned. "Wasn't he with Stacia that evening?"

"We were talking earlier," Joy explained to Shirley, "and we encouraged Evelyn to not write Mr. O'Reilly off as a suspect just because Stacia says so."

"Ah." Shirley nodded her understanding. "I would have to agree."

It still didn't sit well with Evelyn to doubt Stacia, but she couldn't deny there was a possibility that Stacia could have been hoodwinked by the reporter.

The waitress returned with their food. The aroma from Evelyn's grilled salmon made her mouth water. The presentation was also remarkable.

"Are you excited to get home to a finished kitchen?" Joy asked Evelyn after the waitress left.

"I am. I can hardly wait."

Shirley turned her plate so the buttermilk fried chicken was facing her. "What time did James tell you to come home?"

"He said no earlier than eight." And since it was already after seven, she would head home directly following the meal.

"I can't wait to see it." Joy grinned as she picked up her fork. "I'm sure it will be lovely."

"We plan to host a dinner party as soon as we have everything back together." Evelyn also picked up her fork, ready to sample the delectable food before her. "I'll be sure to send out an invitation as soon as we're ready."

They ate their meal in companionable conversation, allowing the topics to drift from their personal lives to their work, to their hobbies, interests, and pastimes. Evelyn loved getting to know both Joy and Shirley better.

After their dessert and coffee, Evelyn said goodbye to her friends and drove toward her home on Short Street. It wasn't a long drive from Magnolias, less than ten minutes, and she smiled when she was greeted with lights streaming from inside the house.

Evelyn parked in the back and collected her shopping bags. She hadn't purchased much but had found a few things she thought would be a welcome addition to their kitchen. A white porcelain bowl, a counter plate rack, and a historic picture of a Charleston kitchen from the 1890s, which she planned to hang directly above the wall oven, where it would be easy to see upon entering the room.

Thankfully, the rain had stopped earlier in the day and Evelyn was able to move from the car to the house without getting her purchases wet.

Her pulse was thumping hard with anticipation as she walked up the back steps. She could hardly wait to see the finished kitchen and to get all her things put back in their proper places. Since they hadn't changed the floorplan of the kitchen or the base cabinets, she fully intended to put everything back where it had been before.

"James," she called as she opened the back door and put her purchases on the sofa close by. "I'm home."

"Wait there," James called to her.

The living room was spotless. Everything looked pristine and in perfect order—Evelyn opened her eyes wide. Where were all the kitchen items? They'd been stacked up along the wall for the past two weeks.

"Where is everything?" Evelyn called out to James.

Her husband appeared in the doorway leading from the hall into the living room. He looked freshly showered, and his beard was trimmed. Instead of jeans and an old T-shirt, he was wearing a pair of slacks and a polo shirt—a little more his style.

But it was his smile that made him look truly handsome.

"Did you have a good day?" he asked.

"Is the kitchen done? Where is everything?"

"What did you buy?" James left the door and walked to the couch, peeking at the purchases.

"James." She motioned to the empty space in the living room. "Where is everything?"

He shrugged.

She laughed and started to move past him. "If you won't show me, I'll go look for myself."

He captured her hand as she went by and joined her as they left the living room and walked down the hall.

"I hope you love it," he said.

Evelyn paused for a heartbeat before turning to look at her new kitchen.

Everything was in place, from the countertop to the trim work. Even the stools that she had ordered, which had apparently arrived today, were butted up to the counter.

"It's beautiful," she breathed. "And it's all done."

"Every last thing is finished." James grinned. "A couple of guys from church came by today and helped me. I wanted to make sure nothing was left unfinished for you when you got home."

Evelyn entered the kitchen and opened the drawer closest to her. It was filled with her cooking utensils—exactly where they'd been before the remodel.

"You'll find everything is returned to its proper home." James joined her in the kitchen. "The only thing left to do is put your purchases in here from today."

Tears stung the backs of Evelyn's eyes as she surveyed the new granite countertop, the new cabinet doors, and the large window. All the appliances fit perfectly, the sink was ready for dishes, and the light fixtures, which hung over the sink and in front of the window, had the most charming green glass shades she'd ever seen. They added just the right amount of color to the black-and-white kitchen with the brown wood floors. A bank of track lights was near the ceiling over the door and gave the space a wonderful glow.

"Do you like it, Evie?" James asked.

In answer to his question, Evelyn embraced her husband and held him tight. "Thank you, from the bottom of my heart, for this gift. It's more than I deserve."

"It's nothing compared to what you deserve," he whispered as he held her close. "I'm just happy it's done and you like it."

"I love it." She gave him a kiss. "And I love you."

"I love you too," he said. "And those stools are perfect."

"Just like the lights."

Now that the kitchen was finished, Evelyn looked forward to coming home each day and enjoying their house as the refuge it had been since they'd purchased it from her parents.

And she could turn her entire attention to the break-in now. She was growing more and more concerned that Stacia hadn't been completely honest with her.

Chapter Sixteen

On Monday morning, Evelyn arrived at Mercy Hospital well before she was expected to open the records department. After a quick stop to grab a cup of freshly brewed coffee from Joy in the gift shop, she went up to Jeanne's room to chat with her about Lord Marshton and to see how she was feeling.

It had been two weeks since the accident, and Evelyn was certain Jeanne was more than ready to leave Mercy Hospital and return home to Atlanta. Hopefully she would soon have a good report from the doctor and would be able to make the move.

"Good morning," Evelyn said as she entered Jeanne's room. Bright sunshine poured through the windows, which were no longer shuttered.

Jeanne was sitting up in bed, her leg no longer in the harness elevating it. She looked like she had recently had a shower, and her hair was blown dry and freshly styled. Her face was also healing nicely, though evidence of the bruising still resided around her eye.

"Wow," Evelyn couldn't help but say. "You look amazing."

"Dr. Tennyson was in yesterday," Jeanne said, "and he told me that he thinks the surgery and antibiotics are doing the trick. He told me I can be discharged tomorrow."

"That's wonderful, Jeanne." Evelyn smiled for her new friend. "And what about care?"

"A home-health aide will visit me once a day for the first week, just to make sure my needs are being met. After that, if all goes well, Dr. Tennyson thinks I can manage on my own with the help of crutches and a walking boot."

"Remarkable. I'm very happy for you."

"So am I." Jeanne's smile was warm and bright. "I owe you a lot of thanks, Evelyn. I reached out to Roy over the weekend to see how Kaley was doing, and we had a good long chat. It was the first time in years that we didn't fight."

Warmth filled Evelyn's chest at the news. "You don't owe me any thanks."

"I do." Jeanne nodded. "You're one of the first people to not grow angry with me and my moods. You've been patient, understanding, and more helpful than I deserve. Your husband must think you're a saint."

"Ha." Evelyn laughed. "I struggle with many of those things, Jeanne, but I appreciate the sentiment. And my husband would be the first to tell you I'm no saint."

"Well, you're an angel of mercy to me, and I can't thank you enough. If it hadn't been for you," Jeanne continued, "I don't think my eyes would have been opened to my boorish ways. I've decided to start working on my attitude and behaviors and investing more into my personal relationships again."

"I'm thrilled to hear that, Jeanne." It was amazing to see God working miracles inside Mercy Hospital. "You have my cell phone number. If you ever need someone to talk to, you can count on me."

"I appreciate that."

Evelyn took the seat next to Jeanne's bed. "There is something I'd like to discuss with you, though, something about the ring."

"Oh?"

"There's a man named Lord—"

"Ms. Robertson." Madison entered the room with a tall, handsome stranger close behind her. "There's a visitor to see you."

Jeanne sat up a little straighter at the sight of the man, her cheeks turning pink.

Madison moved to the end of Jeanne's bed, a smile on her face as she glanced back at the man. "He came all the way from London last night, just to meet you."

"Me?" Jeanne's hand went up to her hair, and she looked a bit self-conscious.

The man extended his hand to Jeanne. "It's a pleasure to meet you, Ms. Robertson." His British accent was strong and aristocratic. He wore a linen suit with a black cotton shirt underneath and shining black shoes on his feet. "My name is Randall Hanover, Lord Marshton."

Jeanne's mouth fell open.

Evelyn's first impression of Lord Marshton in person was that he reminded her of a young James Bond. He had class, sophistication, and confidence to spare. His dark brown hair was combed back into a perfect wave, and his skin was tanned to a golden brown. When he smiled, his white teeth flashed.

"I-it's a pleasure to meet you too," Jeanne said.

Standing, Evelyn also extended her hand. "I'm Evelyn Perry," she said. "Supervisor of the records department here at Mercy Hospital."

Lord Marshton took her hand in his. "I'm pleased to meet you."

"And you."

"This is a pleasant surprise." Jeanne glanced at Madison and then back to Lord Marshton. "To what do I owe this special visit?"

Lord Marshton's piercing blue eyes were filled with undeniable charm. It was clear he was not only used to being the center of attention, but he enjoyed it as he stood there, with all eyes on him. "I've heard that you are in possession of Lord Shaftesbury's ruby ring."

Jeanne nodded. "I inherited it from my uncle just two weeks ago."

"Yes, I have heard." Lord Marshton put his hands behind his back. "I am in possession of the other seven Lords Proprietors' rings and have spent this previous decade locating them. Until recently, I could not determine where Lord Shaftesbury's ring resided. I had my suspicions but could not verify them."

"My," Jeanne said, touching her cheek. "You've been aware of the ring much longer than I have."

"I'm not only aware," Lord Marshton said, his voice growing a bit serious. "But I'm passionate about returning the rings to England, where they rightfully belong—together."

Jeanne glanced at Evelyn, as if to ascertain whether or not this man was for real.

Evelyn nodded, having already done a bit of research on him. She could easily see why he had a reputation as a ladies' man.

"Not only am I a descendant of Charles II but also of Lord Shaftesbury," Lord Marshton continued. "And it has been my deepest desire to restore the ring to my family these many years." His eyes shone with excitement. "Until now, I didn't think that would be possible, so I decided to come here and present my request to you personally."

"Your request?"

"I know this ring means a great deal to you and your family," Lord Marshton continued. "But imagine how much more it means to my family. I am hoping that you will allow me to purchase the ring from you, this very day, so I may return to London with it in my possession. I am prepared to pay you far more than its worth, because, truly, the ring is priceless to me."

Jeanne looked from Lord Marshton to Evelyn and then back again. "I suppose you have more right to it than I do."

Lord Marshton's relief was palpable. He glanced at Madison, who smiled with adoration.

"I brought a check with me," Lord Marshton said. He pulled a checkbook from an inner coat pocket. "I assume this will work for you?"

"Um." Jeanne looked a little discombobulated as she fluttered her hands. "I—I suppose. Do you really want the ring today?"

"Unfortunately, I must get back to London as soon as possible. If we can make this transaction today, I would be very pleased."

Jeanne looked to Evelyn again. "Evelyn will need to remove it from the safe for me. I still don't have my doctor's permission to leave this room."

"Of course. I will happily escort Ms. Perry to the safe after I've paid you." Lord Marshton went to the tray table by Jeanne's bed and set the checkbook down. He wrote a check, tore it out, and handed it to Jeanne.

Jeanne's eyes widened, and her mouth opened. "This is too much," she said, trying to hand the check back to him. "I couldn't ask you to—"

"Nonsense." Lord Marshton put his checkbook into his pocket again and took a step back. "It's the least I can offer. You have made me a very happy man today, Ms. Robertson."

"Likewise," Jeanne said, staring at the check. She nodded to Evelyn. "Could you help Lord Marshton retrieve the ring?"

Evelyn leaned close to Jeanne and said, "Don't you want the check to clear first?"

Jeanne shook her head. "I trust Lord Marshton. Besides, you heard him. He has to leave today."

Evelyn nodded. It wasn't her place to insist that Jeanne be more cautious. She didn't get a look at the amount on the check, but no doubt it would go a long way in helping Jeanne live comfortably.

"Thank you, Ms. Robertson," Lord Marshton said, offering a slight bow. "I'm forever in your debt."

Jeanne nodded but appeared to be a little too stunned to offer a coherent answer.

"This way," Evelyn said as she led Lord Marshton out of the room.

She hadn't anticipated Lord Marshton's arrival, but now perhaps Jeanne could go home and rest easy, knowing the ring was no longer a threat to her well-being.

Or to Evelyn's.

"I hope you don't mind taking the stairs," Evelyn said to Lord Marshton as he followed her out of Jeanne's room. "It won't take as much time as the elevator."

"Of course not."

Madison followed them out of the room but instead of returning to the nurses' station, she stayed right by Lord Marshton's side.

"Do you know each other?" Evelyn asked Madison.

Madison smiled at Lord Marshton, and he took her hand.

"We met when I was working in London last year," Madison explained.

Evelyn's pace slowed as she considered this new information. What were the odds that Madison would take a job at the very hospital where the ring was located? And, more importantly, what were the odds that she would be assigned to care for the very woman in possession of the ring that Lord Marshton had been looking for?

Searching her mind, Evelyn remembered that she'd never seen or heard of Madison before Jeanne was admitted to the hospital. Had that been a coincidence too? It didn't seem likely.

They walked down the grand staircase, and Evelyn led them across the hallway toward the records department, her mind spinning with questions.

But before Evelyn opened the door, she looked from Lord Marshton to Madison. "It's pretty remarkable that Madison ended up at Mercy Hospital, isn't it?"

"That's what I thought when she called me and told me about the ring." Lord Marshton smiled at Madison. "I've been looking for it for a decade, and she found it the moment it reentered the public eye."

Madison clung to Lord Marshton's hand with a little more desperation than necessary. Evelyn couldn't help but wonder if Lord Marshton was the man whom Madison had been engaged to before leaving London. Had she gone looking for the ring to try to win him back? By the way he was allowing her to hold his hand, perhaps it had worked.

"I can admit the truth," Madison said. "As soon as I heard about the ring, I agreed to take the job here. I wanted to make sure it was the ring Randall was looking for before I told him to come all this way."

"Why didn't you tell us?" Evelyn asked. "That didn't need to remain a secret."

Madison's eyes were large and filled with hope as she looked at Lord Marshton. "I didn't want anyone to get suspicious—and I wanted to surprise Randall. If it had gotten out why I was here, I was afraid someone would tell him before I could."

It was all starting to make sense to Evelyn. Madison's singular devotion to Jeanne, her presence whenever Evelyn visited Jeanne's room, and her evasive nature when Evelyn asked about her past.

Evelyn grabbed the doorknob and found that it was already unlocked. No doubt Stacia had arrived—probably curious why Evelyn hadn't come into the office yet.

Had Stacia used her badge to get into the records department with Hunter the night of the break-in? That would explain why the outer door wasn't damaged but the Vault door had been.

Stacia was sitting at her desk, her computer already running, looking at a file in front of her. She glanced up when Evelyn entered with Madison and Lord Marshton.

"Stacia," Evelyn said, "this is Lord Marshton. He's just flown in from London last night to purchase the ring from Jeanne Robertson."

Stacia rose and extended her hand. "It's nice to meet you, Lord Marshton."

"And you." Lord Marshton took her hand and smiled at her.

Evelyn went to the Vault door and used the new key that maintenance had given her. She kept the key on a chain connected to her name badge.

The room was dark, so she flipped on the light switch and allowed Lord Marshton and Madison to follow her inside.

Evelyn had not had time to look for the information Madison had been searching for the last time she'd been in the Vault. But Madison hadn't asked for it again, and Evelyn was starting to wonder if she really wanted the history of Mercy Hospital for her scrapbook, or if Madison had come in looking for a way into the safe. Could she have been the one who tried breaking in?

"If you could give me a moment," Evelyn said. "I'll just get the safe open, and you can be on your way."

Lord Marshton nodded and turned his back to the safe, drawing Madison with him, as Evelyn twisted the combination.

The safe door popped open, and Lord Marshton turned back. The first crack in his suave and confident demeanor appeared as he anxiously looked into the safe.

Evelyn imagined this was a big moment for him. After searching for ten years, the ring was about to fall into his hand.

It didn't take long to locate the ring and the piece of paper with all the owners' names. "It looks like a new name will be added to this list today," Evelyn mused as she removed the items and handed them over to Lord Marshton. "Perhaps you'll want to add Jeanne's name above yours, even though she only owned it for two weeks."

"Yes, yes, of course," Lord Marshton said, though he was so distracted, Evelyn wondered if he even heard what she said.

Lord Marshton held up the ring and turned it this way and that. He showed it to Madison, who leaned in as well.

"It's beautiful," Lord Marshton said as he slipped it onto his ring finger. "And it's almost a perfect fit." He shook his head. "Can you imagine? This ring once sat on Sir Ashley Anthony Cooper's hand."

"It's remarkable," Madison agreed. She glanced at the door. "Shouldn't we get going? Your flight leaves soon."

Lord Marshton admired the ring for another moment and then nodded. "I suppose we should. Thank you for all your help, Mrs. Perry. It's been a pleasure." He shook her hand again and then followed Madison out of the Vault.

"Goodbye," Evelyn said as she closed the safe, but she wondered again if the pair had even heard her.

When Evelyn had the safe secure again, she returned to the office and locked the Vault door.

Madison and Lord Marshton were already gone.

"Jeanne just called," Stacia said. "She's wondering if you could do a favor for her."

"Do you know what she wants?"

"She didn't say, but she did ask for you to go to her room the second you have a chance."

Evelyn glanced around the office, knowing she had a pile of work to attend to, but she decided it could all wait. She would go up and see what Jeanne needed. No doubt the woman was overwhelmed with what had just happened.

"Can you manage in here for a while without me?" Evelyn asked.

Stacia lifted an eyebrow. "You know I can."

Evelyn laughed. She left the records department and headed across the hall to the staircase.

The hospital hummed with activity today. Doctors, nurses, visitors, and other staff members traversed the halls and went up and down the stairs, all of them on a personal mission of some kind. Evelyn loved the energy at Mercy. No matter the day or the hour, something was always happening.

In a few minutes, she was entering Jeanne's room for the second time that day. She smiled. "What can I do for you?"

Jeanne's eyes were still wide, and she still held the check. "Can you believe all of that just happened?"

"It's quite remarkable," Evelyn agreed. "Think about all the events that led up to this moment. Even in the midst of difficulty, God still had a plan."

"This check is a godsend." Jeanne lifted it for emphasis. "I've decided to give half of it to Roy and his family. They need it more than I do."

"Jeanne, that's wonderful."

"I asked you up here to see if you could take this to the bank for me. The sooner I have it deposited, the sooner I can give Roy his half."

It was Monday, which meant Evelyn had more work on her plate than usual. It would take half an hour or so to run the check to the bank, but how could she say no? She could manage to put off her work for thirty minutes.

"Of course I can take it to the bank for you."

Jeanne handed the check to her and, for the first time, Evelyn saw the amount. It was an amazing number—far bigger than Evelyn had even anticipated. "Lord Marshton was quite generous."

"Which is why I feel led to offer half of it to Roy." Jeanne took a deposit slip from her checkbook and filled it out, then told Evelyn which bank to take it to.

"I'll return with the deposit receipt as soon as possible," Evelyn assured her.

"I'm not worried." Jeanne smiled.

As Evelyn walked down the steps, she remembered she had not driven her car to work. It would take even longer for her to walk home and retrieve her car. Maybe Anne was working today. Since she lived a distance out, she always drove to Mercy.

Evelyn pulled out her cell phone and called Anne.

"Hello, Evelyn," Anne said.

"Hi, Anne." Evelyn quickly told her what had happened and asked if she could use her car.

"I'll offer you one better," Anne said. "How about I drive you there myself? I'm almost to the hospital. I can just pick you up at the front entrance."

"That would be wonderful! I'll see you there in a couple of minutes."

Evelyn ended the call and stuck her phone in her back pocket. She stopped by the records department on her way to the entrance and told Stacia the plan as she grabbed her purse.

"Wait," Stacia called out to Evelyn as she was about to leave.

"Yes?"

"Something doesn't make sense to me."

Evelyn paused. "What?"

"It's about Lord Marshton. You said he just flew in last night."

"That's what Madison said."

"But I saw him over a week ago, when Hunter and I were at a nightclub."

"I'm sure you're mistaken. Madison said he just came in from London yesterday."

Stacia shook her head. "No. I'm almost certain it was him at the nightclub. He was with Madison."

"With Madison?" Evelyn frowned. "You saw him at a nightclub with Madison last week?"

"I remember, because I recognized Madison, and I was pretty impressed with her dance partner—who I now know was Lord Marshton. He's not someone you forget easily."

Lord Marshton was in Charleston last week? Then why did they say he had just arrived yesterday?

Then something else shifted, and she realized that Madison had lied to her. "And just a few minutes ago Madison told me she accepted a job here after she heard about the ring, but she was working here before the article in the paper came out." She shook her head. "She had to have known about the ring before that. But how?"

Something wasn't right—but Evelyn didn't have time to figure out what.

Chapter Seventeen

ANNE SAT WAITING NEAR THE main entrance of Mercy Hospital in her midsize sedan. She offered Evelyn a warm smile when their gazes met and moved a backpack and a pair of shoes to the back seat. No doubt they belonged to Addie.

"Thank you," Evelyn said as she opened the passenger side door. "This is saving me quite a bit of time."

"No trouble," Anne said. "I'm not scheduled to work for a half an hour and was just coming in early to grab a cup of coffee from Joy."

Evelyn had set her coffee down in Jeanne's room, yet again, and forgotten it there.

They turned out of Mercy's drive and onto East Battery Street. Evelyn had the address of the bank in her phone and told Anne where it was located.

"Can I ask?" Anne asked.

"What?"

"How much is the check worth?"

Evelyn lifted the check and allowed Anne to see the amount, scrawled out in bold print.

"Whoa." Anne's mouth slipped open. "Is that how much Jeanne asked for?"

"No. She tried to give the check back to Lord Marshton when she saw the amount."

"But he insisted?" Anne shook her head as she turned onto Broad Street, laughter in her voice. "Sounds like something a 'philanthropist' would do."

Traffic was light and it only took them about ten minutes to get to the bank, which was close to Sinclair Antique Jewelry. Anne found a place to park on the street about a block away and they walked to the building.

Even though the money was in the form of a check, Evelyn still felt fidgety holding it. If anything happened to the check, it could be weeks before Lord Marshton would be able to send another, and Jeanne would be so disappointed.

"Here we are," Evelyn said as she opened the door for Anne.

The building was fairly new, tastefully decorated with a modern motif and feel. A teller was open, so Evelyn led Anne up to the counter. The teller's name tag said MARGO.

"How may I help you today?" Margo asked.

"I'd like to deposit a check for my friend." Evelyn pushed the check and the deposit slip across the gray countertop.

Margo picked it up, and her eyes opened a little wider when she read the amount on the check. "This is a substantial deposit—from a foreign account."

Evelyn nodded.

"I'll need to have the bank manager oversee this transaction. Will you excuse me for a moment?"

"Of course."

Margo left her spot at the counter and walked into a room behind her with the check and deposit slip in hand.

The large clock on the wall ticked silently as Evelyn and Anne stood waiting. Neither one spoke.

But the longer it took, the more anxious Evelyn became that Anne would be late for her volunteer shift. "Maybe you should call Aurora and let her know you might be late."

"You're probably right."

"I'm sorry this is taking so long. I should have realized it wouldn't be a simple deposit."

"It's okay." Anne took her phone out of her purse to call her supervisor. "I'll be right back." She walked away to a quiet corner of the bank lobby to make her call.

Evelyn folded her hands on the countertop and smiled at a customer who walked up to the next teller. She let out a sigh and tried to glance into the room Margo had entered, but there was no window and the door was only open a crack. What could be taking so long? Was Margo waiting for the bank manager to get off a phone call? Had they even begun the transaction?

A few minutes later, Anne came back to Evelyn's side. "Aurora was grumpy." Anne smiled. "But she said it's fine if I come in a bit late."

"That's a relief." Evelyn tried not to sound impatient. "I can't imagine what's taking them this long."

"It's a big check—from a foreign account. I'm sure they have several forms to fill out and steps to go through."

Almost twenty minutes after Margo had left her post, she opened the door and was followed by a middle-aged gentleman in a blue pinstriped suit.

"I'm Brian Hadleigh," the gentleman said. "The branch manager."

"It's nice to meet you," Evelyn said. "I'm Evelyn Perry and this is Anne Mabry."

Mr. Hadleigh looked at the check and frowned. He held it up for Evelyn to look at. "May I ask why you brought this check into the bank today?"

Evelyn quickly explained the situation and that her friend, Jeanne, was in the hospital and couldn't come herself.

"I see." Mr. Hadleigh looked at the check again. "And do you know this Randall Hanover?"

"No," Evelyn said. "I only met him briefly when he gave Ms. Robertson the check. Why?"

"I'm sorry to be the one to tell you this, but this check is a forgery." He set it down on the counter. "There is no bank in London with this name and address."

Evelyn stared at Mr. Hadleigh, her breath slowing as she absorbed his words.

"We were able to get ahold of the real Randall Hanover, 13th Earl of Marshton, at his residence in Nottingham, England. He said he is not in Charleston, nor did he write out a check for this amount."

"A-are you saying the man who gave this to me is not Lord Marshton?" Evelyn asked.

"I'm afraid not. Whoever he is, he is most definitely not Lord Marshton."

Weakness stole over Evelyn's legs, and she gripped the counter. She had thought she knew who Lord Marshton was, based on the research she had done online, but she realized, belatedly, that she hadn't actually looked very closely at the few pictures she could find of him. Mostly she'd just read brief mentions in tabloids of his exploits.

"May I ask why this gentleman gave this check to you?" Mr. Hadleigh asked.

"He purchased a very rare and valuable ring from Ms. Robertson."

Mr. Hadleigh spoke slowly and clearly. "And does he have the ring in his possession now?"

Evelyn could only nod, her heart sinking at the realization that Jeanne had been duped. She no longer had the ring *or* the money.

"Ms. Perry," Mr. Hadleigh said, "I am going to call the police. Do you know where this person might have gone?"

"No." Evelyn shook her head. "They said something about a flight."

"They?"

"He and Madison Cummings, a temp nurse at Mercy Hospital."

"Where do you think they may be flying to?"

"Back to London—I think."

"I'll call the police and see what they want to do. Perhaps they'll send some officers to the hospital and the international airport."

"Time is of the essence," Evelyn said.

Mr. Hadleigh used a phone near the teller to dial the police station.

Evelyn had a different idea. She pulled her phone out of her purse with shaking hands.

"Oh, Evelyn," Anne said, regret and disappointment in her voice. "I'm so sorry." She looked at Evelyn's phone. "Who are you calling?"

"Shirley. Remember when she told us she drove Madison home one night? I'm going to see if she remembers Madison's address. While the police do their part, we can do ours."

Evelyn dialed Shirley's number, hoping she had her cell phone on her. Within seconds, Shirley answered. "Hey, Evelyn."

Evelyn tried to calm her voice, not wanting to sound frantic and alarm Shirley. They needed to find Madison and the mystery man before they left Charleston. It might be their only hope of ever seeing the ring again. "Do you remember where Madison Cummings lives?"

"Madison? Why?"

"It's too complicated to explain now, but I need to know."

"Sure." Shirley didn't ask any more questions. "I might still have the address in my maps history."

It took a couple of seconds, but Shirley was able to give Evelyn the exact address. She wrote it down on a scrap of paper.

"Thanks so much! I'll tell you about it later."

"Be careful."

Evelyn hung up the phone and showed Anne the address.

"Do you actually want to go there?" Anne's eyes were wide.

"We need to see if they're still in Charleston, or if they've left. It's only a few blocks from here. We can't wait for the police to get there. Can you take me to Madison's?"

Anne nodded, though she looked a little skeptical. "Sure."

"I'll call Jeanne on the way and explain. Hopefully I can tell her before she learns about this from the police—and prepare her to answer their questions."

After speaking very briefly with Mr. Hadleigh, thanking him for his assistance, Evelyn and Anne rushed out of the bank.

"I hope we can catch Madison and the man to stall them," Evelyn said as she dialed the hospital one more time and asked for the phone in room 2350.

By the time they reached Anne's car, Evelyn had Jeanne on the phone.

"Jeanne," she said, a bit breathless. "The check was fake. The man was *not* Lord Marshton."

"What? What's happening, Evelyn? You sound out of breath. Are you okay?"

"I'm fine. We're leaving the bank and driving to Madison's house to try to stop them." She opened the passenger door and got into Anne's car. "The police are on their way to the hospital, and potentially to the airport. If we find Madison and whoever that guy is at Madison's, I'll call the police and tell them to come there. I wanted to let you know what's happening so you can be prepared to tell the police whatever they need to know."

"O-okay," Jeanne said, her voice uncertain.

"I'm so sorry." Evelyn put on her seat belt as Anne turned on the engine. "We'll do whatever we can to get the ring back."

"Just be careful. I don't want you to get hurt."

"I'll be careful. Call me on my cell phone if you need me. I'll be in touch."

As soon as Evelyn ended the call, she put Madison's address into her cell phone. Almost immediately, a link appeared.

"She's living at an Airbnb," Evelyn said to Anne. "It doesn't look like she was planning to stay here long, does it?"

"Do you think it was all a scam from the beginning?"

"I have a feeling this was a well-laid-out plan, yes." Evelyn pressed her lips together, angry that she had been deceived by Madison. "I have a feeling we know who broke into the Vault."

"Didn't the note that the perpetrator left say they intended to take what was rightfully theirs?"

"Yes."

"Why would Madison or this man think the ring was rightfully theirs?"

"I don't know." Evelyn was determined to get to the bottom of this—but right now, they needed to track down the thieves and get the ring back.

That was the only thing that mattered.

"Which house is it?" Anne asked as she drove slowly down King Street, not too far from Marion Square. Several large, beautiful homes graced the street.

Evelyn glanced at the address for the fifth time, wanting to make sure she got it right. "It should be the white house on the right." She pointed to a stunning home with Greek columns.

"Wow." Anne put her blinker on and pulled her car into the first open space she found. "Can you imagine how much that must cost to rent in August?"

"I would guess that whoever is paying for it has money to spare." Evelyn unlatched her seat belt but didn't make a move to leave the car.

"What's your plan?" Anne studied Evelyn. "Knock on the front door? Do you really think they'll answer?"

Evelyn nibbled her bottom lip as she contemplated what to do next. She had been so keen on coming, she hadn't really thought about what she'd do once she got here. "I want to see if they're here or if they've checked out. If they're here, then we need to call the police immediately and tell them where they can find Madison and her mystery man."

"Maybe try contacting the Airbnb owner. You should be able to find contact info online, shouldn't you?"

"That's a great idea. While I search can you keep your eye on the property to see if anyone comes or goes?"

"Sure."

Evelyn found the Airbnb website again, and it didn't take long to find the contact information.

"Evelyn." Anne placed her hand on Evelyn's arm and used her other to point. "Look."

Up ahead, an Uber car doubled-parked just outside the house.

"Do you think the Uber is here for them?" Evelyn asked.

"The house looks pretty big. There could be more than one unit—but we should be ready to follow them if it's meant for Madison."

"I agree." Evelyn didn't bother to continue looking for the owner of the property. She put her seat belt back on and watched the front door of the Airbnb for movement.

Within a couple of minutes, the door opened and Madison and the man stepped out.

"There!" Evelyn said as she dropped her phone on the floor in her excitement.

"Are you going to call the police?"

"Yes." Evelyn reached for her phone. "Are you prepared to follow them?"

Anne gripped the wheel and nodded, her knuckles white and her face determined.

Evelyn didn't know the police department's number, so as the Uber driver helped Madison put their luggage into the trunk of the car, Evelyn called 911. Her hands were shaking, and adrenaline was rushing through her body. It made typing difficult.

"They're getting into the car," Anne said.

Glancing up briefly, Evelyn nodded. "Don't lose them."

"Where do you think they're going?"

"They have all their bags?"

"It looks like it."

"Then I'd guess they're going to the airport."

Someone picked up the phone. "911, what is your emergency?"

"This is Evelyn Perry," she said, her voice just as shaky as her hands. "There has been a theft of a ruby and diamond ring, and I've located the thieves. I'm currently in my friend's car, and we're following them."

"Ma'am," the dispatcher said, "do not approach the suspects, do you understand?"

Evelyn fumbled with the phone. "Of course."

While the dispatcher asked for more information, including their location, Anne pulled onto King Street to follow the Uber.

"I think they're heading to the airport," Evelyn said to the lady on the phone, who had identified herself as Karen.

"I've put out the call," Karen said. "I repeat: do not approach the suspects."

"I won't." Evelyn didn't think Madison was dangerous, but she didn't have the same confidence about the fake Earl of Marshton.

Traffic was thick as they rode north on Meeting Street.

"They're probably heading toward Highway 26," Anne said as she had to stop at a light. The Uber had not been stopped.

"Don't lose them!" Evelyn said.

"I can see them." Anne sat up higher, clearly trying to look around a car ahead of her. "If they're heading toward the airport, this is the fastest way there."

Evelyn tapped her foot impatiently.

"Ma'am?" Karen asked.

"Yes?"

"The police have been dispatched, and they are on their way to the airport. What kind of vehicle are the suspects in?"

"They're in a silver Ford Fusion."

"Can you see the license plate number?"

"No." Evelyn motioned to Anne. "Try to catch up to them again. I need their license plate number."

"I'm trying," Anne said with a little impatience.

The light finally turned green, and Anne took off with a jolt.

Evelyn used her free hand to brace herself and glanced at Anne out of the corner of her eye.

"Just a minute," Evelyn said to Karen. "I can see the car again."

"Okay," Karen said. "Tell your driver to follow all road laws and to be alert and cautious."

Evelyn repeated the directions, and Anne just gave her a look.

"There." Evelyn pointed to the car. "I can see the license plate now." She rattled off the numbers and letters to Karen.

"Thank you," Karen said.

They weren't too far from the highway now.

"Wait," Anne said with a frown. "What are they doing?"

"What do you mean?" Evelyn asked.

"They're not going toward the highway."

"What's happening?" Karen asked.

"They're not going the way we thought."

"Have they noticed you following them?"

Evelyn watched them take a left and then another quick left.

"Maybe." Her body heat had risen, and she was sweating.

"I think they're onto us," Anne said.

"What should we do?" Evelyn asked Karen.

"The police have been notified to look for a vehicle that fits this description. There are police heading to the airport as we speak and others moving toward Meeting Street. If we're not careful, they will abort their plans. It might be best for you to stop following them."

Evelyn licked her dry lips. What if they lost them for good? What if this was their last chance?

"Ma'am?" Karen asked.

There were few options, and the best people to take over were the police officers. They were trained and equipped for this situation. Evelyn and Anne were not.

"We need to stop following them," Evelyn said to Anne.

"Really?" Anne glanced at Evelyn.

"Yes."

"The police are on this case, Mrs. Perry," Karen said. "If you are in no further need of assistance, I'll let you hang up now."

"Thank you for your help." Evelyn ended the call, letting out a ragged breath as Anne slowed her car and the Uber disappeared from sight.

"Now what?" Anne asked.

"Let's head to the airport."

"Seriously?" Anne's eyes were wide as she looked at Evelyn.

"Yes. I want to be there to see if they're apprehended. I can't go back to work and actually concentrate on anything productive if I don't know how this turns out."

Anne shrugged. "You're right. I don't think I can either."

"We're not too far from the highway." Evelyn set her phone in her lap and watched Anne to see what she would decide.

It didn't take Anne long to take a right turn and head back toward Highway 26 and the international airport.

Chapter Eighteen

THE MORNING TRAFFIC WAS STILL heavy as Anne pulled onto Highway 26 a few minutes later.

"How long do you think it'll take to get to the airport from here?" Evelyn asked.

"Fifteen to twenty minutes, if there are no accidents on the road and no other backups."

Evelyn's heart rate was still pounding as they moved down the highway. All she could think about was Jeanne's ring and the disappointment she'd face if she didn't get it back.

"It breaks my heart to think that the check was a fake," Evelyn said. "Jeanne had hoped to give half of it to her cousin. Now she might lose everything."

"Let's not give up hope. The ring is still valuable."

"What if she never gets it back?"

"We'll worry about that later." Anne put on her blinker and shifted lanes. She wasn't a slow driver, but neither was she one to take unnecessary risks. She drove the speed limit and not a mile over.

"At least she *wanted* to share the money," Evelyn said. "There's something to be said about that."

"God doesn't always concern Himself about earthly treasures," Anne mused. "Like ruby and diamond rings or large sums of money.

He's after our hearts, and if Jeanne has had a change of heart, then she's wealthy beyond compare."

"You're right." Evelyn took comfort in Anne's words. "But it would be nice to have a change of heart *and* a ruby ring."

Anne's joyful laughter filled her car.

Fifteen minutes later, she took the exit to merge onto Highway 526, which they followed until the airport signs directed them to exit.

The Charleston International Airport was not a huge facility, but it was busy and there were many cars coming and going— enough to make Evelyn worry that they'd never find the little silver Ford Fusion.

"Will the police be waiting outside the airport doors?" Evelyn asked.

"They wouldn't want to scare them off." Anne followed the signs directing them toward international departures.

"What if the police don't get here in time? How will we stop them?"

"Evelyn," Anne said in a warning voice. "Don't worry."

Evelyn pressed her lips together, trying desperately not to voice her concerns. They filled her mind to overflowing and were causing her to panic.

"I wonder what carrier they're taking," Anne said as she drove by the signs for various airline companies in the drop-off area.

Pressing herself forward, Evelyn squinted to try to find the silver Ford Fusion. There were so many silver and gray vehicles, it felt like an impossible task. But then she saw it—the Uber they were looking for.

"There!" She pointed. "Under the United Airlines sign."

"There's nowhere to park."

Several no-parking signs dotted the area. It was a drop-off site only.

"Get as close as you can," Evelyn urged.

Madison and her companion left the Uber quickly, while the driver opened the trunk. They pulled out their luggage as Anne came to a stop not too far behind them.

Evelyn remembered Karen's warning not to approach the suspects, but when it looked like the police were nowhere to be found, she reached for the handle and started to open her door.

"Don't you dare!" Anne said as she put her finger on the POWER LOCK button. "You'll get hurt."

"They're getting away!" Evelyn tried the handle, but it wouldn't budge.

"Evelyn Rose Perry," Anne said. "If you get out of this car, I'll jump out and tackle you to the ground. I'm not kidding."

After Madison tipped the driver, he got back into his car and pulled away, and Madison and the man picked up their bags and started to walk toward the sliding glass doors.

"They're getting away, Anne!" Evelyn felt helpless as she watched.

At that moment, the doors opened and four police officers rushed out of the building. Another two came from a spot nearby, where Evelyn had not previously noticed them.

"Look!" Evelyn said, her voice rising several octaves.

"I can see." Anne laughed.

Madison and the man didn't put up a fight. They dropped their bags and lifted their hands in surrender. Madison's face immediately crumpled.

"Now, I'm getting out of the car," Evelyn said to Anne. "I need to go and speak to the police."

"Fine," Anne said. "I'll stay with the car so I don't get a ticket or get towed."

Evelyn jumped out of the car and walked toward the police.

The sounds of cars driving by, people saying goodbye, and others whispering in curiosity, filled Evelyn's ears. The scents of exhaust and warm concrete wafted up to her nose, but she hardly noticed the unpleasant smells.

"Ma'am." An officer on the perimeter held up his hand to stop Evelyn. "I'm afraid I'm going to have to ask you to stay back."

"I'm the woman who called in this complaint," Evelyn said. "I'm Evelyn Perry, and I believe these two have a very valuable ring that belongs to my friend."

"They're being searched right now," the officer said. "I'll need you to stay back."

"Of course."

It didn't take long for the police to find the stolen ring. Evelyn wasn't surprised that he had chosen to carry it on his person.

Evelyn caught Madison's eye at that moment, but Madison looked away, her face filled with shame and embarrassment.

"May I ask who that man is?" Evelyn asked. "I was told his name was Randall Hanover, 13th Earl of Marshton."

"You'll learn all the details after the arrests have been made," the officer said. "We will be contacting your friend to let her know the ring has been found. And as soon as she's able to, she can come and pick it up at the precinct."

Another officer saw Evelyn and came her way.

"This woman said she was the one who called in the complaint," the first officer said to the second.

"I'm Officer Clayton," the second one said. "Are you Evelyn Perry?"

She nodded. "I am."

"Would you be willing to answer a few questions?"

"Yes, of course."

For the next twenty minutes, Evelyn answered all the questions Officer Clayton had for her, while Madison and her friend, whom Officer Clayton identified as Nicholas Bengston, a well-known London socialite, were loaded into the back seat of a squad car.

"I think that will be all," Officer Clayton said to Evelyn. "If we have any further questions, we'll be sure to give you a call."

"Thank you for all your hard work," Evelyn said to him. "My friend will be so happy to get the ring back."

"We appreciate your quick thinking," the officer said. "If it hadn't been for you, they might have gotten onto that plane. Then we would be dealing with an international crime, which is much harder to investigate and track."

"I'm just glad everyone was able to do their part." Evelyn smiled at him and shook his hand and then went back to Anne's car.

"Well?" Anne asked.

"Thank you for waiting. Did you have any trouble?"

"I was asked to move a couple of times, but when I explained who we were, the airport security let me wait." Anne put on her blinker and joined the traffic exiting the airport. "What did you learn?"

"Not as much as I'd like. Officer Clayton did tell me they were able to identify the man as Nicholas Bengston. Apparently, he's a well-known socialite in London, but I don't know his connection to Madison, or to the ring for that matter. We should know more after the police report is filed."

"I can't wait to figure it out. At least we know the ring is safe and everyone connected to it is safe."

"No more break-ins or threatening notes." Evelyn smiled. It felt good to finally know who was behind the trouble.

There were just a few more unanswered questions, but hopefully they'd know more soon.

For now, they needed to get back to Mercy to tell Jeanne the good news.

Half an hour later, Evelyn said goodbye to Anne, who was well overdue for her volunteer shift, and went up the grand staircase to the second floor.

It seemed strange not to see Madison lurking about or to bump into her as she entered Jeanne's room.

"Oh, there you are," Jeanne said, placing her hand over her heart. "Thank God you're all right."

"I appreciate the concern," Evelyn said as she noticed Roy standing in the room. "Hello," she said to him.

"Hello, Mrs. Perry."

"The police just left," Jeanne said. "Can you believe this all happened? I imagine it was a lot scarier for you. All I could do was lie here and fret over everything that was happening. You don't know how unnerving it is to be immobile."

"It's been a very eventful day—and it's not even lunchtime yet," Evelyn quipped.

Roy smiled, but Jeanne didn't seem to appreciate the joke. Her concern for Evelyn's welfare appeared to trump all other humor.

"I'm just thankful you're not hurt," Jeanne said. "I want to thank you for all you did today—and all you've done over the past couple of weeks. The police told us it was your quick thinking and actions that helped them catch Madison and Nicholas before they left the airport. They told me I might never have seen the ring again if you hadn't been involved."

"That's high praise." Evelyn took the seat next to Jeanne's bed. "I'm happy I could help."

"We were told we could pick up the ring tomorrow," Jeanne said, "after I've been discharged from the hospital."

"We?" Evelyn asked.

"Roy and his wife, Helen, are going to take me into their home for a couple of weeks." Jeanne smiled at her cousin. "Then, when I'm able to take care of myself again, they'll drive me back to Atlanta."

"How nice," Evelyn said, offering Roy a smile of her own.

"It'll give me time to get to know Kaley better," Jeanne said. "As long as Roy and Helen can handle two invalids."

"Helen is the most patient woman I know," Roy said. "She wouldn't be married to me if she wasn't."

Jeanne finally allowed herself to laugh, and the sound was beautiful to Evelyn's ears.

When her smile faded, she said to Evelyn, "The police said they should know more about the suspects and their motives by the time I pick up the ring. I heard Nicholas Bengston is quite a rascal. Roy and I looked him up online after we learned his name."

"Oh, really?"

"His father is filthy rich," Jeanne said, "and apparently Nicholas has been in so much trouble, his father publicly threatened to disinherit him last spring when he was arrested after driving drunk and causing an accident that paralyzed a woman."

"My goodness." Evelyn put her hand up to her mouth. "That's horrible."

"It makes me realize all the more how blessed I am that my injuries are minimal."

"Do you remember anything else that happened the day of the accident?" Evelyn asked.

"It's coming back, in bits and pieces, but I doubt I'll ever remember it all." She shrugged. "I don't think I want to remember it all. I have enough information, thanks to you, to help reconstruct the most important parts of the day."

Evelyn nodded. "That's a good attitude to have."

"I'm just thankful I'll be able to walk again." Jeanne smiled. "It could have been much worse."

"I agree." Evelyn rose from the chair. "But I don't want to keep the two of you from visiting. I'll be sure to stop up here tomorrow morning, bright and early, to say my goodbyes before you're discharged. If you think of it, would you mind calling me and letting me know what the police have to say?"

"I will," Jeanne promised.

"If you need anything, please let me know."

"You're an angel," Jeanne said, reaching to Evelyn for a hug. "Thank you."

Evelyn gave Jeanne a quick embrace, and then she took her leave.

She had work needing her attention, though her impatience to find out the details of the heist would keep her distracted until she heard from Jeanne.

On her way back to the records department, Evelyn decided to stop in the gift shop. If ever she needed some coffee, it was now.

"Good morning again," Joy said to Evelyn as she entered the gift shop, already moving to the pot of coffee on the warming plate. "Is all this excitement I've been hearing about true?"

"Probably." Evelyn smiled as she took the cup of coffee and inhaled a large breath before taking a sip. She let out a contented sigh.

All the while, Joy watched her with a curious and mirthful smile.

"What did you hear?" Evelyn finally asked.

"That you and Anne chased down a couple of thieves and aided the police in arresting them."

Evelyn's laughter bubbled out before she could stop it. "It was something like that—but not quite as dramatic as all that."

"Did you chase them down?"

"No. We followed them—but I'm pretty sure they were onto us, so we had to let them go."

"Did you help the police arrest them?"

"No. I called the police and told them I thought the suspects were going to the airport. The police were there waiting for them when we all arrived."

"Did you see it all unfold?" Joy's eyes were wide.

"I did. But they didn't put up a fight or resist in any way."

"Still." Joy shook her head in wonder. "It's pretty amazing, nonetheless."

It *was* pretty amazing to be part of something so exciting.

As usual, being employed at Mercy Hospital proved to be a thrilling ride.

Chapter Nineteen

IT TOOK ALL OF EVELYN'S willpower not to call Jeanne the next day, after she had been discharged. Lunchtime had come and gone, and still Evelyn didn't know the final outcome of the ring or how Madison and Nicholas had concocted the plan to steal it. Jeanne should have been to the police station and left by now, and it was driving Evelyn crazy not knowing.

"Do you have the file you wanted me to copy?" Stacia asked Evelyn as she stood next to Evelyn's desk.

"What?" Evelyn blinked and frowned. "What did you say?"

"The file?" Stacia asked. "I'd like to get it copied, since I'm leaving early today. Remember?"

Evelyn looked around her desk, which was cluttered with unfinished work. She finally found the file Stacia was waiting for and handed it to her. "Yes, I remember you're leaving early—now that you've reminded me."

Stacia smiled and shook her head. "I don't think I've ever seen you so distracted."

"That's because you haven't worked here long." Evelyn chuckled, though her gaze slipped to the clock once again. Had Jeanne forgotten her promise to call her? Would it be weird for Evelyn to call her? She didn't want to bother Jeanne as she was getting reacquainted with her cousin's family.

But the thought of waiting another day or two was too much to bear.

The door opened into the records department and Roy Robertson appeared, pushing Jeanne in a wheelchair.

Evelyn's pulse picked up speed and a knot of nervous energy unfolded in her midsection.

"Jeanne!" Evelyn rose and met her visitors on the other side of the counter that separated the back office from the front. "I didn't expect to see you here again. I thought you'd be happily rid of Mercy Hospital for good once you left."

Jeanne looked a little tired, but happy, as she smiled up at Evelyn. "I wanted to come back here and tell you what we learned at the police station today. And"—she paused as she looked up at Roy and then back at Evelyn—"to tell you the other good news we have to share."

"We would have been here sooner," Roy said, "but we had a stop to make and a little business to attend to—per Jeanne's request."

Evelyn looked from Roy to Jeanne, leaving her question unspoken.

"I had Roy take me to Sinclair Antique Jewelry after we left the police station." Jeanne had a satisfied look on her face. "I asked Abigail if she was still interested in purchasing the ring, but she said she had spoken to the real Lord Marshton, and he was very interested in buying it. He had asked Abigail to be the liaison between us, and she agreed. Roy and I received a tidy little sum for the ring, and we went directly to the bank to deposit the funds."

"And this time," Roy said, "the money was real."

"Oh, I'm so happy." Evelyn smiled.

"Not only are we satisfied with the sale," Jeanne said, "but so is Lord Marshton."

"And Abigail," Roy added, "who was compensated by Lord Marshton for her assistance."

"Now all the rings will be together again," Evelyn said. "Isn't that amazing?"

"It will be back where it belongs," Jeanne agreed. She looked up at Roy again. "I split the money with Roy, fifty-fifty."

"Which was unnecessary," Roy said, "but very much appreciated."

Evelyn was glad to see that the ring would no longer come between these two family members.

"Now, for the rest of the story, as the saying goes," Jeanne said to Evelyn. "The police were able to tell me more about Nicholas and Madison."

This was the information Evelyn had been waiting to hear—though it paled in comparison to the very good news they had already shared.

"What did you learn?" Evelyn asked.

"Apparently, Madison is not a temp nurse." Jeanne lifted an eyebrow. "Though, I'm not surprised, given her poor bedside manner—but that's a different story."

Evelyn hid a chuckle, wondering what led her to make that statement.

"Anyway," Jeanne continued, "Madison met Nicholas when she was in London. The story she told Loretta was true. They were engaged, but Nicholas broke off their engagement a few weeks ago. According to Madison, she was familiar with the ring because Nicholas claims to also be descended from Sir Anthony Ashley

Cooper. He knows Lord Marshton, because they are distantly related, but there was some scandal a few generations ago, and Nicholas believes he should be the legal Lord Marshton. I didn't understand all of it, but needless to say, Madison was under the impression that the ancestral home Lord Marshton inherited, along with the money, should have all been Nicholas's."

"But isn't Nicholas's father wealthy?" Evelyn asked.

"Yes. He's independently wealthy and, like we heard, he disinherited Nicholas, so Nicholas was trying to lay claim to Lord Marshton's title."

"It sounds a bit confusing," Evelyn conceded.

"So," Roy continued, "when Nicholas broke up with Madison, she started investigating the ring and figured out that it was in Uncle Tony's possession, but by the time she found him, he'd already died. She had come to Charleston to see if she could get her hands on it. She heard about Jeanne inheriting the ring and then learned about Jeanne's accident, so she decided to slip into the hospital to impersonate a nurse. After she ascertained that the ring was authentic, she called Nicholas and told him he should come to Charleston. The pair of them broke into the Vault and tried getting into the safe. When they couldn't, Nicholas became irate and messed up your files."

"It must have been Nicholas who left the note," Evelyn said.

Jeanne nodded. "And when they knew they couldn't get into the safe, they came up with the plan that Nicholas would impersonate Lord Marshton and forge a check."

"I see." Evelyn let out a long breath. "But now they're both facing criminal charges." She shook her head, sorry that Madison had decided to get involved in such a terrible plan.

"She did it all for Nicholas," Jeanne said, "and the man will probably dump her again, the moment he has a chance."

"How did they think they'd get away with it?" Evelyn asked.

"They weren't heading back to England," Roy told her. "They were planning to go to Switzerland and sell the ring there."

"Didn't they realize that if they ever wanted to return to England, they'd be caught?"

Jeanne shrugged. "After learning more about Nicholas's past, I'm not surprised he thought he could get away with it. He's been in a lot of trouble before, and his father has bailed him out time and time again."

"Well," Evelyn said. "At least now we know." She smiled. "Thank you for coming back here to tell me this in person."

"It was the least we could do for all the work you've invested." Jeanne reached for Evelyn's hand.

When Evelyn shook it, Jeanne passed a small piece of paper to her.

Frowning, Evelyn turned her hand over and looked at the paper. As she opened it, she realized it was a check.

"As you'll see," Jeanne said, "the check is written out to Mercy Hospital. I want to make a donation, in your name. You may choose where that donation goes."

Tears gathered in Evelyn's eyes. "This is too much—really."

Jeanne and Roy both smiled, but Roy was already turning Jeanne's wheelchair around, to head out the door.

"Goodbye, Evelyn," Jeanne called to her. "I'll be sure to stop in from time to time to say hello when I'm here visiting Roy and his family."

Evelyn walked with them to the door and opened it for them. "Goodbye, Jeanne. It's been a pleasure getting to know you."

"The same." Jeanne waved as Roy pushed her out of the records department.

"Goodbye, Roy," Evelyn called. "Take good care of her."

"I will." Roy nodded, and then the door closed behind them.

A slow, satisfied sigh slipped out of Evelyn's mouth as she felt all the uncertainty and anxiety of the past couple of weeks slip away.

"Well?" Stacia asked. "Are you happy with the outcome?"

"More than I can say."

"Good." Stacia grinned and then went back to her work. "So am I. If it hadn't been for the ruby ring, I would have never met Hunter—and I really think he might be 'the one.'"

Evelyn laughed so hard, tears gathered in her eyes and she had to wipe them away. "Oh, Stacia. What would I do without you?"

Stacia's grin widened, and she joined her laughter with Evelyn's.

It was a good feeling to know the truth, once and for all.

And Evelyn couldn't wait to get home and tell James everything she'd learned.

"Everyone will be arriving any minute," Evelyn said to James as he walked into their kitchen, freshly showered and smelling of Evelyn's favorite cologne. "Can you grab the tray of cheeses in the refrigerator and set it on the counter?"

"I'd be happy to." James came up behind Evelyn and placed a kiss on her cheek. "But before I do, I need to tell the cook how pretty she looks tonight."

Evelyn giggled at him as she accepted his kiss—without stopping her arrangement of the crackers she was putting into a basket. "After the cheeses are out, can you make sure the front light is on? I know the sun is still out, but in case it goes down and I forget, I'd like it to be done now."

James laughed. "Your ability to multitask never ceases to amaze me."

Tonight would be the first time they entertained with their new kitchen. She didn't want to forget a thing. There was a list sitting on the counter that she'd compiled so she didn't miss anything tonight—including the front light.

After James took out the cheese platter and Evelyn set the crackers near it, he left the kitchen.

The smell of baked ziti and french bread wafted up to Evelyn's nose. Garlic permeated the air and made her stomach rumble with hunger. A large tossed salad was waiting in the fridge, along with strawberry gelato in the freezer. Later, while enjoying dessert, they'd have a cup of espresso with the new machine James had surprised her with a couple of days after the kitchen was finished.

Evelyn also left the kitchen to double-check the dining room table. She had set it earlier, but she wanted to make sure the salt and pepper shakers were full.

James was at the door, turning on the light, when the first knock came.

"They're here!" Evelyn said, setting down the full saltshaker. She removed her apron and tossed it into one of the drawers in the hutch.

"Ready?" James asked with a wink.

Evelyn answered him with a grin and joined him in the entry hall as he opened the door to find Ralph and Anne standing on their front stoop, a gift bag in Anne's hand.

"Welcome," Evelyn said, taking the bag from Anne and smiling a warm greeting at Ralph. "You didn't need to bring us anything."

"Of course we did." Anne entered the house, followed closely by Ralph. "It's a hostess gift—and a bit of a housewarming gift for your kitchen remodel."

"Thank you." Evelyn opened the bag and smiled. Inside was a beautiful ceramic measuring cup set.

"It's not much," Anne said, "but I thought it might go with the kitchen."

"It's perfect." Evelyn moved aside so the Mabrys could come all the way into the house.

"Don't shut the door!" Joy called out as James was about to close it.

He opened it wide again and Joy came sailing up the front stoop and into the house, a bright smile on her face.

"Welcome, Joy," Evelyn said.

Joy gave Evelyn and James both a quick hug and then produced another bag for Evelyn. "Just a little something I saw you admiring in the gift shop a couple of weeks ago. When I heard you were remodeling the kitchen, I thought it might be a fun addition."

"You two." Evelyn looked from Joy to Anne. "I didn't expect any gifts."

"Of course you didn't," Anne said. "That's why they're so much fun to give."

The hallway was getting crowded, so Evelyn stepped into the dining room, Anne and Joy close by her side while James and Ralph continued visiting near the front door.

Inside the bag Joy brought was a beautiful ornate ceramic cookbook stand.

"I know you still like to use your cookbooks," Joy said. "So I thought this might be helpful."

"It's perfect! I was admiring this one." Evelyn turned it around to look it over. It appeared sturdy and was heavier than she expected. "This should hold even my biggest cookbooks."

A knock sounded at the door.

"That will probably be Shirley and Regina," Evelyn said with another smile. She had invited Shirley to bring her mother along for the dinner party. They all loved her dearly, and Evelyn knew it wasn't always easy for Shirley to leave her aging mother alone.

James opened the door, and Shirley entered with Regina on her arm.

"Hello," Evelyn said, giving both of them a hug. "Welcome."

"Thank you for inviting me, honey," Regina said. "I haven't been to a dinner party in ages."

"You're always more than welcome."

"What is that delicious smell?" Shirley asked, taking a long, deep breath.

"Baked ziti and french bread."

Shirley's eyes lit up. "I can't wait. But first, a gift." She produced a small box, wrapped in paper with delicate purple flowers on a white background.

"Really," Evelyn said, a little embarrassed. "It wasn't necessary for all of you to bring me gifts."

"Isn't that what a party is for?" Regina asked with a chuckle.

Evelyn set the other gifts on the table and then opened the wrapped box.

Shirley and Regina watched closely, but it was Regina's eyes that sparkled the most.

Inside the box was a small white ceramic box with a fleur-de-lis on the lid. It was the exact same color as the measuring cups and the cookbook holder. "I have a feeling someone coordinated all this," she said with a laugh.

"When I saw how much you liked the cookbook stand," Joy said, "I looked to see if there were any other items in the collection."

"How thoughtful," Evelyn said.

"Look inside the recipe box, honey," Regina said, nodding for her to keep opening the gift.

Evelyn did as she was instructed and found about a dozen cards, already filled out with recipes.

"Those are some of my mama's original Southern recipes," Regina said. "You won't find anything better."

"She even included her famous fried chicken recipe," Shirley said. "And no one gets Mama's recipes outside of the family."

Tears started to gather in Evelyn's eyes. "What an honor."

"You ladies are becoming more like family to my Shirley than most of her real family," Regina said. "So I made copies for all of you."

Joy and Anne exclaimed their delight as Regina pulled the cards from her purse, a light shining from her beautiful face. Shirley just chuckled, but the friendship she felt for Evelyn, Joy, and Anne was evident in her gaze.

It took Evelyn a couple of seconds to pull her emotions together, but when she did, she said, "Would y'all like to see the kitchen?"

"I thought you'd never ask," Shirley said.

Evelyn led her friends into the kitchen, with Ralph and James close behind.

Everyone oohed and aahed over the changes, asking lots of questions and commenting on all the things they loved. James beamed with pride and Evelyn laughed as she shared some of the stories, which were now funny and no longer a source of contention between her and her husband. The failed YouTube tutorial on plumbing was at the top of their list.

Soon, everyone was enjoying the appetizers as Evelyn removed the ziti from the oven to cool a bit.

When it was time to eat the main course, Evelyn told her guests to make their way to the dining room.

"Well," James said to Evelyn as they stood alone in the kitchen for a moment, "was it all worth it?"

Evelyn paused for a moment, inhaling the aromas coming from her kitchen, listening to her friends' happy chatter from the dining room, and basking under the smile of her husband as he watched her.

"Some things are worth the extra effort," she said, the reality of that statement settling on her heart and mind. "Whether that's remodeling a kitchen, preserving the happiness in a marriage, or helping a new friend put together the pieces of a mystery. It's all worth it in the end."

As she and James carried their meal to the dining room, which was full of their friends' laughter, she smiled.

It was indeed worth it.

Dear Reader,

Two years ago, my husband and I had the opportunity to visit Charleston for the first time. My husband is such a trouper! For six solid hours, we walked up and down the streets of the historic district on a self-guided tour. We stopped at several wonderful sites, including beautiful homes, intriguing cemeteries, and magnificent churches. We ambled along the waterfront, spied Fort Sumter in the bay, and learned so much about the amazing history of this gorgeous city.

At the time, I didn't know I'd be writing stories set in Charleston, but my writer's mind was already turning. This third story in the Sweet Carolina Mysteries was inspired by that day in Charleston. As much as I love all the other eras in this fine city, I'm always drawn to the beginning. The English colonization of Charleston was a fascinating time, rife with many obstacles, intrigues, and dreams. I've only scratched the surface in telling the story of the Lords Proprietors of Carolina. Each of these men, along with King Charles II, led amazing lives. I hope I've piqued your interest and you do a little investigating of your own.

Enjoy!

Signed,
Gabrielle

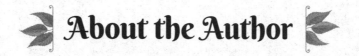# About the Author

GABRIELLE MEYER LIVES ON THE banks of the upper Mississippi River in central Minnesota with her husband and four children. As an employee of the Minnesota Historical Society, she fell in love with the rich history of her state and enjoys writing historical, contemporary, and cozy mystery novels inspired by real people, places, and events. When Gabrielle is not writing, you might find her homeschooling her children, cheering them on at sporting and theatrical events, or hosting a gathering at her home with family and friends.

The Story Behind the Story

My love for new beginnings often takes me back in time to where a city, state, or country began. In *Angels Watching Over Me*, I went back to the very beginning of English colonization in Charleston.

In 1663, King Charles II, who had recently been returned to his throne after the English Civil War, chose to honor eight men who had faithfully served him. Those eight men included the Earl of Shaftesbury (Sir Anthony Ashley Cooper) and the Earl of Clarendon (Edward Hyde). The king granted these eight men a charter to establish the colony of Carolina, and they became known as the Lords Proprietors of Carolina. None of these men ever set foot in Charleston, but Sir Anthony Ashley Cooper was tasked with laying out the Grand Model, which included the Fundamental Constitution of Carolina, as well as a settlement and developmental plan. Colonization began in 1670, and because of the incentives given to the colonists, there were over 6,600 settlers in Carolina by 1700.

Each of the Lords Proprietors were given other gifts from the king, including land, titles, and political power. The rings I included in this story are purely fictional, but it would not have been outside the realm of possibility. In the story, Sir Anthony Ashley Cooper's ruby ring is stolen by Edward Hyde, which act is also fictional, but in real life, the two men were sworn enemies, and eventually Edward Hyde was exiled from England by the king.

Unfortunately, King Charles II did not have any children with his wife, Catherine of Braganza, so his brother, James II, took over the throne upon his death. Though King Charles II did not have any legitimate children, he did claim over a dozen children by seven different mistresses. Some of these children were given titles, and the late Princess Diana was descended from two of them, the Dukes of Grafton and Richmond. When her son, Prince William, one day takes the throne of England, he will be the first of King Charles II's descendants to do so. It's amazing how connected we remain with history.

Good for What Ails You

ALL-NATURAL CLEANING RECIPES

Homemade All-Purpose Cleaner

   ½ cup white vinegar

   2 tablespoons baking soda

   10 drops tea tree, lavender, or lemon
      essential oil (for their disinfectant
      properties)

Mix vinegar, essential oils, and a little water before adding baking
soda in a clean spray bottle (glass is best). Then fill to top with water.
I use about a 12 oz bottle. Gently shake to mix ingredients, and then
spray, wipe with a cloth, and allow to dry.

Homemade Disinfectant Wipes

   1 cup water

   ¼ cup vinegar

   8 drops tea tree oil

   8 drops eucalyptus essential
      oil

   8 drops lemon essential oil

   Empty "wipes" container
      (baby wipes, for example)

   15–20 squares of cloth (old
      T-shirts work well, as do
      old dish towels or similar
      material)

Fold and place the cloth squares into the empty wipes container and set aside.

Combine the water, vinegar, and 3 essential oils in a mixing bowl, stirring until well mixed.

Pour this mixture over the cloths in the container. Once the cloths are soaked through, they are ready for you to pull out and use.

Launder and repeat as often as the cloths hold up!

*Read on for a sneak peek of another exciting book
in the Sweet Carolina Mysteries series!*

A Change of Art
BY LESLIE GOULD

JOY ATKINS STOPPED IN THE middle of the Grove, on the grounds of Mercy Hospital. Ahead was the Angel of Mercy statue. Overhead was the lush canopy of an eastern redbud tree, thick with heart-shaped leaves.

All around in the peaceful setting were more trees, pots of flowers, and tables and chairs arranged for staff, patients, and visitors.

On three sides of the Grove were the hospital buildings. Joy turned toward the lobby, clutching her bag in one hand and a bundle of zinnias from her garden in the other. As she started toward the entrance door to the hospital, she breathed out a prayer of gratitude.

God had provided a new home for her in Charleston, South Carolina, and a new job and community at the hospital.

As she stepped into the lobby and started toward the gift shop, a new painting in the hallway leading to the emergency department caught Joy's attention. Had another month gone by already?

Abrielle Fleury, the proprietor of Belina House Gallery, changed the artwork every month. She had gotten off to an early start today. It was only a quarter to seven.

The paintings of summer flowers by local artists were gone, and it looked as if the theme for September was Charleston architecture. The first painting was of the Colonial-style Old Exchange Building. The second was of the Gothic Revival Huguenot Church, which Joy knew Abrielle attended. The third was of an Italianate-style three-story building with flower boxes filled with white angel's trumpet. Joy stepped closer. It was the Belina House. She smiled. That was Abrielle's art gallery, which Joy had been meaning to visit.

The fourth painting was titled *The Fleury Estate*. It was of a Georgian-style home behind a gate, probably built in the late 1700s or early 1800s, surrounded by a lovely garden.

"Joy!"

She turned toward the voice. It was Abrielle, her blond hair piled high in a bun and her brown eyes, framed by dark eyebrows and lashes, bright and lively. She wore a turquoise blouse, a black flowing skirt, and heels. She stood with the posture of royalty.

"Hello," Joy responded. "I was just admiring the artwork."

"These are some of my favorite pieces." Abrielle, who was at least a half foot taller, smiled down at Joy. "From my family collection. All of the properties are dear to us."

Joy pointed to the fourth painting. "Is that where you grew up?" Abrielle nodded.

Joy asked, "And where Claire lives now?"

Abrielle answered, "That's right. The property has been in the family for centuries—Daddy moved into the guest cottage a year ago, so Claire and Lloyd live in the big house by themselves now. Doc Fleury, one of the founders of the hospital, lived there for most of the 1800s."

"Is that Dr. Arthur Fleury? The one in the portrait that's been restored?"

Abrielle nodded. "Everyone calls him Doc Fleury, to this day. Even his descendants. The plan is to unveil the portrait at the art auction and then hang it in Garrison's office." She smiled. "It's going to be delivered in a few days. We've been doing some other work with the same consultant, although I haven't given Claire all the details yet."

Claire, who'd been away part of the summer, was one of Joy's volunteers in the hospital gift shop. However, Claire had invited Joy to join the art auction planning meeting and attend a brunch for the group the next day—at that gorgeous home in the painting.

"What a lovely property, and how wonderful that it's been in the family for so long."

Abrielle nodded and pointed toward the painting of her gallery. "The Belina House Gallery has only been in the family for a century. We're celebrating one hundred years this month."

"Wow." Joy stared at the painting.

"I live on the top floor," Abrielle added.

Joy put her hand to her chest. "How enchanting." She couldn't imagine having deep roots in an old city like Charleston. Yes, she grew up in Houston and lived there as an adult, but her parents weren't from there. They'd moved to the city as newlyweds.

And how nice that Abrielle and Claire had each other too. Joy had a sister—Hope—but they weren't exactly close. Joy felt a twinge of envy. "Well," she said to Abrielle, realizing she'd become lost in her own unhealthy thoughts, "I'd better get things ready in the gift shop."

Abrielle picked up the box of wrapped paintings. "I have to get going too. I'm expecting a call about three paintings we're having authenticated. It's rather exciting."

"That sounds fascinating."

"It is. I'll tell you all about it tomorrow. I'll be at the brunch too." Abrielle took a step toward the front door and then stopped and turned toward Joy again. "Oh, and Claire plans to stop by and talk with you about the art auction this morning."

Joy waved and said, "I can't wait to see her." Claire had spent August on Lake Champlain, in Vermont, at her husband's family home there—something they did every year.

Claire had volunteered in the gift shop a handful of times before she left, just enough for Joy to know she considered the woman a friend.

Moving to Charleston to be close to her daughter, Sabrina, and grandchildren had definitely been the right decision for Joy. And getting to know women such as Claire and Abrielle was an added blessing, along with her hospital coworkers. Evelyn Perry, who worked in the records department, had already become a close friend. And Anne Mabry, the volunteer extraordinaire, whose husband was a hospital chaplain, was also part of her new group. Shirley Bashore, a nurse who worked everywhere from the emergency department to the surgery floor, rounded out the group. Well, almost. Shirley's spitfire of a mother, Regina, had become one of Joy's favorites too.

Approaching the gift shop, Joy gazed through the wall of windows at the shelves of colored glassware—red, green, indigo, and azure blue. She unlocked the door and stepped out from under the painted-sky ceiling of the lobby, into her own spectacular domain of beauty.

She had worked hard to order just the right pieces, anticipating what visitors, guests, and employees needed, and then displayed them to draw customers into the shop. The collection of candles filled the air with the scent of lemongrass, and the items hanging from the ceiling—Japanese lanterns and origami cranes—added texture to the shop. And all the glassware bounced color and light around the shop. Her planning had paid off. The place was bright and vibrant.

After she secured her bag in the bottom drawer of her desk and put the zinnias in a vase full of water by the cash register, Joy put on her smock, inhaled the aroma of the pot of coffee that was brewing, and saw to the details of opening the shop for the day.

After she finished, Joy pulled her phone from the pocket of her smock. She'd texted Sabrina the evening before to see if she and her family would come for Sunday dinner after church. There was still no response.

At eight, as Joy flipped the sign to Open, Claire came waltzing through the door in a navy blue dress with a wide skirt and heels. She wasn't as tall as Abrielle, but she still towered over Joy by a few inches. Claire did have the same shade of blond hair as her sister, the same dark eyes, and the same book-on-top-of-her-head posture. But instead of wearing whimsical blouses with skirts like Abrielle, Claire wore tailored fifties-style dresses, skirts, and sweater sets. She also wore bright red lipstick.

She gave Joy a hug and then kissed her on one cheek. "It's so good to be back!"

Joy returned the hug and then said, "It's great to have you back. How was Lake Champlain?"

"Wonderful!" Claire said. "Of course, it nearly broke my heart to be away from our grand girl that long." Her first grandchild had been born in June. "So I've been spoiling Talia every single minute since we got home."

Claire held up her phone and showed a photo of herself with the baby. The little one had a pink bow on her bald head and a serious expression on her face.

"She's darling," Joy said.

"She's getting baptized on Sunday." Claire slipped her phone back into her bag. "You should come. Have you attended our church yet?"

Joy shook her head. The historic Huguenot Church had been on her list of churches she wanted to visit.

Claire clapped her hands together. "Come on Sunday."

"You might be tired of me, after the brunch tomorrow," Joy teased.

"Never." Claire beamed.

"I'm not sure if I have plans yet or not," Joy said. "If I don't, I'll keep it in mind."

"Wonderful," Claire said.

"Just one question." Joy clasped her hands together. "Is the service in French? Because *je ne parle pas français*."

Claire laughed. "You're in luck. Only one service a year is in French, and it's not this Sunday. Now, as far as tomorrow..." She went on to discuss the brunch. She'd called Joy the day before, asking Joy to be on the committee because one of the members had bowed out at the last minute to be with her pregnant daughter in Ashville who was on bed rest. "Anne and Evelyn will be there," Claire said. "And so will Roger."

Joy raised her eyebrows. She'd heard about Roger Gaylord—a new benefactor to the hospital—but hadn't met him yet.

Claire grabbed Joy's forearm and gave it a squeeze. "We're going to have so much fun!"

Joy didn't hear back from Sabrina until the next morning, as she approached the gate across the walkway to Claire's home for the eleven o'clock brunch. Sorry, Sabrina texted. Sunday dinner won't work. We already have plans with Rob's family. Maybe next week?

As she put her phone away, Joy decided she'd take Claire up on attending church for her granddaughter's baptism. If she couldn't spend time with her own family, she might as well spend time with Claire's.

She squared her shoulders and straightened her jacket, ready to press the button on the box by the gate.

"Joy!"

She turned around. Evelyn and Anne, along with Anne's granddaughter, Addie, hurried toward her. Lili, Addie's mom and Anne and Ralph's daughter, was serving in Afghanistan, so the little girl was living with her grandparents.

Anne's blond hair shone in the morning light, and Evelyn had her white hair pulled back in a barrette that matched the dragonfly pin on her lapel. Both women wore blouses and skirts, and seven-year-old Addie wore a yellow sundress.

Joy hoped her pantsuit wasn't too casual. She did have a gauzy scarf around her neck that added an element of elegance. "Hello, y'all!" she called out.

"Hi!" Anne and Evelyn responded.

Addie yelled. "Howdy!"

Joy smiled at all of them and then waved at Addie, who ran ahead, her dress twirling around her knees and her sandals flapping the sidewalk.

"Have you buzzed the gate yet?" Anne asked.

Joy shook her head.

"Hold on. I know the code."

As Anne punched in the number, Evelyn said, "I've always loved this house. It was built for the Fleury family, who had a shipping business with ties to Europe."

"Interesting," Joy said.

"Yes, they were—still are—Huguenots, otherwise known as French Calvinists. When Louis XIV forced many of them from French society, some of the Fleury family went into hiding in France for a time. But one branch of the family arrived in Charleston in the late 1600s."

Intrigue filled Joy. "Now, that's fascinating."

The gate clicked open and Anne, followed by Addie, led the way onto the property. Joy knew a little bit about the Huguenots. Many found freedom of religion in the New World, along with so many other faith groups that arose out of the Reformation.

"Oh, look at Claire's Japanese maple tree," Evelyn said. "Isn't it gorgeous?"

It was to the right of the path in a well shaded garden—and about three feet high. The leaves, all bright red, shimmered in the morning light, casting shadows over hostas, coleus, and coral bells.

"Claire definitely has a green thumb." Evelyn held up her hand. "Unlike me."

Joy laughed. Evelyn had many skills, including organizational and historical sleuthing, but gardening wasn't on the list.

"We should go around to the patio," Anne said, pointing toward the left as she reached for Addie's hand. Ralph, Anne's husband, was working his once-a-month Saturday shift at the hospital. All of the women were happy to have Addie tag along on outings.

Joy's gaze shifted from the perfectly kept grounds to the house as she walked. It was three stories and made of bricks with cream-painted columns framing the front door.

They followed the pathway to another, smaller gate. As Anne opened it, she called out, "Hello!"

"Come on in, y'all!"

The three women and Addie stepped through the gate onto a large patio, dotted with potted palmetto trees and lush plants. Claire, who wore a black polka-dot dress, stood with a stack of cloth napkins in her hands. She wore her hair in a flip, right at her shoulders. She greeted the women with a sweet, "Welcome."

A large table was set with cutlery and plates. Food—scrambled eggs, bacon, fruit, and pastries—covered another table.

Two men chatted by a fountain near the back door. Abrielle placed a bouquet of cosmos on the food table, and Claire put the napkins around at each place setting on the table.

As the women chatted, the men, one of whom wore gray slacks and a blue shirt, approached. His dark eyes shone, and he gave Joy a warm smile.

"Roger Gaylord," he said, extending his hand.

Joy took it and said, "Pleased to meet you. I'm Joy Atkins."

"Pleased to meet you also." He smiled again. "You work at the hospital, right?"

She nodded. "In the gift shop."

Claire then introduced her husband, Lloyd Walter, to Joy.

Claire added, "Lloyd can only join us to eat. He has to rush off to Savannah to look in on his Aunt Mae."

Abrielle's head shot up. "What about Talia's baptism tomorrow?"

"I only plan to spend the night," Lloyd said. "I'll leave early in the morning."

Joy knew it was only a two-hour drive. He could easily be back for the baptism.

Claire turned toward Lloyd. "Honey, would you please say a blessing for us?"

After the prayer, everyone filled their plates and then sat around the table. From her place, Joy could see a guest cottage, most likely where Claire and Abrielle's father lived, on the edge of the back garden, and to the left of it a garage that looked as if it had been a stable at one time.

"Isn't Daddy joining us?" Abrielle asked.

Claire shook her head. "He had some errands to run this morning."

"He's out walking?"

Claire nodded. "He's fine." She glanced toward Joy. "Our father is eighty-four but in good shape. He had an irregular heartbeat, but his new medication has corrected it."

Joy smiled. "What a relief." Claire and Abrielle were fortunate to still have their father alive.

Addie arranged strawberries on her plate while the discussion around the table turned to the art auction. Everyone else at the table had been involved in the past. Joy listened intently, trying to catch up. The auction would be held at Belina House Gallery in one week. Abrielle and her staff would hang the exhibit next Friday. A local caterer was donating the food—a collection of canapés—and drinks at cost for the event. Claire, with Anne's help, had seen to the details of all of that. The tickets had already been sold. It sounded as if all of the details had been seen to.

"What can I do to help?" Joy asked.

"Well, besides attending the infamous art auction dinner for the planning committee on Thursday, here"—Claire gestured toward the house as she grinned—"we need you to stand by the back door of the gallery and direct people into the workroom, where one of the food tables will be. Mostly we don't want anyone going in or out of the back door, for security reasons. And would you like to help arrange the flowers the morning before the event? Our usual florist just went out of business." She made a sad face, which quickly transformed into a happier one. "We could visit the gallery today, and I can show you exactly what we'll need."

"I'd love to," Joy answered.

"Perfect." Claire beamed. "Roger will be on duty in the hallway during the event too."

Joy glanced toward Roger, who was taking a small notebook and pen from his shirt pocket. He started to jot down a couple of notes.

Abrielle's cell phone rang. "Excuse me," she said. "I've been waiting for this call and need to take it."

She stepped away from the table toward the guest cottage. When she returned, Claire gave her a questioning look and Abrielle gave her a quick nod and then said softly, "I'll fill you in later."

But then Abrielle had another phone call, a short one, and when she returned she said, "I need to get to the gallery." She turned to Joy and then to Claire. "I'll see you two soon." She told the others goodbye and slipped through the patio gate.

Anne, Addie, Evelyn, and Roger all needed to leave right after the brunch, but Joy helped Claire clean up. Then the two walked the eight blocks to the gallery, past the Dock Street Theatre and onto the cobblestones of Queen Street. A right turn took them straight to Belina House Gallery.

Just like in the painting, the Italianate building was painted white with black trim, and the window boxes overflowed with white angel's trumpets.

Claire bounded up the steps, the skirt of her dress swaying back and forth. Joy imagined the Fleury sisters as girls, running the blocks between their house and the gallery. Claire opened the door and called out, "Hello! We're here!"

A young man with a shock of dark hair and bright eyes smiled. "Claire! How was your trip?" He stepped out from behind the counter.

Claire gave him a hug and a kiss. "It was wonderful," she answered. "But I'm happy to be home!"

She turned toward Joy. "This is our friend, Joy Atkins. She manages the gift shop at the hospital." She gestured toward the young man. "And this is Grey Monte. Abrielle's assistant extraordinaire."

"Nice to meet you." Joy extended her hand.

Grey had a firm grip. He appeared to be in his late twenties and had a sweet smile.

"Abrielle's in the office, on the phone with the authenticator again."

Claire's eyebrows shot up. "Again?"

He nodded. "It's the third call since she arrived."

"So bad news?" Claire asked.

"It seems to be mixed," Grey answered.

Claire grimaced. "We'll head back that way."

As they walked down the hall, Claire said, "We have three French paintings from the early 1870s. Abrielle missed this, but an art dealer we've worked with saw the paintings and became convinced they're very early Theodore Joubert paintings."

Joy tried to pull the name *Joubert* out of the files of her brain, but she came up empty. "Sorry, I don't know who that is."

"Don't worry—lots of people who aren't in the art world don't," Claire said. "He was a French painter, 1870s through 1880s. On the outer edges of Impressionism—he studied with the some of the greats. That sort of thing. He has some nice Paris scenes and landscapes with figures. A few portraits. He died in the late 1880s at the age of forty-two, so fairly young."

"What are the paintings of?" Joy asked.

"Three young women—*Abrielle Overlooking the Village*, *Belina in the Garden*, and *Claire at the Church Steps*."

Joy stopped. "What?"

"Right?" Claire smiled. "We're named after the paintings."

"You and Abrielle and the gallery?"

Claire turned her head. "Something like that… Anyway, it turns out Joubert had three sisters. An art authenticator who also does restoration work told us that. Can you guess their names?"

Joy smiled, wryly. "Abrielle, Belina, and Claire."

"Exactly. The family story was that the paintings were a gift from friends in France, but over time the name of the French family was lost to us. When the art dealer said he thought the paintings were early Jouberts, research showed he had sisters with names that had been in our family since the 1800s." Claire smiled again. "That was the first clue that he might be the painter."

"Goodness," Joy said. "What a mystery."

Claire nodded. "Hopefully the authenticator has been able to sort it all out."

Claire stopped walking. "It's a bit of a quandary. If all three were done by Theodore, which we're still waiting for the final word, that means they're worth a lot of money. But the authenticator said it also might implicate our great-great-great-grandfather, Doc Fleury, in the theft of the paintings."

Joy froze. "The same Doc Fleury who was one of the founders of the hospital? Whose portrait is being restored and will be unveiled the night of the auction? The portrait that will be hung in Garrison's office?"

Claire nodded. "There's a theory that's been floating around the internet by an anonymous blogger about an unaccounted for early Joubert that went missing sometime in the early 1870s."

"That's a big deal, if Doc Fleury stole the paintings, or if it's even assumed he did."

Claire shrugged. "I'm sure he didn't. He's always been described as a man of character. And besides, even if he did, it would have happened a hundred and fifty years ago."

Joy had done enough nonprofit work to know it could be a big deal, if the information reached the wrong hands—or the right hands, if in fact he had stolen the paintings. "What do you know about him?"

"He was one of the founders of the hospital, as you know. A pillar of the Huguenot Church." She shrugged and then lowered her voice. "Just between you and me, I've never been that interested in family history, so I actually don't know that much about him."

"Claire!" someone yelled from the next room. "Claire! I hear you out there. Get in here!"

Claire grabbed Joy by the arm and dragged her into the office. Abrielle sat on the desk, her long legs crossed with her phone in her hand. "So," she said, "I just got off the phone with Pamela DePass. She said she can only authenticate *Belina in the Garden* as a Joubert."

"Then who painted the other two?" Claire asked.

"She doesn't know. Most likely someone who knew Theodore, perhaps someone who painted with him and spent time with him. Maybe one of his classmates even, who visited the family. It turns out he had four brothers and five sisters all together."

"Wow," Claire said. "Were any of them painters?"

"Pamela hasn't found that information yet. The sisters likely wouldn't have been. Women usually only did landscapes back then and that sort of thing. But perhaps one of his brothers was."

"Are the paintings really that different?" Claire asked.

"As much as I was hoping all three were Theodore's," Abrielle said, "I can see it. I mean, we grew up thinking the same artist did all three, so it's hard to adjust to, but I can see the difference."

"So," Claire said, "does that mean Pamela thinks Arthur Fleury only stole one of the paintings?"

Abrielle slid off the desk. "She said the only concern of the art world would be if he stole *Belina in the Garden*. No one would care about the other two. Hopefully no one will make a big deal out of it."

Joy bristled. "Oh, someone will. And from a PR standpoint for the hospital, it could be bad. The unveiling of Doc Fleury's portrait is taking place the night of the auction. If it comes out in the news that he's suspected of stealing a Joubert, that won't be good for the hospital."

"Or for the gallery," Abrielle said.

Claire wrinkled her nose. "Or for our family."

Abrielle opened her mouth and then closed it. Finally, she said, "You're right, Joy. Absolutely. This won't be good. And Daddy will be crushed. Doc Fleury has always been his biggest hero."

"I suppose we should get to the bottom of whether Doc Fleury stole the Joubert or not," Claire said.

"Right." Claire sighed. "Maybe there's information stored away somewhere that would clear him."

Abrielle nodded. "Maybe at the college." She turned toward Joy. "Someone in our family a long time ago donated Doc Fleury's papers to the South Carolina Historical Society archives, but they're stored in the college library."

"Oh." The college was close. Just a few blocks away.

"Well," said Claire. "Where are you keeping the three sisters these days?"

"In the safe, of course." Abrielle stood. "Want me to show you the differences in *Belina in the Garden*? Then we can talk about the auction—and how to figure out if Doc Fleury was a thief or not."

Claire nodded.

Joy was relieved the two were taking the accusation against Doc Fleury seriously.

Abrielle headed for the door with Claire behind her. Joy followed along. She looked ahead to the end of the hall and the back door, where she'd be stationed the night of the auction.

Claire increased her pace to keep up with her sister. "How much did she say the painting is worth?"

"That depends on quite a few factors that she hasn't determined yet," Abrielle answered, stepping through a doorway to the left.

Abrielle flipped a switch, and soft lights came on. Joy noted there were no windows. There were two large worktables, supplies, and a large safe at the front of the room. Abrielle entered the combination, leaning down as she did, and then pulled open the door.

There were a few small paintings. Joy had imagined the paintings of the three sisters to be much larger.

Claire peered over her sister's shoulder. "Where are they?"

"Gone." Abrielle turned toward her sister, her face ashen. "They were here last night."

Claire's voice wavered as she took a step backward. "Was the alarm set when you opened up this morning?"

"Yes. We didn't open until noon. I disarmed the alarm. I unlocked the door. Everything was in order."

"Well something wasn't in order." Claire pointed at the safe. "We've been robbed."

A Note from the Editors

WE HOPE YOU ENJOYED ANOTHER exciting volume in the Sweet Carolina Mysteries series, published by Guideposts. For over seventy-five years, Guideposts, a nonprofit organization, has been driven by a vision of a world filled with hope. We aspire to be the voice of a trusted friend, a friend who makes you feel more hopeful and connected.

By making a purchase from Guideposts, you join our community in touching millions of lives, inspiring them to believe that all things are possible through faith, hope, and prayer. Your continued support allows us to provide uplifting resources to those in need. Whether through our online communities, websites, apps, or publications, we strive to inspire our audiences, bring them together, and comfort, uplift, entertain, and guide them.

To learn more, please go to guideposts.org.

Find more inspiring stories in these best-loved Guideposts fiction series!

Mysteries of Lancaster County

Follow the Classen sisters as they unravel clues and uncover hidden secrets in Mysteries of Lancaster County. As you get to know these women and their friends, you'll see how God brings each of them together for a fresh start in life.

Secrets of Wayfarers Inn

Retired schoolteachers find themselves owners of an old warehouse-turned-inn that is filled with hidden passages, buried secrets, and stunning surprises that will set them on a course to puzzling mysteries from the Underground Railroad.

Tearoom Mysteries Series

Mix one stately Victorian home, a charming lakeside town in Maine, and two adventurous cousins with a passion for tea and hospitality. Add a large scoop of intriguing mystery, and sprinkle generously with faith, family, and friends, and you have the recipe for *Tearoom Mysteries*.

Ordinary Women of the Bible

Richly imagined stories—based on facts from the Bible—have all the plot twists and suspense of a great mystery, while bringing you fascinating insights on what it was like to be a woman living in the ancient world.

To learn more about these books, visit Guideposts.org/Shop